Richard Paul Russo's Orbit debut, UNTO LEVIATHAN, won the prestigious Philip K. Dick Award in 2002 under its original title SHIP OF FOOLS. He is the author of many acclaimed SF novels, including the Carlucci series, and lives in Seattle, USA.

Find out more about Richard Paul Russo and other Orbit authors by visiting the Orbit website at www.orbitbooks.co.uk

By Richard Paul Russo

UNTO LEVIATHAN

THE ROSETTA CODEX

RICHARD PAUL RUSSO

www.orbitbooks.co.uk

ORBIT

First published in Great Britain in December 2005 by Orbit

Text design by Kristin del Rosario

A CIP catalogue record for this book is available from the British Library

ISBN 1 84149 298 1

Printed and bound in Great Britain by
Mackays of Chatham plc

Orbit
An imprint of
Time Warner Book Group UK
Brettenham House
Lancaster Place
London WC2E 7EN

www.orbitbooks.co.uk

for Candace

PROLOGUE

Disguised as a freelance star freighter, the *Exile Prince* entered the Costamara System and made for Conrad's World, the system's only habitable planet. Like any other freighter, it approached Conrad's World with loaded holds and formal trade contracts, but was also outfitted with weaponry and defenses no freighter was ever authorized to carry, and passengers who would normally never travel on such a ship.

Two days out from Conrad's World, the *Exile Prince* transmitted its manifest—legitimate and accurate, if incomplete—along with encrypted registrations and certifications from the Independent Traders Collective. The orbital docking station returned a preliminary authorization.

One day out, Captain Jan Olveg had two long conversations with the station master. After the second conversation, the station master transmitted final authorization codes to dock and unload the *Exile Prince*'s cargo.

Four hours out from the station, three combat fighters emerged in battle vectors from the shadow of Ambrose, Conrad's larger moon, and attacked the *Exile Prince.*

Although they were still in zero gravity, Sidonie and Cale sat strapped into their acceleration couches, the woman's outstretched hand resting on Cale's arm. Just five years old, Cale did not understand what was happening, did not understand why they were strapped in, but he felt safe with Sidonie. She'd been taking care of him since he could remember; sometimes he accidentally called her "Mother," and though she would gently correct him, she always smiled and didn't seem to mind. Now she softly squeezed his arm and smiled at him, but it wasn't her normal smile and he wondered what was wrong.

The couches jolted from an explosion, and Cale stared at her, eyes wide, but remained silent.

"It's okay, Cale," Sidonie said in a hushed and soothing voice. "We'll be okay."

The stateroom door slid open and Cale's father moved into the cabin, bringing with him the sharp tang of burning plastic and distant electric cracks of sound.

"Papa!" Cale cried. "What's happening?"

His father was tall and stocky and his thick black hair was more than half gone to gray—a handsome man with lined skin. His clothing was a rich indigo, undecorated except for the family crest of gold and crimson just above his heart—a hooded falcon gripping a world in each set of talons against a background of stars.

"Someone's attacking the ship," he said.

"Why?"

"I don't know." He turned to Sidonie and said, "Take Cale to the *Kestrel.* It's too dangerous here." She nodded and immediately began unstrapping herself from the couch. "I'll have Captain Olveg launch decoys," he muttered, more to himself than to her. "I'll have him do any damn thing I can think of."

Sidonie pulled herself to Cale's side, released the restraints, and helped him out of the couch.

"There's only one real city on Conrad's World," Cale's father said. "Morningstar. The *Kestrel* is programmed with flight paths, evasive maneuvers, access codes. If anything happens to the programming and you have to fly the *Kestrel* manually, head for Morningstar. Don't land anywhere else on Conrad's World. The air space above Morningstar's restricted and aggressively protected." He wrote something on a pocket slate and handed it to her. "Verbally transmit these emergency access codes if necessary."

Cale tried to move forward and tumbled through the air, limbs flailing until Sidonie caught and steadied him; he still wasn't used to zero gravity.

"Aren't you coming with us, Papa?"

His father shook his head. "Later," he told his son. "I have to stay with the ship and help." He looked into Cale's wide, deep green eyes, then wrapped his arms around his son, pulling the boy tightly to him. "I'll follow as soon as I can," he said. "You go with Sidonie, all right?" Cale nodded, and his father looked back at Sidonie. "Once you get to

Morningstar, find Adanka Suttree. Remember that name. It's important."

"Adanka Suttree."

"He's my brother. That's the name he's using here. Find him, and stay with him. He'll protect you both. If I . . ." He stopped, released Cale, and straightened. "When this is over, I'll come for you and Cale. If I don't come soon, Adanka will know what to do. Whatever he tells you, treat his words as if they come from me."

Sidonie nodded, then took Cale's hand in hers. Cale's father looked once more at him. "Cale, you must remember something. It's very important." Cale nodded, his brow furrowing. "Do not tell anyone your last name. Never mention the name 'Alexandros,' not until I see you again. If someone asks you what your last name is, say you don't know. Your last name's dangerous now. Do you understand, Cale?"

"Yes, Papa." He paused and added, "My name's Cale. Just Cale."

"Good. Now go, quickly."

"Bye, Papa."

"Goodbye, Cale. I'll see you soon, I promise." Then, with a halting voice said to Sidonie, "Take care of him."

"I will."

She gripped Cale's hand tightly and led him out into the passage, and Cale looked back at the tense and hard face of his father, afraid he would never see him again.

Gusting winds and turbulence buffeted the *Kestrel*; the wing-jet dipped and bucked, shimmied sideways. They could see little more than dark gray. Thick storm clouds engulfed them. Sidonie turned to Cale. "Don't be afraid," she said.

Cale shook his head, regarding her with complete confidence. "I'm not."

But Sidonie seemed to be afraid. She turned back to the now nearly useless controls, pulled and twisted at the stick, and punched light panels with her fingers. The roiling clouds continued to rush past them, and she said quietly and tautly, "We're dropping too fast."

A break in the clouds opened to their right. Cale craned his neck around and glimpsed the towers of tall buildings in the distance behind them: a big city, glass and metal reflections like flames in the rising sun. Far, far away and getting farther every second. He thought they were trying to get to that city and all those bright buildings. He thought his father was going to be there soon. But not his mother, she was back at their home and he hadn't seen her in a long time and he didn't know when he would. The clouds enveloped them again and they continued to hurtle farther from the city.

Suddenly they were beneath the clouds, and the land below them appeared. Mountains stretched endlessly in all directions, broken by plains and valleys, large tracts of blue-green forests; a river snaked through a jagged shadowed canyon then widened and meandered through golden flat grasslands; far ahead and to the left sprawled a vast dark blue lake like a giant gas nebula. All of it coming up at them much too swiftly.

Sidonie struggled with the controls, hissing out words that Cale couldn't quite understand. The wing-jet passed over a peak of black rock and continued to drop. There was no place to land. They cleared another peak, this time with a far smaller margin, and a flat and barren mesa spread out below them, networked by gullies and ravines, pocked with dry and spindly scrub. Steep rocky slopes rose to one side, and the mesa dropped precipitously away on the others. Sidonie worked at the controls, and the *Kestrel* dropped toward the earth. "I'm going to try to land us here," she told Cale.

She twisted around and checked once more to confirm that Cale was securely strapped in, tugging at the harness clasps. "Hold on tight," she said, then returned her attention to the controls. Sand and rock in striated reds and yellows rose up to meet them, mercifully flat and even. Mere seconds before impact, the ground opened up and became a narrow and jagged ravine. The *Kestrel* bucked violently twice and then dropped into it. Sidonie cursed and pulled at the controls. Cale's stomach lurched as a pocket downdraft hammered the wing-jet to the earth and they were both thrown forward against their harnesses as the *Kestrel* tore along the bottom of the ravine. Cale cried out, metal squealed, objects crashed and shattered, the straps cut into his skin, something crushed away his breath, and his vision silvered. . . . The pilot's chair broke free and tumbled past him, Sidonie screamed, the fingers of one hand scraped Cale's face as he spastically reached out for her. Everything slammed to a halt, silver went dark, and he blacked out.

They came over the ragged rise, boots scraping rock and scrub as they shuffled their feet. They numbered seven—five bearded men and two women—and the sky above them was a bright pale blue with blossoming white clouds. The hot and gold sun beat down on them, baked the earth beneath them.

The lead man saw the wreckage, stumbled, then halted, holding up a hand. Charred and smoking metal lay scattered along the ravine, with the largest section wedged between a cracked boulder and an uprooted tree. He worked his way carefully down the unstable slope, and the others followed.

Cale watched them approach, standing shaky and nauseated and stunned amid shattered steelglass and crumpled flooring, no memory of getting out of his seat. Blood ran from two gashes in his forehead and he blinked at the men and women; he opened his mouth, but closed it again without making a sound. Sidonie was only semiconscious behind him. She was covered in blood streaked with viscous black fluids, and she moaned, eyelids fluttering like the wings of a dying insect.

The men carefully pulled him out of the wreckage, freeing him from a tangle of blue fabric bands that clung to his skin and clothes, and gave him into the care of the two women. Then they cut the fabric bands from Sidonie and dragged her carelessly across jagged metal, ignoring her cries as they scraped fresh wounds across her side and legs. They laid her out on the ground beside the torn and twisted wreck.

Discussion ensued over what to do with the wreckage. Cale listened intently, as if their decision was important. One of the men suggested they tie ropes to the main section of the wreckage and drag it back to the village. The others looked at him, spat, and laughed. Another suggested they torch it. The leader finally decided—they would shuttle back and forth over the coming weeks, routing by on their scavenging runs, and take whatever was useful back to the village a little bit at a time.

As Cale watched from between the two women, who held him in place, the men gathered around Sidonie. They dragged her down the scraggy ravine until they came to a flatter section of earth sparsely covered with grasses. For a minute or so they stood wordlessly over her, looking down at her motionless form, then they stripped off her clothes, tossing them into the dirt as if she would never have use for them again.

The men then lay atop Sidonie, humped and thrashed against her, one after another. One of the women dug her fingers deeper into Cale's shoulder, holding him back. At first Sidonie's semiconscious cries intensified, and her hands and arms flailed weakly, uselessly. But it wasn't long before she stopped moving; soon after that, a final wheezing gasp broke weakly from between her lips; then the only sounds were the grunts and coughing sounds made by the men.

When they were done, and the last had fastened his belt tight around his waist, the leader, who had gone first, kicked Sidonie in the side of the head. He found a large, flat stone nearby, and with the help of two of the others picked it up and carried it over toward Sidonie. They held it over her head and Cale cried out, some awful and wordless sound. The men looked at him, then casually released their grip and dropped the stone onto her face.

The five men turned and, without a glance back at Sidonie's body, made their way toward Cale and the women. Cale's harsh cry had subsided, but his mouth remained open. He felt paralyzed, unable to move his feet. The leader of the men smacked Cale's ear and barked something. The men climbed out of the ravine and the women followed, dragging Cale between them.

BOOK ONE

ONE

They came across the water at night. There was no moon, but the sky was cold and clear and the stars were bright slivers of shining ice. The strangers came in four boats, six to each, and they rowed as quietly as possible; oars dipped gently into the cold black water, pulled deep and through, then carefully rose and swung forward, water dripping invisibly, almost silently from the dull wide blades.

Shivering, the boy watched from the shelter of rocks. He wanted to warn them, but he was afraid of what Petros and the others would do to him. They had beaten him regularly over the years—because he had no father to do it, they said, no mother to scold him or slap his face. He worked hard for them, did whatever he was told, but it never seemed to be enough.

The boats were headed for the short, narrow strip of sandy beach. The boy crouched out on a spit of land that jutted into the lake, a clutter of rocks and driftwood and dead grasses. The boats would have to pass by on their approach to the beach. He could hear the creak of wood, the faintest splash of water, and he could see shards of starlight reflecting from metal and shining eyes.

The boy was tall for his age—thirteen or fourteen, no one knew for sure—and lanky. He crouched lower behind a large rock. The first boat slid past, so close he could have jumped into it. He counted the people—two rowing and facing backward, four staring fixedly forward—and looked for weapons, but the floor of the boat was too dark. It didn't matter. It wouldn't be enough for what they were about to encounter.

The second and third boats passed, then the fourth. So quiet. Tiny splashes and flashes in the black of the water. Their stealth was futile.

The first boat slowed as it neared the beach and the rowers pulled in their oars as wood hulls scraped against sand and gravel. Moments later the beach lit up with a burst of flames.

Petros and the others had ignited a string of fires just back from the water's edge, wood coated with oils and resins. Orange and scarlet flames roared and cracked and spit into the night sky like some great malevolent beast. Unable to stop in time, the second and third boats landed on the beach beside the first as a volley of flaming arrows shot between the fires, across the open sand and into the midst of the attackers. Some of the arrows missed their targets completely or deflected away and fell into the water with loud hissing, but others dug deeply into the wood or clattered still aflame inside the boats.

One arrow plunged into the back of an oarsman. He lurched forward in stupefied amazement, then jerked back with a harsh cry, the arrow tail lodging in the boat as he fell, the head driving up and through him until the shaft broke apart as he rolled onto his side and dropped from view.

The boy remained motionless on the point, huddled in a coarse blanket, watching, listening to the screams that tore the night. More arrows flew, now accompanied by shouts and burning spears and flaming, oil-filled glass vessels that burst on impact and spread thin sheets of blue and orange flames, engulfing the boats.

The fourth boat had managed to stop just before beaching, and now moved slowly in reverse, the rowers frantically and awkwardly shifting direction, pushing the oars instead of pulling, struggling against the resistance met by the flat stern. *Go,* the boy thought at them. *Go!*

The people in the first boats scrambled for weapons, for clubs and blades, long staffs and bolas, stumbling into each other, unbalanced, panicked and confused. Leaping and howling, Petros and the other men rushed through the gaps between the fires and attacked with spears and knives and cudgels. Blades bit deep into flesh; knotted wood cut the air and crushed bones. The beach became an inferno of smoke and screams and flames and blood, the bitter stench of burning flesh, and cries of victory; rising above it, strings of burning embers climbed toward the sky like the dying swarms of lantern bugs in the late summer nights. Sickened, the boy turned away.

But he watched the one boat that might still escape.

A small fire burned in it, but was quickly extinguished. When they were several boat lengths away from the beach, the oarsmen, now composed and synchronized, dug in on one side, turning the boat around, then began pulling desperately with the oars. Several more flaming arrows launched toward them, but only one made contact, and it bounced harmlessly off the side of the boat and into the water.

The boy's decision was almost unconscious. As the boat neared the spit of land, he stood upright, shrugged off the blanket, clambered onto the rock, and dove into the lake. The cold stunned him for a moment, and he slid through the water like a slowly sinking statue. He opened his eyes, but was as good as blind. For several long moments he did nothing, nearly accepting the bottom of the lake as his final destination. He had no will, no desire, no sense of loss. Then some spark of life returned and he recovered; he pulled with his arms and kicked with his legs, and swam awkwardly for the surface.

His boots filled with water. One at a time he kicked them from his feet. Finally he began to rise through the cold and dark. A driving ache in his chest, strange inner glistenings of silver in his vision. His arms and legs felt dead and useless, but he managed movement, upward progress until at last he broke the surface.

Water came with his first breath, choking him. For a moment he couldn't see the boat, and he was afraid it had already passed him by. Then he heard a splash, turned his head, and saw it no more than fifteen feet away; but it was moving quickly now. He swam toward a point ahead of it, and in ten strokes he was within reach.

The boy kicked hard, rising slightly out of the water, and

grabbed the side of the boat with one hand. The boat's momentum continued, dragging him through the water, straining his arm and shoulder. He pulled himself up enough to get a grip with the other hand and cried out. "Help me!"

The help he received was an oar cracked across his hands, then again across his skull. He fought the instinct to let go, his vision shifting slightly.

"Help me!" he cried again.

The oar came down hard on his left hand and he released its grip, but held on with his right. His face smashed against the wet dark wood, the fingers of his left hand scrabbled for purchase somewhere, anywhere.

"Wait!" a voice whispered forcefully from inside the boat. "He's just a boy!"

The boy couldn't see anything but darkness; he craned his head around, tried to look above him, saw something like moving shadows.

"I don't care what he is." A deep, scared voice of a man. "He's one of them and they're slaughtering us back there."

You would have slaughtered them first if you'd had the chance, the boy thought. "No," he choked out, "I'm not one of them."

The boat had slowed, and now there was almost no forward movement; it rocked slightly with the shifting of people and water.

"Pull him in or bash his skull," a third voice said. "I don't care. But do it quick, whatever you do. We have to get the hell out of here."

"Please," the boy cried desperately. "Take me with you."

"He's just a boy," the first voice repeated.

He didn't know which way it would go. His fingers were numb and started to slip.

Then the boy felt a large hand grip his forearm, and he was pulled up and out of the water, the boat tipping as he was dragged in over the side. He scrambled the rest of the way into the boat and sprawled face up in the bottom, his breath ragged. The cold bright stars in the sky and the face of a woman looked down at him. He began to shiver violently. The oars creaked and dipped into the water, pulling, and the boat slowly picked up speed.

No one spoke for a long time. The sounds of the slaughter receded until he heard nothing but harsh grunts, muttered curses, the steady splash of water. Still on the bottom of the boat, unable to move, he sensed they were safe.

"What's your name?" the woman asked.

His mind tried to work through the cold and the shivering. Petros and the others had given him a name, and they had called him other things; but he had always kept his own name deep inside his heart. Now it was there for him to take on again, and he brought it forth.

"Cale."

The woman nodded. "That's a good name." She laid a blanket over him, tucked it in tight. "A strong name."

He didn't feel strong. He felt very weak. But he was escaping, and he had his name back. The stars seemed even brighter now above him, shimmering in the black sky. Eyes of the night, someone had once told him. Cale closed his own eyes, and soon he was dreaming.

TWO

Rain had been falling for days and the village roads ran with rust-colored mud. Cale sat at the window of his room watching the downpour in the gray afternoon light; mud and water flowed and swirled through ruts and sinkholes, over river rock and crushed gravel, streaming toward the lower end of the village. He was grateful for the respite from work that the storms provided. It had been almost three years since the night he dove into the water and convinced the fleeing attackers to take him with them, and six months since he'd arrived at this village. He no longer suffered the beatings and abuse that Petros and the others had inflicted, but the villagers worked him hard, and until the rain had come he had been perpetually exhausted. Scraping, sanding, and painting boat hulls; cleaning crustaceans and shellfish by the hundreds; digging pits for new latrines; hauling rocks from the dry riverbed an hour away and then working them into the roadways. Blisters, scrapes, and cuts; sore muscles, aching spine, and burning eyes.

He looked across the road and up several huts, hoping to catch a glimpse of Aglaia. Pale yellow candlelight flickered in her bedroom window, then steadied. Shadows moved, and a dark shape filled the window for a moment, then she put her head out into the rain and looked at him. Before, he would have pulled back, but now he didn't move and they stared openly and frankly at one another. She was older than he was, but that no longer intimidated him. Her hair was long and dark, almost black; her eyes were large, and as dark as her hair. Cale thought she was beautiful. Although they had been watching each other for weeks, exchanging furtive glances, or more rarely the long mutual appraisals such as this, they had never spoken—the villagers kept him away from the older girls, the younger women.

A sound broke through the pouring rain, a kind of sucking and splashing. Cale turned to see a man straddling the back of an enormous four-legged animal, riding steadily up the muddy road and into the village. The man was clean-shaven and wore a wide-brimmed hat and a long, shiny black greatcoat that repelled the rain so intensely that it seemed to leap away from him. Several bulging leather satchels hung across the animal both behind and in front of the saddle. Surefooted despite the slick and uneven ground, the great beast marched with its maned head held high, as if proud of both itself and its rider. As the man rode past, he turned and looked at Cale, raised his hat in greeting—revealing a large, glistening shaved head—and rode on.

Aglaia was no longer in sight, the candle extinguished, the window dark and empty. Man and beast rode steadily through the village, then pulled up just before they reached the last of the dwellings. The man glanced to the left, turned the animal, and they disappeared between two huts. Cale remained at the window a long time, but the rider did not reappear.

Storms pounded them nonstop for three more days. No one mentioned the man until Cale asked. Marta, the woman who provided his room and meals, said only that the man's name was Blackburn and that he was staying with Dextram, the village headman. Marta's brother, a bitter and unhealthy man called Walker, whose hair periodically fell in patches from his scalp, scowled at her and said, "Not another damn word."

On the fourth day after the man arrived, the rain let up and there was regular work again. Cale spent the morning down at the lakeshore, cleaning, scraping, and sorting split blade-clam shells in a light drizzle. Faint vibrations in the ground beneath him. Regular beats. Cale looked up to see the man approaching atop the great maned beast. He still wore the wide-brimmed hat, the black greatcoat that reached his calves. The animal's massive, metal-shod hooves kicked up mud with each step, and its head shook and whipped the reins, which Blackburn held loosely in his hand.

He kicked loose a stirrup extension and dismounted; he seemed small next to the animal, the top of his hat only reaching midneck. He looped the reins around the branch of a dead, fire-scarred log and came forward. Cale rocked back on his haunches, bloody hands resting on his knees, and looked up at the man.

"Rough work," the man said.

Cale shrugged, rubbed his nose with the back of his hand. Now that the man was on foot and away from the huge animal, Cale could see that he was tall, though his build was obscured within the folds of the coat, and his skin was weathered. The man sat on a tree stump; water dripped from the brim of his hat. Cale thought he smelled tobacco smoke.

"You weren't here the last time I came through," the man said. "They tell me you've been here less than half a year." When Cale did not respond, the man said, "They tell me your name is Cale."

"What's *yours*?" Although he knew.

"Blackburn. *Is* your name Cale?"

Cale hesitated, then reluctantly nodded.

"What's your surname?" Blackburn asked.

Cale shook his head.

"Can't remember, or don't have one?" *Or won't tell me?* was the question unsaid but understood by both of them.

"Don't know," Cale said. The drizzle had washed away most of the blood, but he still felt a sting in the thin slices across his fingers and palms. Walker, Marta's brother, stood on the crest of a low dune back from the water's edge, wet stringy hair whipped by the wind; he stared at Cale with his permanent scowl. "I need to get back to work," Cale said.

Blackburn turned and looked at Walker. "It's all right. No one will object if you're talking to me."

"Until you're gone, maybe."

"No, not even then. Because they know I'll be back." He returned his attention to Cale. "I understand your people live on the other side of the lake. That you left them a few years ago."

"They weren't my people."

"No?"

"No." Cale stopped, but Blackburn gazed intently at him, waiting to hear an explanation. There was something about the man, the way he listened and watched, that invoked in Cale the desire to tell him anything he wanted to know. Cale fought against that urge, determined to reveal as little as possible.

"They found me," Cale said. "When I was young."

Blackburn smiled. "You're young now."

"Very young," Cale replied.

"Found you where?"

Cale shrugged. "Lost. Up on Glass Mesa."

"What were you doing up on Glass Mesa?"

"I don't know. I don't remember. I was hurt." He almost said he had been in a crash of some kind, but he managed to hold back.

Blackburn glanced at Cale's forehead. "I saw the scars. I assumed they were more recent."

"The only recent scars are on my back," Cale said without thinking.

"Do they beat you?" Blackburn asked. "Flog you?"

"No, not here." He wished he hadn't said anything. "Where I was before."

"Ahh, that's why you fled." Blackburn sighed heavily. "They may not beat you, but you aren't treated much better here."

Cale didn't reply. What could he say?

"You are little more than a slave."

Cale vaguely understood the word, though he wasn't sure why, or where he had heard it before.

"That's all you'll ever be if you stay," Blackburn added.

That was probably true, Cale thought. But he did not see that there was anything he could do about it. He leaned forward and reached into the sack of shells he had already scraped clean, then withdrew a handful. He sorted through them, checking for size and shape, tossing a few into the crate on his left, the others into the one on his right.

Blackburn got to his feet, shaking the water from his coat and hat. He looked out over the lake and up into the low gray clouds overhead, then returned to the large animal and unlooped the reins. He led the beast a few steps closer to Cale, who scrambled to his feet as the two approached; the animal towered over him and seemed to grow with each stride. Blackburn pulled up a few paces away, but even so, Cale could feel the steam from the animal's breath.

"Don't be afraid," Blackburn said. "She won't hurt you." He grinned. "Not unless I give her the command. Then she would tear you to pieces. She could stamp you to death, then rip out your throat just for pleasure."

"That's supposed to reassure me?"

Blackburn chuckled. "She's a wonderful animal. Have you ever seen a drayver before?"

Cale shook his head.

"Ever seen an Earth horse? A picture of one, I mean."

Again Cale shook his head.

"A drayver is larger and meaner, but it's about half horse. They used the genetic sequence of Earth horses and combined it with a wild animal that's native to this world, and this is what they ended up with. A magnificent creature. Mostly what you see here on Conrad's World are those small, scrawny creatures they call ponies, but they're really only half-assed horses. Failed experiments, I think, but far more numerous. Drayvers are twice their size, and a lot better adapted to this planet than the damn ponies." Cale knew what the ponies were—traders often rode them or used them to pull their wagons—but other than that he had no idea what Blackburn was talking about. Blackburn ran his hand firmly along the drayver's neck, tugging at its long coarse mane. The drayver bowed her head and nuzzled Blackburn's face, breath steaming; when she pulled back, his cheek was shiny with saliva, which he gently wiped away. "Her name is Morrigan," Blackburn said. "Come closer, she likes to meet new people."

Cale hesitated, then took a couple of steps. He was still frightened, but he did not want Blackburn to know. "Morrigan?" he said.

Blackburn nodded. "It's an old Earth name. Means something like 'Queen of the Demons.' Which she surely is when she gets angry. Rub her neck, she likes that."

Cale reached out tentatively; he had to stretch his arm to run his hand along her neck. The thick coat was softer than he had imagined, the muscle beneath it warm but firm, twitching at the contact. She lowered her head, nudged his brow, then nibbled at his hair. The drayver's breath was hot and moist and almost sweet, a strangely comforting smell.

Morrigan snorted and stamped her hoof, and Cale stepped back. He eyed the drayver, but when she made no other threatening movements, he turned back to Blackburn.

"What's the mystery about you?" Cale asked.

"What do you mean?"

"No one wants to talk about you. No one wants to tell me why you're here or how long. But I've seen people going into Dextram's house to see you." He hesitated. "They go, but . . . but they don't like you."

Blackburn smiled faintly. "No, they don't. They don't like me, but they would be extremely unhappy if I left right now, or if I never returned."

"Why?"

"I have things they want. Things they need."

"What things?" Cale asked.

But Blackburn just shook his head again. "You don't need to know about that. You'll have plenty of time in your life to discover the more depraved aspects of human character. No need to hurry it." He glanced at Walker, then turned back to Cale. "We'll talk again," he said.

Cale nodded, but said nothing. He watched Blackburn walk away then purposefully climb the dune and stop at Walker's side, Morrigan snorting and tossing her head. Blackburn leaned close to Walker, and his lips moved. Walker's left eye twitched, but he did not otherwise respond. Blackburn nodded once, then walked on, descended the far side of the dune, and disappeared. Walker remained atop the low dune for a few moments, glaring at Cale, then he, too, turned and walked away. Cale reached for another handful of shells.

Three nights later, just after supper, Blackburn stopped by the hut and asked Cale to accompany him to the village tavern. Cale declined, but Blackburn insisted, grinning at

Marta and Walker. "The boy needs to break loose once in a while," he said. Neither Marta nor Walker returned the smile or otherwise responded.

Outside, the air was crisp and clear and the stars shone bright and crystalline above them. Cale sealed up his coat and stuffed his fists into the pockets.

"A beautiful night," Blackburn said. "Autumn is firmly arrived, and winter approaches." He sighed. "It's going to be a terrible winter."

"How do you know?"

"I've seen the omens," Blackburn replied with a smile that quickly faded. "They bode ill. It will be terrible and cold, and violent storms will batter the land."

As they passed Aglaia's home, Cale glanced at her window, but it was dark, the cloth panels drawn. He realized he had not seen her since Blackburn's arrival.

"What do you do during the winter?" he asked. "Keep traveling?"

"As long as I can," Blackburn answered. "But when the worst storms arrive, no one should be unsheltered. I have several places to go. Depends on where I am and what sort of company I want for weeks on end."

At the far end of the village stood the tavern, a stone building with two massive hearths; smoke rose from both chimneys. Orange light flickered in the low windows. Cale had been inside only once, soon after he had come to this place; he had not been allowed in since.

"You're going to cause trouble for me," Cale said.

This time Blackburn did not respond to Cale's complaint except to open the tavern door and push him inside. Thick and heavy heat overwhelmed Cale for a moment, dizzying him. Blackburn steadied him, chuckling softly. Ten or twelve men and women sat at tables throughout the large room, most of them staring at the two newcomers. Quiet. The crackling of the two fires and someone coughing. The slide of a boot. The smell of wood smoke and tobacco and lantern oil and the faint aroma of malt and yeast. A tension in the air, the sense of anticipation. Someone began to talk to his companions, and people returned to their drinks and conversations, but the tension didn't break.

Blackburn led Cale to a corner table near the smaller fire. He gestured at Pig, the tavern owner, and held up two fingers. Pig squinted and scratched his elbow; he was a fat man with a round face, his skin spongy and mottled. He turned to a large barrel, drew two mugs of drink, and brought them over to the table. When Blackburn tried to pay, Pig refused to take either barter chits or coins.

"You know you drink free," Pig said with a frown.

"I'll pay for Cale."

Pig looked down at the floor, shook his head, and walked away.

Cale looked down at his drink. Steam rose from thick, russet foam. "What is it?"

"Oh, a kind of milk stout nog. You haven't been in here before?"

"Not to drink."

"You ever drink alcohol?"

"Just once." Four years earlier, Petros had forced him to drink glass after glass of wine the clan had made. They were celebrating something at night down on the lake shore, fires burning, everyone drunk, Tanya and Zarra pounding on drums and providing a beat for people to dance to. Petros made Cale drink until the faces and waving arms and leaping flames spun around him and then the others forced him to dance, pulling him in circles, holding him upright when he could not stand on his own. Only when he began vomiting did they let him go. Much later, Mosca, Petros's brother, came into his bed and tried to force himself on Cale. Fortunately Mosca was so drunk he could barely control his limbs and Cale had sobered enough to fight, scratching and biting at Mosca until the man fell back and Cale escaped into the night. The next day Mosca whipped Cale with a rope until his back ran with blood.

"Drink up," Blackburn said.

Cale sipped at the drink. It was warm and sweet and bitter all at once, bubbling tartly on his tongue, and then a different kind of warm as it ran down his throat and into his stomach. He drank again.

By the time they started on their second mugs, Cale felt light-headed, yet suffused with a numb comfort and sense of contentment. He watched the flames in the hearth, concentrated on the profound orange and crimson glow of the wood and embers beneath the grate.

"You don't talk much," Blackburn said.

Cale looked at him, but did not reply except to shrug.

"You don't say much, and you don't reveal much about yourself," Blackburn continued. "Sometimes that indicates depths of thought. A quiet but cautious and careful intelligence." Blackburn paused. "And sometimes it indicates stupidity." He cocked his head. "Which is it with you?"

Cale still did not respond. He drank deeply.

"I think I know," Blackburn said.

"You think you know a lot," Cale said.

"I know more than most people on this miserable world. I know more than the ignorant bastards in this godforsaken village. But I also recognize how little that is, how much more there is to know and to learn. Which is why I'm here on this backwater planet instead of on some more civilized world, or traveling among the stars."

"I don't understand."

"I'm still learning, especially about human beings, and this is a better place for it. For now. Less is hidden by the veneer of civilization."

Cale still did not completely understand, and he wasn't sure that what little he *did* understand made sense, but he let it go.

"I said once before that you were little more than a slave here," Blackburn reminded him. "And that it was all you would ever be if you stayed."

"I remember."

"You're better than that."

"How do you know?" Cale asked. "Maybe it's all I'm good for."

Blackburn shook his head. "Come away with me," he said.

Cale tipped his head to the side, and the motion dizzied him. "What do you mean?"

"I'm leaving in a couple of days. I'll take you with me."

"They won't let me go."

Blackburn nodded. "That's why you need to go with me. They probably wouldn't try to stop us, but we'll go at night. There's room on Morrigan."

It was tempting. But it was also frightening. Cale was not so much afraid of the villagers as he was of something in

Blackburn. He did not know what that was, but he knew he was afraid. He was also thinking about Aglaia.

"They offered to sell you to me," Blackburn added.

"But you want me for nothing."

Blackburn shook his head firmly. "I don't *want* you at all. I just want to help you."

Cale drank again, draining the mug. He welcomed the warm thrumming that coursed through his limbs, the heaviness. He wanted to lie down in front of the fire, close his eyes, bask in the heat. He wanted Aglaia beside him, wanted to be able to reach out and lay his hand upon hers.

"I guess maybe I'll just stay here," Cale eventually said.

Blackburn stared at Cale, his gaze unwavering, then finally nodded. "I see now that it's more difficult for you than I realized. But someday you will decide that you have no choice. That you have to get out of this place or die." Then he cocked his head, as though with some growing realization. "You don't understand why most people live out here, do you? Out here in primitive conditions, away from towns and cities. You don't realize that most of them have no choice, do you?" Cale shrugged, and Blackburn continued. "Yes, that explains much. I am here by choice. I can go back anytime I want. Most people out here can't."

"Go back where?" Cale asked.

"Across the Divide."

"The Divide," he said, not quite a question.

Blackburn nodded. "It's inaccurate, but that's what it's called. A divide is a high ridge of land, like a mountain range, a barrier between two areas. The Divide is a barrier, too, but it's just the opposite of a ridge—it's a vast, incredibly deep crevasse that splits this continent from one end to the other. A great crack in the earth. This part of the continent, west of the Divide, is a prison. The worst of the criminals in Morningstar and other parts of the Eastern Continent are exiled across the Divide. Murderers, rapists, men and women with multiple convictions for assault and other violent crimes. Political dissidents. Unrepentant troublemakers. Drug dealers who aren't executives in the pharmaceutical consortiums. The list goes on.

"They're sent across with almost nothing. Clothes and food and rudimentary tools. No advanced technology. No weapons. The airspace is rigorously monitored so no flights across can be made, and there's heavy security at the Divide bridges. The authorities are very thorough. Nonprisoners are allowed to cross to this side, go back and forth, though not many people want to. Traders, mostly."

"Like you."

"Like me. A market has been established over the years. A somewhat legitimate network, and an illegal one as well. Contraband is smuggled across the Divide. And there is a demand for trade goods that exist only here. There are plants that grow wild on this side of the continent, valuable minerals. Exotic foods, particularly aquatic."

Cale thought about all the shellfish he had opened and cleaned, and wondered what was special about it. Something, apparently—the cleansed shellfish were processed and sealed into tiny containers that were then shipped out with traders.

"Two bridges have been built across the Divide, and they are wonders indeed, as you will one day certainly see. The only way back to the east and out of this pesthole, to Morningstar or any of the other towns or settlements, is over the bridges. But to cross them, you must be tested."

"Tested how?"

"Genetic analysis. The authorities maintain the genetic records of everyone exiled to the west. First-generation descendants, as well as the exiles themselves, are all forbidden to cross. Second-generation descendants are permitted to return to 'civilization' if they wish." He stopped. "You don't know what genetic analysis is, do you?"

"No," Cale said.

"Well, I can't explain it to you. But they scrape some skin from you, take some hair and blood, and analyze it. They can tell if you're a convicted prisoner sent into the west, and they can tell if you're a descendant of a prisoner, and what generation."

"What if you're not descended at all from any exile?" Cale asked.

"Do you know that you're not?" he asked him in return.

Cale didn't answer except to shrug.

Blackburn smiled slyly. "You're not from this world at all, are you?"

Again, Cale didn't answer.

"Here's some advice for you," Blackburn said. "When you do eventually leave here, head east. When you reach the Divide, if you meet anyone nearby, ask them which way to the nearest bridge. If you don't find anyone, head south. Get to a bridge, and cross it."

"What will I find?" Cale asked.

"Better places than this, that's for damn sure." Blackburn looked down into his own empty mug. "Better places than this." He turned to Pig and gestured for two more drinks.

* * *

Two days later Cale stood beside a ruined boat he was dismantling for salvage, and watched Blackburn depart. Blackburn rode tall astride the drayver, the great beast holding its own head high and rigid as they passed between two lines of villagers watching them with envy and resentment. Cale expected Blackburn to look for him, but the man did not once turn his head. Blackburn and Morrigan just kept riding out of the north end of the village, then along the lake shore. Just past the last dock, Blackburn turned the drayver away from the water; they marched into the trees and were gone.

THREE

She waited for him at the edge of the lake. When Cale came over the rise and saw her shadowed form in the bright orange moonlight, surrounded by translucent strands of pale mist, his breath caught and he felt a fluttering deep inside his chest.

It was an hour past midnight and the air was cold, damp from the mists drifting in from the lake like the phantoms of long dead aquatic creatures. Burnished gold scales of light reflected from the lake's surface. Water lapped quietly on rocks and pebbles; the docks creaked with a melancholy regularity. Behind him, the village was silent, and dark except for the light in Crazy Mary's hut.

As Cale approached, Aglaia stepped toward him and

they both stopped when they were an arm's length apart. The moon was behind her and her face was in shadow, but her eyes shone in the darkness.

"So you understood," she said.

Of course, he wanted to say. If he hadn't understood her message, he wouldn't be here. But he remained silent and nodded once.

They walked along the shore for a time. He was careful not to touch her, but her presence was like a static charge in the air, and he smelled an aroma he could not identify or name, except that he knew it was *her*; he thought he could feel heat radiating from her skin.

They did not talk at first. He did not know what to say, and perhaps she didn't, either. Something splashed out on the lake, but when he turned to look, all he saw were quickly fading ripples. The moon glowed like the low flames of a fire, but it generated no warmth, and Cale shivered inside his jacket.

"Winter's coming," Aglaia said.

Cale nodded, wondering if she expected a response from him, but he still did not know what to say.

"I'd like to leave someday, like Blackburn," she said, turning to him. "Wouldn't you? I'd like to get out of this rotten place."

"Where would you go?"

"Morningstar," she replied.

Morningstar. Blackburn had mentioned it, too. The name sounded familiar, but he didn't think he had heard it from Petros or any of the others there. Not from anyone here, either.

"What's Morningstar?" he asked.

"A city. A real city with millions of people."

Millions. Cale could not conceive of how many people that truly was, and he could not imagine what a city with that many would be like. He had vague recollections of cities, from his infancy, but those memories were so fragmentary, and so actively suppressed, that they did not provide him with anything concrete. He doubted Aglaia had any real idea, either.

"Why don't you just go, then?" he asked her.

She shook her head. "It's not so easy to leave this place. I couldn't do it on my own. And I don't know where it is or how to get there. Blackburn's been there, though. I think he comes from there."

"How often does he come through here?"

"Twice a year."

"Have you thought about asking him to take you with him?" Thinking of Blackburn's offer three weeks earlier.

She made a sound that might have been a laugh, but there was something disconcerting about it. "I'd be afraid," she said. "Not to *ask* him. I'd be afraid he'd say yes and take me."

They stopped, and when he looked back he could not see any part of the village, not even Crazy Mary's light. The trees grew close to the water here, and he looked at the dark forms rising above them, listened to the hushed sounds of tiny animals within those shadowed woods. Did she want him to help her get away? Did she want him to leave and take her with him?

"Why would you be afraid of Blackburn?" he asked.

"Do you know what he brings?"

He shook his head. "No. Do you?"

"No. But it makes some people scary for a while. After

they see him, you have to stay away from them or they'll do things to you."

"What things?"

Aglaia shuddered and shook her head.

"What about one of the other traders that come through? Like that family that came through a few weeks ago with the knives and coffee and tobacco?"

"Most of them are scarier than Blackburn," she said. "And that family, did you see the two girls? They were sick and they had all those open sores and scars and I don't want to know what else was wrong with them." She sighed and gazed out over the water, and her face was half hidden in shadow. "Cale," she said.

"Yes?"

She turned back to him. "Kiss me."

Cale could not move, he could not speak. He felt his heart race, felt the thumping at his ribs and the throb of the pulse up his neck, rushing in his ears. She touched his hand with her cold fingers and leaned toward him. Her eyes remained open, watching him. Finally he moved forward and brought his lips softly against hers.

Lost and uncertain but strangely unafraid, he put his arms around her and pulled her to him, reveling in her warmth and smell and the moist heat of her mouth. He felt dizzy and short of breath and weak. They separated, cold air flowing between them, and she led him into the darkness of the trees.

Cale could see nothing but shadows and darkness, misting slices of moonlight, but Aglaia seemed to know where she was going, so he followed.

"Here," she said.

Faint moonlight filtered through the branches to illuminate a small, circular clearing with a cloth mat and blankets laid out on flat ground. Aglaia knelt on the edge of the mat and gently tugged at his hand. Cale knelt beside her and they kissed again, but now he was scared. Maybe not scared, but anxious. Afraid he would not know what to do. *Certain* he would not know what to do.

"Wait," he said. "I . . . I don't . . ."

"It's all right," she said. She brushed her fingers softly along his cheek. "Just lie here with me. Just hold me, Cale."

They lay together fully clothed under the blankets, hardly moving. He could not see her face, but he could smell her, could smell the damp and musky odor they both produced as they held each other, the odor trapped by the blankets. He could hardly believe he was here with her.

"We can take off our clothes," Aglaia said.

Cale did not move, he did not say a word.

"Cale?"

"Yes."

"Are you all right?"

He nodded. He helped her out of her jacket, then slowly, gently, he untucked her shirt and pulled it up along her body; she twisted and raised her arms so he could slide it up over her head. He laid it carefully on the mat beside them, then put his arms around her once more, running his hands along her warm smooth skin. His breath caught again, and he thought his heart stopped for a moment. Lost, wonderfully lost.

A cracking and a wavering light stopped him. "What?" she whispered. Bright light washed across his face, someone yelled; crash of footsteps, more shouting. Light danced crazily all around them. *Move!* Cale told himself, but he held Aglaia more tightly to him. The blankets pulled away, cold air rushing in. Aglaia cried out. More light, lanterns swinging in the darkness, shouts and cursing. Cale released her and tried to rise.

Someone grabbed Cale's arm and yanked him around and he sprawled onto his back, jerking at a grip that would not let him go. Shifting light and shadow and yelling figures all around him. Two more hands grabbed Cale's free arm and then he was being dragged off the mat, across the ground, then spun around and dragged over rocks and branches. He could not see faces. Lantern light flashed inches away, blinding him. "Cale!" Aglaia's voice.

He fought his way to his feet, stood upright for a moment, but they threw him down again. Where was she? What were they doing to her? "Cale!" He pulled and jerked his arms, twisted and kicked without success. He craned his head around, saw Aglaia huddled on her knees with the blankets wrapped around her and her father standing just behind her, both hands holding her firmly in place.

When he realized she was all right, when he realized what was happening, Cale ceased struggling. The men maintained their grip on his arms and he hung between them on his knees.

There were seven or eight men, including Aglaia's father, Dextram, and Walker. No women. Four lanterns on the ground burned steadily now, casting long shadows up into the trees. Aglaia stared at Cale with anguish in her eyes, in her trembling mouth. He saw hatred in the faces of the men around him, hatred cut through with fear and guilt.

The two men holding Cale pulled him up to his feet and

Walker approached with a cudgel in his hand. It occurred to Cale that they might kill him.

Walker jabbed the cudgel into Cale's chest; the cudgel was formed from a thick branch, the blunt end a knot that was twice the size of a man's fist. Walker leaned in close, his breath yeasty and foul. The sweat on his face glistened in the lantern light. He put his cracked lips against Cale's ear and whispered. "He's not going to help you now, that bastard. He can't do a damn thing, nothing this time. You think about that."

Walker stepped back, spat, then swung the cudgel against Cale's ribs. Cale cried out, twisting violently. The men released him and he dropped to the ground, holding his side. On one hand and knees he backed slowly away from Walker only to be blindsided, kicked in the head, jolting his vision. Then came Walker and the cudgel again, this time driven into his shoulder, collapsing him.

He curled up, pulled his arms in tight against his sides, tried to tuck his head down deep between his knees, his forehead pressed into the dirt. Another kick, something slammed across his back. A slight pause, then they all seemed to join in and soon the blows landed steadily and frequently—boots and cudgels and sticks and fists and rocks. Cale thought he heard Aglaia crying out, pleading with them to stop, but perhaps he just imagined it because that was what he wanted to hear.

The beating stopped. Cale realized that it had actually ended sometime earlier, but he had been so lost in a mental place of refuge, a trancelike state, that he had not noticed.

He did not move. He listened. Yes, they were still there. Labored breathing. Shuffling footsteps. A hacking cough.

Whispering in the trees above him. Aglaia weeping softly.

He hurt everywhere. He could not pinpoint particular areas of pain, and there was a strange numbness laid over it all, but there seemed no longer a distinction between his body and the steady driving ache that coursed through it.

Cale opened his eyes, but still did not move. He was afraid to move, afraid to raise his head. The light wavered about him, laced with shadow; dizzy, he felt he was slowly turning, and the light was rotating around him in the opposite direction. He closed his eyes; the spinning grew worse, and he opened them again. The world steadied—a fragile stability.

With a long, deep, and painful breath, Cale slowly raised his head, fighting against the threatening vertigo. His vision was slightly blurry, shifting in and out of focus. The men surrounded him, but back several paces now, faces almost empty of expression, eyes glazed and hardly seeing him. He raised his head farther, his vision clearing and holding steady, and he marked the lumined branches of the trees capped by dark shadow, tipped his head back until he was staring straight upward through the ring of spiked treetops, at the shining stars glittering brightly and peacefully in the night sky.

"Cale!" Aglaia cried.

He lowered his head and saw Walker stepping forward with the cudgel raised. For a moment he could not move, then Walker swung the cudgel at his face and in that instant Cale turned and ducked and the cudgel smashed into the back of his skull with an explosion of light, and he pitched forward to the earth.

* * *

When he came to, Cale wasn't sure he was alive. All he could see was diffuse dark gray and brown; and for a few moments he felt no pain.

He lay facedown in the clearing, the taste of dirt in his mouth. As soon as he turned his head, the pain returned, knifing up his neck and driving in and behind his eyes. Cale slowly rolled onto his back, the pain returning all through his body, and stared at the gray sky above him, the treetops swaying gently in a breeze he did not feel. Dawn or dusk? he wondered. Dawn, he hoped.

He sat up, then worked his way to his feet, feeling a sense of accomplishment when he stood. He looked and felt like one resurrected. Dried blood matted the hair on the back of his head, marked his face and hands like crusted birthmarks. He knew his skin was severely bruised under his clothing, and was glad he could not see it. A deep breath brought a sharp, intense pain to his ribs and tears to his eyes.

A few paces away, propped against a chunk of rotting log, was a rucksack. Cale looked at it, then turned away and staggered to the nearest tree. He unbuttoned his trousers and pissed onto the rough bark, fighting nausea and closing his eyes against the pain in his kidneys; he was afraid to look, certain he would see blood in the urine.

He returned to the rucksack and knelt beside it. Strapped to the bottom was an almost new, insulated bedroll; attached to the sides of the rucksack were four empty plastic water flasks. Cale looked through a few of the bulging outer pockets and discovered two firestarters, a ring of barter chits, a small pouch filled with coins, two knives, a hand-fishing kit. Next he inspected the contents of the two main compartments, searching carefully without unpacking them. There was a cooking kit, cold weather clothes including gloves and a cap, food, and a leather bag with his few personal belongings. There was more, packed well inside, but a complete inventory could wait.

Cale was surprised by their generosity. Or was it guilt?

He stood and turned, and through the trees he could see slivers of the lake, the water like floating pieces of chipped stone. He would be glad to leave the lake behind.

The sky was a little lighter now. Dawn, then. A faint breeze blew in under his coat; he shivered, then pulled the coat tight, sealing it. He remembered the warmth beneath the blankets and Aglaia's smell and the feel of her warm smooth skin under his fingers. Maybe this was better for both of them. He shook his head; it was something to tell himself. It might be better for him, eventually, but he wondered if she would ever be able to get away now, if she would ever get to Morningstar.

The rucksack was heavy, but the straps were padded and did not cut much into his tender shoulders. Cale limped out of the clearing and headed south, away from the village and the lake and the last twelve years of his life.

He could have taken the roadway and trail, but he did not want to chance meeting any of the villagers, as unlikely as that was, so he stayed in the dense woods and hiked on without rest. The sun rose, and wide shafts of golden light angled through the trees, lighting the way and providing a faint warmth. Cale was only vaguely aware of his surroundings; he walked in a trance of dull pain and numbed thoughts, his feet avoiding holes and loose rocks without conscious direction.

Near midmorning he came across a narrow stream of cold, clear water. Cale cleaned off the dried blood and dirt, cuts stinging; he drank deeply, then filled the water flasks. Although he felt no hunger, he ate some of the cheese that had been packed for him, and chewed painfully on a piece of dried fish. He sat beside the stream for some time, dizzy again. He watched the water flow past him, listened to it bubble over stones and roots, breathed in the warm aroma of tiny pale blue flowers that spread their petals to the sun. Then he shouldered the rucksack and continued on.

The sun was almost directly above him when he encountered a well-traveled path through the trees. He stood at the crossroads, fighting against the pain and weariness, looking along the path in both directions, trying to think. Deciding he was far enough from the village by now, he stepped onto the trail and followed it south. For a time the land rose, though not steeply, and the trees grew taller and farther apart. The air cooled, most of the sunlight blocked by the dense branches, but the woods were peaceful and quiet and the whisper of the breezes through the leaves high above him was comforting.

He crested the mountain and began to descend; the trail wound back and forth down the steeper southern slope. The trees became sparser and the sun warmed the hillside. A flock of loud, cawing terratorns flew by, casting dozens of moving shadows across his path. Unseen creatures scuttled beneath the undergrowth as he walked past, leaves and twigs shivering as they sped away from him. The warmth and the steady movement eased away some of the pain, soothed the ache in his muscles.

The trail emerged from the woods and intersected a wide dirt roadway heading east and west, heavily rutted by the wheels of carts and wagons. Here the roadway curved around the hillside on an outcropping of rock, and the view to the south was expansive, overwhelming in its breadth. Cale overlooked a mountainside that descended to meet lower hills in the distance, which in turn became flatlands that extended as far as he could see. To the east, the mountains continued and curved around to the south, bordering the eastern reaches of the plains; the mountains continued to the west as well, but ran parallel to the flatlands. He could not make out where either of them ended.

The sun hung low in the sky, coloring the narrow strips of cloud with magenta and bloodred. Cale saw no one on the roadway in either direction, and heard not even the faintest sounds of travelers. Blackburn had told him to go east. He looked again in that direction, where, according to Blackburn, the Divide lay, and presumably the city of Morningstar. *Better places than this,* Blackburn had said. He wondered.

He adjusted the pack on his shoulder, drank from one of the flasks, then turned to face the setting sun and headed into the west.

FOUR

He was several weeks in the mountains, gradually making his way west. The days grew cooler, the nights often freezing; mornings now he woke up to frost, or puddles completely iced over. But no matter how cold the nights were, the insulated bedroll kept him warm and dry.

The first snow found him atop a ridge of uneven black rock, looking out over mountains that stretched beyond the range of his sight. The flakes were light and cool and soft as they landed on his skin; they tasted fresh and dry, even as they melted on his tongue.

A shiver worked through him—not from the cold, but from a momentary touch of fear. *A terrible winter,* Blackburn had said. Cale turned to the south, but could no longer see the end of the mountains in that direction, either. He should have headed south to begin with, he thought, or maybe even east, as Blackburn had told him. Too late now. He slowly turned full circle, searching all directions. He had to get out of the mountains, and soon. For no reason that he could articulate, continuing to the west seemed his best option; the south had once been, but no longer.

That first snow did not stick, the skies cleared, and for the next three days there was bright sun and mild afternoons. More than that, it seemed that the highest mountains were now behind him, with the peaks gradually declining before him. Then another icy front blew through with dark roiling clouds, and a cold heavy snow fell, and kept falling for two days, laying a bed of hard and dirty ice upon the ground. Winter had finally arrived.

He came across another road, rutted and uneven and poorly traveled, and he followed it for several days as it wound through the mountains. Food grew scarcer, or more unrecognizable—he was reluctant to eat plants he had never seen before. Game, too, became more difficult to find, though he feasted one day from a pond well-populated with yellow, fat crawling creatures twice the size of his foot that were slow to move and easy to catch. He spent the following morning and afternoon smoking as much meat from them as he could carry, then moved on.

Two days later, in the cold early morning, he came upon a dead man hanging upside down from a tree beside the road. His shirt fell around his armpits and neck, exposing a belly crusted with thin ragged lines of dried blood, and his swollen arms and hands hung down so that the broken fingers nearly touched the ground. Black and brown stingflies crawled in and out of the man's blackened mouth and nostrils, and his eye sockets had been torn and gouged, though Cale could not determine whether that had been done by scavengers or by those who had killed him; either possibility seemed equally plausible.

An hour down the road, Cale passed another dead man hanging from a tree. Perhaps the two dead men were warnings; but for whom, and why? Travelers on the road, or those who might live around here? Perhaps both. Better to be safe, he decided. He left the road, and continued on through the dense, cold woods.

Snow fell for days without letup. Cale soon found himself struggling through drifts that reached his thighs and occasionally his waist. If there was a trail or roadway anywhere, it was impossible to locate. There was no sun, the sky an almost featureless gray and white above him, and he lost all sense of direction. Downhill was the only direction he followed now. If he could get out of the mountains, if he could reach the flatlands he had once been able to see, it might be warmer, there might be less snow or no snow at all. He thought often about Blackburn's warning about this winter—that it would be terrible, long, and cold, that to survive it he would need to find shelter to wait out the worst of it. He should have been prepared.

Time passed strangely, as though he had entered some alternate world where it stopped or became nonexistent. Sound, too, seemed to vanish except for the huff of his breath and the crunch and sliding of snow as he pushed through it. The trees became brown and white skeletons, paralyzed by ice.

Cale came across a shallow cave and camped inside for two days, drying out his clothes before a fire and trying to stay warm in his bedroll. His mind was numb with hunger. One morning, bundled in the bedroll and looking at the cold ashes of the fire, a clear and certain thought formed—*If I stay here, I'll die.*

He dressed in dry clothing, packed everything carefully, then left the cave and pressed on through the still falling snow.

The ground leveled and the sky brightened as he stepped between two trees and into a clearing. His heart sank when he saw he was on the floor of a narrow valley, mountains rising again on all sides.

The snow wasn't as deep here, barely above his knees, but that was little compensation for the despair he felt as he looked at the ascending slopes all along the valley. Then, far down the valley, a thin column of rising smoke caught his eye, its source a third of the way up the opposite hillside. From this distance he could not make out any details, but he thought he could see a dwelling of some sort sheltered by a rock overhang.

An hour later he stood directly below the dwelling, watching the smoke rise from a round metal chimney, curl around the overhang, then continue to rise until it merged with the clouds above. A steeply roofed cabin nestled against a rock cliff face that angled out from the slope, providing some shelter. The windows were shuttered. Off to the side was a small shack.

It took him nearly an hour to climb up the hillside through the snow. Darkness was falling. The flat shelf upon which the cabin rested was larger than he had first thought. Cale listened intently, but all he heard was the snapping of a branch, the hiss of snow sliding across stone, and a faint whistle of wind. The cabin was nicely sheltered, protected from the wind and the worst of the snow, a pocket of quiet and calm.

He stepped up to the cabin door and knocked. No response. He knocked harder and called out. "Hello! Anyone here?" When there was still no response, he tried the door, but it was barred or bolted. "I just need a place for the night," he said loudly. "I need some rest. I'll leave in the morning." Cale banged on the door one final time, then turned away and approached the shack.

The shack wasn't locked. Inside were gardening tools and shelves filled with boxes and two small wheeled carts; a damp, earthy odor. Wood was stacked several rows deep against the back wall. Cale shut the door. In the dry and quiet darkness, exhaustion overwhelmed him. He stood motionless, hardly thinking, went back outside to relieve himself, then returned and laid out his bedroll. He undressed, hung his clothes on the tools to dry, crawled into the bedroll, and dropped immediately into sleep.

When he woke, it was light outside, but the storm had worsened, and even here in the shelter of the overhang the wind whipped the snow in a frenzy of chaotic patterns, occasionally twisting upward so that the snow seemed to be returning to the clouds from which it had fallen. Cale stood in the doorway and watched the storm. The cabin was unchanged—windows shuttered, door secure, smoke rising from the chimney. Someone was inside, he was certain of that, but he couldn't do anything about it. He also couldn't do anything about the storm; he closed the door against it and retreated to the back, where it was slightly warmer. He wasn't going anywhere in this weather.

Later that day there came a pounding on the shack door, and a voice shouting above the storm. "Come on out!" A woman's voice, he thought.

Cale pushed open the door and looked out. A figure bundled in a heavy coat, head wrapped in scarves, stood a few paces away and pointed an object at him. Probably a weapon.

"You're hardly more than a kid," the woman said. She shook her head. "Pack up your things, then come on inside. But don't get too close to me or I'll burn a hole right through you."

Cale believed she wouldn't hesitate. He quickly gathered his belongings, then walked ahead of her to the cabin, opened the door, and stepped into the warmth of the interior.

Aside from a number of shelves filled with books, the cabin was surprisingly bare. One large chair, two smaller ones at a plain wood table, a sleeping mat in the corner. A large wood stove, atop of which steamed a kettle, a basin, a few basic cooking utensils. Oil lamps, two now lit with all the windows shuttered. A stack of wood. No decorations on the unpainted walls other than a single disturbing icon—the figure of a naked man nailed with arms spread to two crossed pieces of wood.

The woman removed her coat and scarves, then tucked the weapon into her belt. She was much older than he had expected, thin, with wrinkled, weathered skin. Hair short and coarse and almost completely white. Eyes that now looked kindly upon him.

"I'll make us some tea," she said.

She was an anchorite, she told him, and she had lived in the cabin for six years. It had been built long ago by an old man who had given it into her keeping when he decided it was time to go off and die.

She had no name. Or rather, she had given up her name when she had left civilization and come here to . . . well, what she came here to do was her own business, she told Cale. When he asked her if she had come from Morningstar, she said she had come *through* Morningstar, but would not elaborate.

"I've left all that behind," she told him.

"Why?"

She shook her head.

Three days after Cale arrived, the woman announced what they both had already silently accepted—that he could stay until the worst of the storms were over. That would be at least seven or eight weeks, she informed him. Possibly much longer.

If he stayed, she told him, he would have to agree to certain conditions, though they were not many. When she asked for silence, even if it was for an entire day, he would comply or leave. He would bring wood from the shack each day and help with the cooking and keeping the cabin clean.

He would not go naked in her presence. Anything else she might ask of him—and she did not expect there would be much—he would comply or leave. Did he agree? He agreed.

"The days will seem long," she said. "But reading helps pass the time, and it is edifying as well. You may read any of these books." She gestured at the bookshelves around the cabin. "The only books you may *not* read, the books you *will* not touch, are those in this case." She stepped to the small, three-shelf bookcase beside her chair, brushed her fingers lightly across the dark, worn spines. "These are sacred texts." She turned back to him. "But everything else is open to you."

"I can't read," Cale admitted.

The woman seemed surprised. "Not at all?"

Cale shook his head. "I think I could once, a little. A few words. When I was young."

"Can't write either, I suppose," she said with a sigh. "Not even your name?"

"No."

She sat in the chair and looked at him, shaking her head to herself. Then she got up and paced back and forth from one end of the cabin to the other, brows furrowed. Cale wondered what was distressing her. He couldn't read, but it didn't trouble him much, and it was not her problem.

"I can't do it," she finally said, looking at him.

"Do what?"

"Teach you to read."

"I didn't ask you to."

"But you *should* be able to read. You're an intelligent young man, I can see that. But I lack the patience to teach you."

"That's all right."

The anchorite shook her head. "No, it's not all right." She sighed again, then nodded slowly. "What I *will* do, though, is read to you," she said.

The storms drove through the mountains, one after another. The valley, narrow with steep slopes, was relatively sheltered, the cabin even more so, but still there were times when the wind shook the cabin and rattled the stove pipe and screeched through the tiniest gaps in the walls. There was nowhere to go, nothing to do.

She read to him, and new worlds opened up all around him. She read from books of stories, excerpts of novels and epic poems; from books of science and history and art; from philosophical inquiries into the nature of human beings, the reality of the universe, and the meaning of existence.

She recited poetry by Sartorian, Emily Dickinson, Anwar Munif, T. S. Eliot, and the Widows of Landsend.

She spent one evening singing the Hive Chants of Marker's Colony, swaying slightly with eyes closed and arms outspread as if in supplication. Cale felt mesmerized, though the words made no sense, jumbled together without logic, without meaning, yet flowing naturally from one to another with feeling and purpose.

History: "An Analysis of the Insurrection of Cygnus 7," by Bronso of Ox. *Angels of Expansion*, by Mia Motono. *Exiles*, author unknown.

Archaeology: Two slender books speculating on the nature of the Jaaprana aliens, who had apparently become extinct long before human beings had begun their expansion outward from Earth, and whose existence was evidenced only by scattered ruins on several worlds humans had themselves later colonized.

Science: *The Interrogatories of Samuel*, questions about the nature of physical reality answered by other questions. *Man, Machine, and the Sarakheen*, concerning the biomechanical advances made by the Sarakheen, human beings who turned themselves into cyborgs.

The old woman began to read from her sacred texts. She explained that they were the canonical texts and authoritative commentaries of most of the major religions, and some of the minor or obscure sects. Over the next several days she gave him an overview of the major religions, read texts from each, but although it had become clear to him that she had chosen this solitary existence for religious reasons, she never discussed her own beliefs, and Cale thought it would be rude to ask.

The religious books interested him less than the others she had read, however, and the woman appeared to sense that, because after a few days she abandoned her sacred texts and returned to the other books in the cabin.

She read aloud a book called *Invisible Worlds*, which at first appeared to be a kind of travel guide to other planets, filled with descriptions of exotic and wonderful places; but Cale gradually realized that few, if any, of the worlds described in the book could actually exist. This realization did not diminish his enjoyment of the book, nor dampen his desire to travel to those imaginary places.

One day she acted out the scenes from several dramas, moving about the cabin, gesturing, modulating her voice for each of the different characters. Another day she brought out several large volumes of art reproductions, and explained painting, sculpture, and other art forms to him as she leafed slowly through the books.

Philosophy. Natural sciences. Sociology, which the anchorite said she read more for amusement than insight, but which Cale found fascinating for the descriptions of large numbers of people living together in cities on different worlds.

Astronomy, cosmology, and physics, all of which were so far beyond his comprehension as to be nearly meaningless.

More novels and stories, which Cale relished most of all.

The anchorite read, and Cale listened.

The day he left, the sun was bright and the sky was clear, but the air was still cold with a crisp edge that tightened the skin on his face. The anchorite had presented him with several gifts the night before: a water-testing kit, which she insisted could save his life; packets of dried meat and fruit; a hand light; and a small Bible. "One day you will be able to read it," she had said. "Until then, it may provide some small measure of protection. For your soul."

Cale stood at the edge of the rock shelf and studied the snow, which still blanketed the earth, though now with a thinner layer. His rucksack was heavier than when he'd arrived, but seemed lighter. He was ready to leave, though he would miss the old woman and all those books.

He had learned much during his weeks with the anchorite. The biggest change was a new and growing awareness of the world . . . no, not just the world, but an entire universe that existed out there, somewhere, a universe filled with worlds and cities and people and technologies, beliefs and ways of thinking and views of life that he could not yet truly imagine. The woman's books had provided only glimpses of that universe, but they were enough to instill in him a yearning to explore it. But he wasn't sure he was ready for that yet. For there was also the fitful and incomplete awakening of the memories of his life before the crash, which produced more confusion than anything else.

"Where will you go now?" the woman asked.

Cale turned. She stood in the cabin doorway, watching him. He knew she was both glad and sorry to see him go. "I haven't thought about it, yet."

"Going west from here you come out of these mountains pretty quickly, not more than four or five days on foot in good weather. But what you get to is wasteland. A barren desert that seems to have no end, at least not one you can see. I don't know that anyone can survive out there for very long."

"So I've come about as far west as I can."

"Just about." She appeared concerned. "This is no place for you, Cale. If you want to live with decent people, go east. Cross the Divide. You don't have to go all the way to Morningstar, but at least get to the other side."

"I think I'll go west," he said. "I guess I want to see that endless wasteland first."

"Why, Cale?"

He shrugged. "It feels important, somehow."

"And after that?"

"Then I'll make my way east. To the Divide."

She walked toward him, and suddenly seemed ill at ease. "I will never see you again, Cale."

"I might come back."

"No . . . you won't." She reached out with her hands, took his between her warm and gnarled fingers. "Take care of yourself, Cale. It's a terrible world out there." For a moment he thought she would step forward to embrace him, but she didn't move, and he sensed her discomfort. He gently squeezed her hands.

"Goodbye," he said. "Thank you."

She withdrew her hands, then turned and walked back to the cabin. She stepped inside, and closed the door.

Time to go. Cale turned from the cabin and started down the slope.

FIVE

For several days on the lower slopes of the western foothills, Cale shadowed a caravan of families. Ponies half the size of Morrigan pulled wheeled carts and wagons while the men and women and older children walked beside the laboring beasts; a few elders and small children rode in the carts, wedged between crates and bundles and furniture and other belongings lashed securely to the vehicles. One old woman cloaked in heavy folds of black cloth rode in a chair mounted high atop a cart near the center of the caravan, like some ancient matriarch guiding the remnants of a once prominent clan. Cale counted thirteen vehicles, close to forty animals, and nearly seventy-five people—a small village on the move.

The narrow road was rutted and muddy, and the animals strained at their harnesses, breath steaming in the cool air as they struggled with their footing on the slick earth. Several times some of the men and women would have to join efforts with the animals, pushing at the carts to free them from deep ruts or heave them up and over a ridge or hump in the road. The old woman lurched from side to side, jolted up and down, but never seemed disturbed by the motion.

In the afternoon of the fourth day, Cale emerged from the trees on a rise above the caravan, and took in his first full view of the barren plains stretching westward. The anchorite's description had not completely prepared him for the utter desolation and vastness of the flatlands that now lay spread before him like the basin of a colorless universe, or one of the anchorite's several versions of Hell.

As he stood regarding that great expanse, however, he began to distinguish colors and features that had at first appeared to be nonexistent—pale rust-colored rocks; pockets of dry, spindly scrub; shallow and shadowed depressions that might once have been stream beds; striated sands of bleached reds and purples; far in the distance, a splotch of color that might have been a small butte; and farther still a crater of indeterminable size. But as the anchorite had said, no sign of hills or mountains as far as he could see—it seemed that this wasteland truly stretched into a strange, lost infinity.

Three days later, the caravan reached the edge of the flatlands, and in the early evening camped at the base of the foothills beside a spring. Cale remained in the brush on the slope above them and watched their fires burn in the night; the drifting smells of cooking food made his cheeks ache.

He chewed on a piece of dried meat and drank cold tea, and reflected on the anchorite's warning that no one could long survive in that wasteland.

In the morning, after an hour spent filling enormous containers from the spring, the caravan set out, headed almost directly west, following their own long shadows across the sands. With no place to hide on that open expanse, Cale knew he would have to reveal himself, or let them go. He hesitated, considering his options, then scrambled down the hillside. He stopped at the spring to refill his water bottles, then stood and watched the departing caravan with a sense of loss. He was certain the anchorite was right, and that out on that desert these people would find only their deaths.

He headed east. In the early summer he came upon a deserted town at the edge of a dry lake bed. Sixteen small dwellings built of stone and wood formed an irregular ring around a larger building near the center. Nothing moved, and the silence rose from the town like a warm, dense fog.

Cale squatted on a hillock, looking down on the ruined dwellings. Roofs sagged, broken shutters hung askew from their hinges, chimney rock lay scattered on the ground. He watched for a long time, until midday when the shadows nearly disappeared, then he clambered down the rocky slope and entered the empty town.

Heat shimmered up from the ground, reflected off the walls. Cale blinked the sweat from his eyes. No breeze stirred the air. He did not at first enter any of the dwellings, but circled several of them and searched the shadowed interiors through open doorways and windows. He coughed at the smell of rancid dust, a harsh grit he kicked up with each footstep.

Three of his water flasks were empty, but there was no sign of a well anywhere in the town. Although he had little hope of finding water inside any of the dwellings, he dug the hand light out of his rucksack, squeezed the beam on, and entered one of the small buildings.

There was only one room; the air was dry but heavy and stifling, as if there had been no circulation inside since the town had been abandoned. Bright motes of dust hung almost motionless in the light. Scraps of faded, curled paper hung on one wall, flanked by two chains of oxidized metal.

In the corner farthest from the doorway lay a human skeleton, the bones discolored by bits of dark and desiccated muscle or sinew. The hands and arms were folded across one another atop the figure's chest, as if the inhabitant had died peacefully, but its skull had been crushed in by a huge mallet that still lay nestled within the shattered bones.

Once outside, he breathed freely again. He looked into a few of the other buildings, saw pieces of broken furniture, scattered bones, two more nearly complete skeletons, and the smaller skeleton of a six-legged animal. He saw no signs of food or water, but even if he had he would not have dared to eat or drink.

Cale approached the larger central building and studied it. There were a number of large windows on either side of its length, and two open doorways at one end. Sunlight slanted in through two holes in the roof, irregular beams that illuminated rotting benches and a pedestal tipped onto its side. He set the rucksack on the ground, then stepped through the doorway.

The wooden floor was surprisingly firm beneath him, more solid than any of the other wood he had seen in this town. His footsteps were loud but did not echo as he expected. He righted the pedestal; set into the top surface was a wide metal bowl. When he looked up, the sun shone through a ragged hole in the roof and directly into his face. Cale moved on.

He worked his way among the rotting benches, stepping over broken candles, pieces of colored glass, a black leather shoe. For some reason he was reminded of pictures of church sanctuaries the anchorite had shown him. At the far end of the room, the floor stepped up twice and he stopped before a long stone structure that might have been an altar. A strip of rich, deeply colored fabric lay across the stone, dark purple and indigo patterns lined in bloodred, the ends weighted with brass cubes. He stared at the fabric, and gradually made out the image of a woman holding up clasped hands in prayer.

The high stone wall behind the altar was etched with strange, alien glyphs unlike anything he had ever seen. The anchorite had shown Cale several alphabets, including the odd letters she had said were Greek, Arabic, Hebrew, and Cyrillic, as well as the Asian ideographic systems, but nothing in any of her books had even vaguely resembled these figures. He was reminded of the tracks of terratorns, and patterned blades of grass. Standing before the wall, he felt a power in the glyphs, as though the words they formed, when spoken, could conjure up the dead.

When he finally turned away from the wall, he froze as he saw for the first time a large painting at the other end of the building, above the front doorway. The painting depicted a tall, massive armored figure emerging from the impenetrable darkness of a cave mouth surrounded by a star-filled night sky. Shining silver spines bristled from the arms and legs of the blue-black armor, gleaming in the starlight. Most of the head was obscured by the cave's shadows, but a strip of reflected light illuminated the lower half of the face—where there should have been a mouth there was only smooth pale skin. Cale glanced back at the wall of glyphs, then looked back at the painting, sensing some kind of invisible connection between the two.

He hiked out of the deserted town and onto the dry, gently sloping lake bed. Large splotches of tiny white crystals spread across the bottom of the dry lake like diseased skin; each step left a distinct footprint, but he saw no tracks other than his own. He passed small white bones and the bleached ruins of old boats. In the distance, storm clouds darkened the sky above the nearest foothills.

There was a small, shallow pool at the center of the lake bed, surrounded by a few clumps of reeds and several short, scraggly berry shrubs. Day-bats looked up at him from across the pool, green fleshy wings shivering; they hopped back fluttering from the water's edge, but did not take flight.

Cale knelt beside the pool and filled the water tester, then added the drops from the two small bottles. The water in the tester column remained clear. He filled his flasks, then drank deeply from the pool.

He considered staying the night by the pool, but when he looked up at the sky again, the storm clouds were nearer and he could see the slanted wall of dark rain descending from them. The clouds roiled with the winds, and a breeze picked up around the pool, bending the reeds. The day-bats squawked and rose with a frenzied flapping of wings and flew off toward the deserted town. Although he did not welcome the thought of spending the night in one of those buildings, Cale decided he had better go back.

By the time he reached the town, a colder gusting wind swirled dust and dirt up from the earth, and he could feel the storm at his back. He put the rucksack inside the large central building then went back outside to secure it as well as he could against the storm. He was able to cover many of the windows with cracked or broken shutters, but he could close up only one of the two doorways, and there was nothing he could do about the holes in the roof.

Minutes later the storm hit the town with a tremendous downpour and bursts of lightning and thunder. Cale cleared an area in the front corner of the building, on the side with the closed door and away from the two ceiling holes, and set up camp for the night. He assembled the stove and cooked up a stew with the last of the smoked meat from a lame buckbaby he had killed a few days earlier. While the stew simmered, he went to one of the open windows and watched the storm.

The sky had darkened further, but Cale could not tell if that was from a worsening of the storm, or night beginning to fall. When lightning flashed, the dwellings of the town seemed to momentarily come to life, lit somehow in those moments from within as well as from without, sharpening their shadows, which now seemed to move.

Watching the rain and the mud sluicing between the buildings, Cale was reminded of the day he had first seen Blackburn riding atop Morrigan through the downpour and into the village. He thought about Aglaia, and the way he had watched for her each day, hoping to catch her eye, not suspecting how badly that all would end.

A flash of lightning lit up a drenched and ragged figure stumbling among the dwellings. When the light faded, Cale could still make out the figure, though now as a dim shadow moving among other motionless shadows. The figure disappeared, either behind or into one of the dwellings, then reappeared running and splashing through mud, headed toward him.

Cale retreated into the corner, shut down the stove, then pulled the larger hunting knife from his rucksack and crouched behind one of the rotting benches. The figure staggered through the doorway and stood dripping and breathing heavily just inside the building. As he shook himself and stamped his boots, another flash of lightning illuminated his face, which glistened with moisture. Ropes of hair hung from beneath the man's hat, and a long thick moustache framed his open mouth and prominent jaw. He wore a knee-length slick plastic poncho that dripped water steadily onto the wood floor.

In darkness again, the man stood almost motionless, his head turning slowly from side to side. There was just enough light for Cale to make out his outline, his movements, his eyes. The man sniffed once, then twice more long and deep.

"Somebody's here," the man said. His voice was dry and cracked. "I smell food. Good eats, yeah?" Then he slowly lowered himself into a crouch not unlike Cale's.

A long wordless time passed, the rain producing the only sounds: splashing the mud, clattering on the roof tiles, and spraying through the holes in the roof and onto the floor.

"Not going to hurt no one," the man said. "Just need a dry place to sleep. Wouldn't mind some of that food, though. Haven't eaten too much for a while, yeah. Got no weapons, just my knife, that's all."

Another long silence passed. The man put his hands on the floor, then shifted from the crouch into a sitting position.

"Not going nowhere," he said. "Too damn wet and dark out there, and those other buildings are too damn spooky. Just take my chances in here." He removed his hat, hit it twice against the pedestal. "Not giving up my knife, either. I'm not stupid." Then he gazed slowly around the long room. "Maybe no one's here, maybe they cooked their food and ate and then left and I'm all alone." Cale thought he saw the man smile and shake his head. "Don't think so, though."

Either way, Cale thought, he wasn't going to get much sleep tonight. He got to his feet and he must have made a noise because the man turned toward him.

"Somebody there, yeah?" the man said.

"I am," Cale said.

"You going to kill me?"

"No."

"How many are you?"

"One," Cale replied. "But one's enough."

"Meant what I said," the man assured him. "Don't wanna hurt anyone. Don't wanna *be* hurt." He stood. "Could use some food, though, if you got any to spare."

"I guess I do," Cale told him.

The man's name was Sproul and he had not eaten in two days. He was grateful for the offer of food, but disappointed that Cale had no tobacco or "distilled spirits." They lit a couple of the broken candles for light, then pried the metal bowl out of the pedestal, set it on the floor, and built a fire in it for warmth. Sproul hung his poncho before the fire to dry, then pulled off his boots and socks and set them on one of the benches near the flames. Under the coat, he wore a long vest with bulging pockets and catches and loops too numerous to count; a canteen hung from a leather strap around his neck. "I can carry just about everything I need in this thing," he said, patting the full pockets.

But he had lost his bedroll in the mountains, he told Cale as they ate. Lost his bedroll and his animal traps and his pack with his pipe and tobacco and a metal flask of whiskey when he had slipped trying to cross a river. He had fallen in and nearly drowned in the rapids. If it had been winter he would have died, but he had managed to get out of the mountains, living on fruits and jawberries and the scraps of animal kills.

They broke and fed pieces of wood into the fire, and after a while they didn't talk anymore. Not trusting Sproul, Cale determined to stay awake through the night. But sitting before the warmth of the fire with his back against the wall and his knife in his hand, surrounded by the soothing sounds of rainfall, he soon fell asleep.

He was awakened by Sproul gently shaking his shoulder. Cale scrambled back, gripping his knife tightly.

"Hey," Sproul said. "Not going to hurt you. Just need your help is all."

"Help with what?"

"That." He nodded his head toward the far end of the room. A candle burned near the stone altar. A slice of faintly glowing blue light emerged from the stone. "Can't get the top slab off, yeah? Too damn heavy. Slid it a little, but about broke my back doing that."

Cale looked at Sproul, who shrugged and gave him a guilty smile. "You think I ended up in this place by accident?" He shrugged again. "We can be partners."

"Partners in what?"

"That," he said again, gesturing at the altar. "There's treasure in there."

"What kind of treasure?" Cale asked.

"Don't really know. That's what I'm trying to find out. But it's something a lot of people have thought was worth killing or dying over."

"Then I suppose you'll try to kill me after I help you."

Sproul shook his head. "No. Don't want to kill no one. Been enough death already." He paused, and his cheek twitched. "I lost my brother in that goddamn river along with everything else. Didn't say anything about him before because I thought you might think I killed him."

"And you didn't?"

"No. I *told* you. Never killed anyone, and don't plan to. Not for anything, not even for this crazy treasure."

Cale believed him. He didn't know why he should, but he did. He got to his feet and said, "All right, let's see about this treasure."

The storm had abated somewhat, but wind and rain still gusted in through the open windows and the holes in the roof. Cale followed Sproul to the altar and the flickering candle. The rich fabric tapestry that had covered the altar lay in a crumpled heap on the wooden floor. Sproul had moved the slab just enough to allow the blue light to leak out through a crack no wider than Cale's smallest finger.

"Strange, yeah?" Sproul said. "How something could glow like that. But it's not radioactive. I checked." He held up a black metal disk with tiny windows and pulsing green figures. "See?"

Cale didn't, but he wasn't going to let Sproul know his ignorance, so he just nodded. They took hold of the slab, gripping the lip that extended from the altar on all sides; Cale at one end, Sproul at the other. The stone was smooth and cold on top, warm and rough below. Cale bent his knees, adjusted his grip, then straightened his legs when Sproul said, "Now."

Muscles strained, pain knifed Cale's back, and a finger joint popped loudly. The slab came up, and more glowing blue light fanned out to the sides.

"Damn!" Sproul gasped out.

They shuffle-stepped to one side, then Sproul lost his grip and released the slab. As the long great stone dropped, Cale let go and leaped backward. The slab crashed to the floor, crushing and cracking the wood, but remained intact.

Lambent azure light seemed to flow up and over the sides of the altar like liquid, pouring down to the floor and rising slowly upward to the ceiling above them. Cale wondered if he was hallucinating, or if some distracting trickery was involved, a protective device at work inside the altar.

Sproul stood transfixed in the gleaming blue radiance, his eyes weirdly luminescent.

"Treasure," he whispered.

Then all the strangeness faded, and all that remained before them was a plain, faint glow of light. Cale looked into the open altar.

Blue faceted stones formed a nest for a large book bound

with a shiny coppery material. Sproul plunged his hands into the stones, then withdrew them, holding one large stone in each upturned palm. He grinned at Cale.

"What are they?" Cale asked.

"Don't know, but they must be rare, must be worth a fortune, all the people searching for them. Killing for them."

Killing, again. Cale wondered how many people had been killed in the search for this. He picked up the book, which was astonishingly heavy. He sat on the top step with it, near the candle, and held the book in his lap. The candlelight flickered across the covers so that the coppery material seemed to be in flux, transmuting before him. There were no markings, no letters or designs of any kind. Tentatively holding the corner between thumb and finger, he slowly raised the front cover.

The pages appeared to have been fabricated from incredibly thin sheets of metal rather than paper like the anchorite's books. The markings, which looked disturbingly like the incomprehensible glyphs on the wall behind him, were etched completely through the metal sheets, so that each leaf was like a stencil. He sliced his finger as he turned one of the pages, and blood dripped onto his pants, but he ignored the cut.

Sproul's shadow fell across the book. A rough, dirty hand held three large blue stones before Cale's face.

"Look at them," Sproul said. "More than enough for both of us. Our lives will never be the same."

When they left the next morning, Sproul carried all of the blue stones himself, distributed throughout the numerous pockets and pouches of his vest. Cale carried the book in his rucksack; the extra weight pulled at the shoulder straps.

They set out under clear skies. They would traverse the dry lake bed, replenish their water supplies at the pool, then head for the nearby foothills to the east. Sproul said he knew the best way to the Divide and the northern bridge. He wasn't sure how they would get the gems across, but he said he had some ideas.

As they left the town, Cale stopped and looked back at the central building. He felt as though someone, or something, was watching them. Observing and judging them, as if they had committed some foul deed. Cale thought that perhaps they had. *Desecration.* A word he had learned from the anchorite. He turned away from the building, and followed Sproul out across the dead dry lake.

SIX

Sproul coughed up blood, bright red spattering the dry and dusty earth. His hands shook and he was feverish. He drank deeply from his canteen, which seemed to provide little comfort. His curses were weak and hoarse.

They were five days out from the deserted town, camped in the shelter of a tilted stone slab. Crouched with his back against the cool stone, Cale surveyed the barren expanse before them, watching the waves of heat rise like visions of delirium. He looked back at Sproul, who knelt half in shade, half in the late morning sun, eyes nearly closed and dripping with sweat.

"You need to stay in the shade," Cale told him.

Sproul blinked several times, nodded halfheartedly, and

crawled back to lay beside the slab, dragging the canteen with him. "This damn heat," he said.

"Can I do anything for you?"

Sproul rolled his head slowly from side to side and closed his eyes without a word. Oozing sores had first appeared on his hands the second day out, and by the following morning had spread to his arms and legs, a few working their way up his neck. His skin became flushed and sensitive, and a painful fever coursed through him. Sproul refused to stop and rest, however, and they struggled through the morning until they reached the shelter of a dry riverbed, where they slept until sunset in the shade of a fallen tree partially buried in the crumbling bank.

Temporarily revived by sleep and the cool darkness, Sproul resumed a steady pace. For most of that night he had been lucid and seemed certain of the way, but before the first light of dawn had even appeared he became delirious and disoriented, staggering chaotically from one direction to another until Cale had spotted the large stone slab jutting up from the earth and guided Sproul to it. They had remained here since, Sproul becoming more and more ill, their water supply dwindling.

"Where do I go for water?" Cale asked. It was not the first time he had asked, but like the previous time, Sproul didn't reply. Sproul had said he knew where water was, knew the way east to the Divide, so Cale had followed. Now they were in the middle of a barren desert—not as vast and desolate as the wasteland the caravan had embarked upon, but hotter and drier, and at the moment promising to be just as deadly—with no signs of water, and nothing hopeful in sight. The shortest way, Sproul had said. The quickest.

Across this small strip of desert, north and east to the low hills barely visible on the horizon. It would save several days of travel, Sproul had said, and he knew where they could find water on the way if they needed it.

"Water," Cale said again.

"Not a problem," Sproul finally replied. "I know where it is." But he did not open his eyes, did not move, and said no more.

Cale squatted beside Sproul and regarded the fevered face, the trembling eyelids and cracked lips. Sproul was dying; he probably knew it as well as Cale did. They were both waiting for him to die.

Sproul opened his eyes, his gaze unfocused, or focused on something far beyond Cale. "I'm being punished for my brother," he said.

"You told me you didn't kill him."

"Might as well have. He didn't want to come here, he didn't want any treasure. He was happy with his zoological studies and his fossil collection, his quiet life. But I couldn't do it . . ." He stopped, shutting his eyes tightly against some spasm of pain. He gasped, coughed, then resumed. "I couldn't do it alone, so he came with me, and now he's dead."

"It's not your fault," Cale said. He wasn't sure that he believed that, but he wanted to comfort Sproul, ease his suffering.

He opened Sproul's canteen and reluctantly trickled what was left into the dying man's mouth. Sproul's lips quivered, and his dark and swollen tongue convulsed, made a choking, sucking noise.

Cale glanced at his water bottles, wondering how much, if any, of his own water he would spare for a man who would soon be dead. Two of the four bottles were empty, and a third was less than half full. He had no idea how many days it would take to find water; without Sproul's guidance, Cale did not know where to begin looking. Turning back to Sproul, Cale realized he wanted the man to die quickly. He understood why, but the thought still produced a terrible ache of guilt deep inside him.

The afternoon sun had worked its way around the large stone slab and now touched the top of Sproul's head, highlighting his hair with a golden sheen. Cale remained motionless, locked in place by an inertia born of despair, and watched the sun slowly, inevitably advance across Sproul's hair until at last it touched his feverish skin. Then Cale finally moved, took hold of Sproul's boots, and gently dragged him back into the shade.

"Where do I go for water?" Cale asked, barely able to keep from shouting it at him. Then in a whisper added, "Damn you, anyway." He wasn't sure why he bothered to ask. He had asked Sproul the same question four or five times over the last two days, and never got an answer.

He could not wait any longer, or he would die, too. Cale set out from their camp in search of water—a spring or pool, even a seep of some kind, anything at all. He traveled in a spiral, working his way outward, searching the ground, the faint shadows of stones and scrub, shallow depressions and draws.

Cale was surprised when, three hours later, he came

across a deep, circular pit, at the bottom of which lay a small pool of water. He stood at the rim of the pit, looking down on the water. He had not really expected to find any; he had expected to die a dry and painful death.

On hands and feet, he slid down the steep bank and crouched beside the pool. He didn't bother testing the water; he didn't want to know if it wasn't safe, for he had no choice. Cale lowered his face to the pool and drank. The water was tepid and slightly acrid, but he drank and drank until his belly felt bloated and nauseated. The pool was shallow, but maintained a constant level even as he filled the bottles and Sproul's canteen. He sat beside it for a few minutes, letting the water settle in his gut. No stomach pain, no cramping. Maybe it would only kill him slowly. And maybe it was perfectly safe. He secured the bottles and canteen, then climbed up out of the pit newly alive.

By the time he returned to their camp the western sky was a deep bloodred flowing into the darker violet-blue of approaching night, the stars mutely coming to life. Sproul's breathing was labored, yet strangely shallow, and his body radiated a rank odor. Cale spoke to him, but he didn't respond.

He splashed water over Sproul's face, and the dying man blinked his eyes and opened his mouth with a dry croak. Cale raised Sproul's head and dripped water into the open mouth, but he could not manage to swallow any of it; the water dribbled out the side of his mouth and ran through the caked dirt along his neck. After trying for some time without success, Cale lowered Sproul's head, then sat beside him to wait.

* * *

He dug the grave in the cool, predawn light. The stars above gleamed brightly in the dark blue sky, and he was reminded of the stars that shone down upon him as he lay cold and shivering in the boat the night he had escaped from Petros and the others. Such a long time ago.

By the time he finished, he was tired and sweaty. He tossed aside the rock he'd used, and stood. The grave was shallow, but he didn't have the strength or the tools to dig any deeper. Cale dragged the body to the grave and pulled it in face up; the limbs were just beginning to stiffen. He left all of the blue stones in Sproul's vest. He wanted to keep the book, but it seemed somehow dangerous. With some reluctance, he removed the book from his rucksack and laid it on Sproul's chest, then covered the body with dirt and rock.

Cale stood over the mounded earth, wondering if there was some ritual he should perform, words he should speak. Wondering if anything like that mattered, and if so, for whom. The dead or the living?

He looked up and out at the sun, which hung just above the foothills. East . . . head east. It had become like a chant, almost inescapable. East. Where else was there for him to go? Nowhere. He shouldered his rucksack, glanced one final time at Sproul's grave, then set forth into the rising sun.

SEVEN

The following days seemed like an interminable fugue state; Cale wondered if he had contracted Sproul's illness, and if he, too, would die.

Two days after he had buried Sproul, Cale completed the desert crossing and reached the low hills Sproul had been guiding them toward. He was nearly out of water and weak from hunger, but just before sunset he heard bubbling sounds, and followed them to a small creek that emerged from a tumble of rocks, flowed above ground for several dozen paces between clumps of grasses and low ferns, then disappeared into rock again. The water tested clean; drinking revived him somewhat, and he made camp for the night on the other side of the hill.

By the light of Ambrose, which was not quite full, Cale returned to the stream and waited in ambush. As he expected, animals came to drink, in ones and twos, taking turns as if on a schedule. Eventually a lone campobar—a slow and slow-witted animal half Cale's size, with mottled fur and heavy-lidded eyes—lumbered to the edge of the stream, settled its heavy haunches on the already crushed grasses, and lowered its head to the water. Cale sprang from the shadows with knife drawn, wrestled the dazed creature to the ground, and cut its throat.

Two mornings later, his rucksack filled with smoked meat, Cale set off over the dry hills. The heat here was just as great as out on the open desert, but as he continued he began to sense moisture in both the ground and the air, an impression confirmed by a gradual increase in the variety and abundance of plant life. Isolated clumps of grass became long strips and wide patches; spiny, skeletal brush gave way to succulents, and then to dense bushes dotted with green and violet berries. Near midday he came upon a dark, clear pool in a deep stone basin; an hour later he crossed a shallow stream running through a jagged ravine. Both times the water tested safe.

By late afternoon the moisture in the air had become a light ground mist or fog, and a peculiar haze had developed overhead, obscuring the sun and smearing its outline. He crested a low ridge and stopped, gazing out upon an extensive marsh stretching far in all directions, its boundaries lost in the denser fogs that shrouded it.

The marsh was beautiful but disturbing, and too much to take in all at once—stands of tall, drooping tree ferns unlike any he had ever seen before; pockets of meshed leaves and branches that floated atop the water, drifting with the fogs; islets of mud and grass and squat trees whose roots rose above the surface; aquatic creatures that revealed themselves with ripples or tiny splashes, the occasional flip of an appendage, the surfacing of a pair of translucent eyes; and the broken limbs of dead trees reaching up from the water as if in futile supplication.

Cale descended the other side of the ridge and approached the marsh. The haze and mists sucked the light out of the air so that the marsh appeared to be in a state of perpetual dusk. A sour, pungent odor of rotting vegetation wafted to him and the air was cool as well as damp. He knelt on a bed of blackened moss and unpacked the water tester. When he added the drops from the second tiny bottle, a deep red swirl appeared in the tube of marsh water—unsafe.

He headed north, keeping the water on his right; he didn't like the marsh, didn't like the chill it produced, but one way or another he had to get around it. An unsettling silence hung over the still waters; darkness fell earlier than he expected.

That night, seated before a fire he'd built for warmth both physical and psychological, he watched the silent ground lightning arcing out across the black waters in thin filaments of golden fire. A haunting cry from some invisible creature called throughout the night, each time from a different area of the marsh. He slept fitfully.

Late the next morning, the faint disk of the sun barely visible in the haze above the marsh, Cale spotted a boat far from shore, drifting between the islets and floating green mats, an open skiff manned by two figures. He stopped and watched them for some time, confused—they appeared to be drifting aimlessly with unseen currents, for Cale did not see either of them paddle or otherwise attempt to control the boat. He eventually called out to them, but there was no response. They drifted generally north and west, so he kept pace with them, walking slowly along the shore as they gradually came nearer. Twice more he beckoned, but they still did not respond.

The skiff disappeared for several minutes behind a densely thicketed isle. At first Cale thought they might have tied up, even disembarked, but eventually the boat reappeared; the bow swung around as it cleared the isle, caught in some current, and headed almost directly toward him. An older man and a boy not much younger than Cale sat stiffly upright in the skiff. As the boat neared, he saw why they had not responded—they were both at least several days dead. They were propped up and bound to poles mounted on the seats. Their clothes were torn and filthy, their exposed flesh slashed and punctured, but their eyes, which were kept open by slivers of wood, were hideously intact, and seemed to stare directly at Cale.

Another invisible current caught the boat and spun it slowly around, the two figures now mercifully facing away from him. The skiff drifted away from shore, now headed south and east. Cale shivered, then with legs shaky and weak turned and resumed his way north. He did not once look back.

After that, he stayed far from the shore, and didn't make any more fires at night, though he kept the marsh in sight as a landmark. Two days later, he finally reached the marsh's northern limits. The dark waters and swampy ground ended at a long stretch of uneven, rocky terrain, which in turn transitioned to a field of waist-high grasses bending and hissing in a gentle warm breeze. Cale walked into the field, savoring the warmth of the sun that eased away the marsh's chill. The grasses parted before him with each stride, then sprang back into place once he had passed.

For the first time in many days he felt at ease and content. In the middle of the field he unshouldered the rucksack, drank some water, then lay on his back, the grasses warm and soft. Bright blue sky above, edged with puffs of white cloud; comforting whisper of the grasses surrounding him; solid earth beneath. No hurry, he told himself. No hurry to get anywhere, no hurry to end this wonderful feeling. He closed his eyes, basking in the sun like a lazy desert creature, and dozed, mentally drifting, half awake and half asleep, and fully at peace.

East again, and wondering how far he had to go, how many more days, or weeks. Cale had a destination in mind—the Divide, or Morningstar—but it didn't feel any more real than the days when he had traveled in the mountains with no destination at all. Grasslands became rolling hills, then more grasslands, then another barren wasteland, an arid expanse of what might once have been some vast inland sea. He saw no way around it, so at dawn he set forth, bark-like layers of dried mud cracking and crumbling under his boots.

Sometime later, a distant figure moved out on the eastern horizon, a speck in the midday sun, moving from south to north. After two more hours of walking, the figure wasn't much larger, but Cale now changed his route—toward the southeast—hoping to avoid the distant traveler. Almost immediately, however, the figure changed course as well, as if to intercept him; again Cale altered direction, and again the traveler changed course. Accepting the inevitability of their meeting, Cale gave up and marched on, now with knife in hand.

Another two or three hours and the figure resolved into two—one man large and bent, pulling a kind of barrel on wheels; another man, thinner and wearing a straw hat, crouched inside the barrel. Just before sunset, Cale's shadow long and thin across the barren earth, he met the two men.

The man pulling the cart was an imbecile. He squatted in the harness and turned his expressionless face to Cale, his jaw slack and his watery eyes dull. His clothes were filthy rags, but his feet were shod with finely worked leather boots. The other man, barefoot and wearing only shorts, scrambled out of the barrel and waved gaily at Cale.

"Well met, fellow traveler." The man scuttled forward and shook Cale's free hand. "My name is Aliazar. And yours?"

"Cale." He carefully sheathed the knife at his waist, within easy reach.

Aliazar nodded in approval. "That is my brother, Harlock. You needn't say hello to him, for he doesn't speak." Then he leaned forward and whispered in Cale's ear. "He's an idiot, but I don't like to say that before him. He probably wouldn't understand, but he might, and I don't want to hurt his feelings. Life is difficult enough for him." Aliazar's breath was warm and foul. He straightened and pointed to a bleached, leafless tree a ways to the north. "We were going to make camp for the night there," he said. "Will you join us?"

* * *

The tree was dead, though still upright. Aliazar built a large fire against its trunk, and by the time darkness fell, the entire tree was ablaze, a flaming beacon in the night. They had to move back from the intense heat. Desert creatures appeared at the edge of the light, gazing at the burning tree as though worshipping their preternatural god. Harlock sat swaying before the fire, humming.

"Perhaps he will have a vision," Aliazar said. "He has them, sometimes."

"How do you know?"

"He tells them to me."

"You said he didn't talk."

"Only then. While he's in the middle of a vision he starts to speak and he tells me what he sees. You would be fortunate to hear him." Aliazar sighed and closed his eyes. "Sometimes I think he's seeing the future."

"Yes?"

"Mmm. He told me we would be meeting *you,* for instance."

"He did?" Cale wasn't sure if he should laugh, or be distressed.

"Well, I *think* so," Aliazar said. "Someone that might have been you." He vigorously scratched his scalp under the straw hat. "I've been waiting for some days now to encounter a solitary traveler. So I was not surprised to see you."

"What did he say about me?" Cale asked. "Or about this solitary traveler."

"Nothing, really. A king in disguise, he said. But I imagine that was some sort of riddle. Unless you *are* a king."

Cale smiled. "No."

They ate, Aliazar retrieving food and cooking utensils from the barrel, which appeared to contain an incredible assortment of goods. Harlock ate messily with his fingers from a bowl of stew that his brother gave him. When the meal was finished, Aliazar heated a pot of mulled wine and poured them each a cup, including one for Harlock, who gulped his wine, draining the cup in seconds, and held it out to be refilled. Aliazar obliged, grinning at Cale. "He likes to take a drink." After drinking the second cup as quickly as the first, and having his cup refilled once more, Harlock returned his attention to the blazing tree, sipping slowly now.

A few minutes passed, and Harlock stopped humming, though he continued to sway from side to side. He dropped his cup, then tilted his head back, eyes wide and rolling, and cried out, a long, loud, and mournful wail.

"Here he goes," said Aliazar. He watched his imbecile brother with rapt attention.

Harlock reached toward the flames, the wail continuing. Cale knew he had to be imagining it—an effect of the firelight, perhaps—but Harlock seemed to grow, his arms and hands lengthening, neck and head elongating as he stretched toward the heat and light. The imbecile's skin shone, taking on a glowing golden cast, and he trembled before the blazing tree, mouth open and tongue moving in and out as though searching desperately for water. Then he began to speak.

"Metal burns . . . metal burns . . . metal burns . . ." His voice trailed off, but he continued to repeat the same two words, now silently mouthing them.

Harlock lowered his arms, and his head came back down so that he gazed into the heart of the fire. His eyes were barely open now, and he appeared drugged or entranced or otherwise caught up into some other level of awareness.

Cale turned to Aliazar, but the man remained completely focused on his brother.

Harlock began to speak again, and though his voice was soft, the words were clear and distinct.

"A screaming comes across the black and starless night. Fades. Night? Always night, always day. Artificial light . . . artificial darkness . . . artificial life. A jewel around a star. Inside the jewel. . . .

"Silence. You enter, unmasked. The chamber has no end. Pale azure lights, the dense shadows of immense forms, massive instruments of . . . ? Energies to tear the universe, to break down the stars. Or . . . ? Resurrect the dead. Resurrect the living.

"I am at your side."

He stopped speaking. Frothy saliva dripped down his jaw. A hand rose, then fell again. He whimpered, coughed, and resumed.

"A great chariot awaits. You carry the stone with you. The key.

"The screaming again. The earth opens, eternal fires come forth. You ride within the chariot, lightnings trail in your wake.

"I am at your side. She is at your other side. She has no face.

"You carry the stone . . . you carry the stone.

"The jewel. We enter unmasked . . . I leave masked. You carry the stone and bring the great machines to life.

"You tear my head from my neck.

"You carry the stone."

The imbecile cried out, arched his back with arms thrown out to the side, then collapsed and huddled against the ground, eyes closed.

Aliazar turned to Cale. "He's finished."

When Cale woke the next morning, Aliazar and his brother were gone. Bewildered, he wondered briefly if he had imagined them. The tree was a blackened, skeletal ruin, gray smoke rising into the pale blue sky; wheel ruts in the dried mud curved away from the tree and headed north. He felt drugged, and guessed that Aliazar had put some narcotic in his wine. He sat before the smoldering tree, still disturbed by the imbecile's vision.

Cale wondered if anyone could truly see the future. It seemed unlikely. Glimpses, perhaps. A *possible* future, maybe. He could not believe that the future was completely predetermined. Some of the anchorite's religious writers seemed to believe in such a future, but just as many did not, so it appeared to be an open question. For himself, he did not see much purpose in pressing on with life if everything was predetermined.

Still, the imbecile's words, the intensity of his voice, were impossible to ignore. Cale would not forget those visions; he did not *want* to forget them. He felt they had some connection to this world, if not the future itself. He thought he could use them as guideposts or warnings. Something to keep him focused and cautious, and help him through all the unknowns that lay ahead.

He rose to his feet and surveyed the land around him. No one in sight, no signs of human life anywhere except a scattered cloud of dust far to the north, the wake of Aliazar and Harlock's passage. Alone again, but Cale was glad they were gone.

EIGHT

The village was laid out along the western bank of the river, about forty small dwellings that appeared to be well-constructed and well-maintained. Nearby were several large, cultivated plots striped or otherwise patterned with various shades of green and yellow. From his vantage point in the foothills, Cale watched distant figures moving about the village and plots. There was a safe, comfortable feel to the place, but he was wary—he would observe for at least two days, maybe three, before approaching.

Early in the afternoon, Cale nodded off in the heat, fragments of a dream trying to gain hold. A noise intruded, shattering the dream, and he jerked fully awake, scrambling to his feet while at the same time trying to identify the sound he'd heard. He froze, staring at a young woman who stood a few feet away with a weapon trained on him. The weapon looked like a tiny bow rigged to a hand-held apparatus with a small arrow poised to be fired from it.

The woman seemed to relax slightly. "You're younger than I thought," she said.

Cale didn't move, and he didn't say anything. He didn't think she was much older than he was. The woman lowered her weapon, and a hint of smile worked into her mouth.

"You've been up here all day," she said. "Alone. What are you looking for?"

"Just watching," Cale replied. "To see if it was safe."

She nodded as if what he said made perfect sense. "Not planning to attack us, then?" A bit more of a smile, now.

"No," Cale said.

"Good, then," she replied. "Let's eat."

From a pack she'd stashed partway down the hill, she produced a variety of foods, more than enough for both of them, and refused to let him share any of his. Her name was Lammia Sarko, and she was taking her turn as one of the village sentries. Although slightly shorter than Cale, she was strong and lean and he was certain she could overpower him even without her weapon. They ate, drank some diluted wine, and sat looking out on the village as the sun rose hot and bright above them. Lammia was talkative, and Cale was content to listen.

She explained to him that the village was a community of political dissidents. They had been sentenced across the Divide, not for criminal acts, though most of them had committed their share of civil disobedience, but for their political activities. Like most of those in the village, her parents were both Resurrectionists, and had been exiled here more than thirty years earlier. Lammia had been born here.

"What are Resurrectionists?" Cale asked.

"You don't know about them?"

Cale shook his head.

"The Resurrectionists are trying to unearth and restore the remains of an alien civilization that used to live here on Conrad's World, long before we arrived. Morningstar is actually built on top of the ruins. Some people think the first people here wiped out the aliens and destroyed their city, then built Morningstar over it to hide all traces of them, though my parents don't think that's very likely. The Resurrectionists just want to learn what the aliens were like, and maybe learn what happened to them."

Cale thought about the desert village and the wall of glyphs, and the book now buried with Sproul. "Why do you need to post sentries?" he asked.

"We work hard to make a decent life here. Most of the people on this side of the Divide don't give a damn about decent life, and would be happy to just take everything we've got, everything we've worked for."

"Then why are you telling me all this? Maybe *I'm* here to steal from you."

"I don't think so," she said. "I'm a fairly good judge of people. I think you're just looking for a place to live. I think you'd like a community of your own, a place to call home."

Maybe so, Cale thought, but it wasn't that simple. "I'm headed for the Divide," he told her.

"You can cross?" she asked.

"I think so."

She nodded wistfully. "I'd like to be able to go with you.

Morningstar's a terrible place in many ways, but this . . ." She gestured expansively at the village and the valley. "This is just existing. I'd like to join the Resurrectionists, like my parents. I'd like to bring my parents back, and we could all be with the Resurrectionists." She stopped and sighed. "But none of us will ever go back."

A distant, muted horn sounded. Lammia turned and looked to the north, brows furrowing. The horn sounded again. She turned back to Cale, studied his face, then shook her head. "Not you," she said. "You don't know what this is, do you?"

Confused, he had no response for her. The horn sounded a third time, and now they both looked in its direction. At the far end of the valley, a group of twenty or twenty-five riders on ponies emerged from the trees and bore down on the village.

"No . . ." Lammia moaned, drawing it out as she got to her feet. She ran down the slope toward the village.

The villagers out in the cultivated plots hurried back to the town, while those already there ducked into buildings to retrieve weapons, then gathered behind the barriers at the northern end of the village. Lammia was already halfway to the village by the time Cale started hesitantly down the slope after her.

The riders neared the village, shouting now, arms raised and holding weapons Cale had never seen before. Trailing them was a single rider on a much larger animal, the rider dressed in a greatcoat and wide-brimmed hat—Blackburn. He appeared to be more observer than participant, riding steadily toward the village but in no hurry.

Arrows flew toward the riders, and smaller bolts from

crossbows like the woman's. The riders responded with several bursts of small explosions and crackling sounds, accompanied by puffs of smoke and arcs of colored light not unlike the lightnings that had snapped across the surface of the marsh. A crossbow bolt pierced the neck of one of the riders and he pitched from his mount. A thump shook the air, followed by a much larger explosion and screams as a section of the village barrier burst apart and two bodies flew backward.

Six riders split off from the main group and skirted the village to the west, cutting down two of the villagers who were still on their way in from the fields. Then they swung around and approached the village from the south, where there were no defenders. They rode unimpeded into the village, and moments later two of the huts had burst into flames.

Cale reached the bottom of the slope, and could no longer make out what was happening. He saw flames rising from the village, black smoke and the blurred motion of ponies and riders and men and women running frantically; he heard shouts and popping explosions, more screams and loud cracks, pounding hoofbeats and whistling, and a terrible inhuman wailing sound that came from one of the riders' weapons. He stopped at the foot of the hill, afraid, gazing with stupefaction through the billowing smoke and swirling ash.

Off to the west, away from the fighting, Blackburn sat on the drayver and regarded the scene before him. Without thinking, Cale threw his rucksack to the ground and ran toward man and beast. He was barely aware of his surroundings. His attention was on the figure of Blackburn ahead of him, Blackburn atop Morrigan, Blackburn who now turned toward the person running at him, raised a weapon, and aimed.

Cale kept running without pause or hesitation, because he did not know what else to do. Blackburn must have recognized him, for he lowered the weapon and waited.

Breathing heavily, Cale staggered to a stop just a few paces away. The big man looked down at him and smiled. "It's you."

"Stop them!" Cale shouted, his voice hoarse and dry. "Stop them!"

"I can't."

"They're slaughtering them!" Wheezing, doubled over with pain in his side.

"There's nothing I can do."

Cale turned back toward the village and dropped to his knees. He did not want to see, but he could not avert his gaze. Most of the dwellings were now ablaze, and the smoke was thick and black. Streaks of red and golden fire lanced through the smoke, and a fountain of emerald sparks shot up out of the village, climbed in several directions at once, then showered down and faded. Much of the activity was so chaotic and obscured by smoke that he couldn't make out visual details, but the sounds were distinct and horrifying—the pounding of the ponies' hooves, so intense at times it seemed as though an entire herd of them, sixty or seventy or more, raced through the village; the screams of terror and pain from people and animals, tearing through the air; the crackling of burning wood, and the crashes of roofs and walls collapsing; and the popping explosions of gunfire. Then, slicing through the pervasive odor of charred wood, came the smell of burning flesh and blood.

As if to confirm this perception, one of the villagers staggered out of the smoke, his left arm hacked or blown off at the elbow, blood pumping from the ragged stump and splattering across the earth. The man stumbled, righted himself for a moment, took one more step, then pitched forward and lay still.

The fighting gradually wound down. The screams abated, the gunfire became sporadic, and the terrible wailing of the mysterious weapon subsided until it silenced altogether. The riders now moved deliberately through the smoke and burning buildings. Cale saw no signs of the villagers except for the obscured forms of bodies sprawled on the ground.

One of the attackers emerged from the village and rode toward Blackburn and Cale. When he reached them, he thrust his bearded chin toward Cale and spoke to Blackburn in a language completely unfamiliar to Cale. Blackburn replied in the same tongue, and the two men spoke back and forth. Eventually the man turned his pony and rode back to the village.

"It's over," Blackburn said. "They won't harm you."

Cale got to his feet and started toward the village.

"You don't need to see all that," Blackburn said. "Wait here, we'll make camp later."

Cale ignored him and walked on.

The stench was terrible; Cale could not identify all the acrid smells, nor did he want to know what they were. The first body he saw was the man who had staggered into view missing part of his arm. The blood pooled thick and dark beside the body, already aswarm with fat black flies. Farther on, the barely recognizable detached limb lay crushed and broken in a clump of blood-soaked grasses.

He wandered through the burning village like a lost and troubled amnesiac. The dead lay everywhere, a few partially inside buildings that still burned, the flesh blackening. Sound faded away, as if coming from a great distance, replaced by a ringing in his ears. Cale felt sick and weak, and his eyes stung from the smoke.

Most of the attackers were on foot now, looting the dead and those buildings that had not yet been set afire. They either ignored Cale or grinned at him, pointing and making gestures he could not interpret but which he felt certain were obscene. They all appeared somehow inhuman.

He found Lammia at the river's edge, face up with one arm and leg in the river; blood colored the water with dissipating swirls of red. Most of her chest had been blown open. Her dead wide eyes surprisingly held neither judgment nor condemnation. Cale knelt beside her and gently tried to close those eyes, but the lids would not stay shut—her eyes remained open in silent witness to all that had occurred.

After recovering his rucksack, Cale hiked upstream and made camp beside the river. The village continued to glow orange and red in the dark gray light of dusk, and occasionally new flames would come to life, springing up from the embers to consume some stray piece of wood. The attackers had set up their own camp on the outskirts of the wasted village, gathering around two large fires to eat and drink; their laughter carried across the night air, and Cale wished he had gone even farther upstream.

He sat before his own fire, numb and unable to eat, and wondered if he would be able to sleep. He wasn't sure he *wanted* to sleep, afraid of the nightmares certain to visit.

Blackburn appeared on foot after dark had completely

fallen, leading a saddled pony by a set of reins. "Can I join you?"

Cale didn't look up from the fire. "Seems to me you can do just about anything you want to do, except stop a massacre. Unless maybe you were actually directing it yourself."

"It had nothing to do with me," Blackburn said.

Cale looked at him, started to say something, then shut his mouth and shook his head.

"I'll go if you want me to," Blackburn said.

"I don't care."

Blackburn tied the reins to a bush just back from the fire, then sat across from Cale. "I'm surprised to see you still on this side of the Divide," he said. When Cale didn't reply, he went on. "The pony's for you. They lost a few men, and have a couple of extras. She's a good mount. You're not that far from the Divide now, but the first bridge is a long way to the south. With the pony, you can get there in a matter of days rather than weeks."

"You didn't even try to stop them," Cale said.

"How could I?" Blackburn replied. "One man against all of them. They would have killed me, too."

"I doubt that. They seemed to come to you for counsel."

"No. Arkon just wanted to know who you were, and what he should do with you. I told him you were a friend. I saved your life."

Cale stared at Blackburn, then slowly shook his head. "You're with them. If nothing else, you're with them."

"I'm just an observer. I told you that before. I'm out here trying to understand people, watching them, studying the full range of human behavior, even the extremes."

"Especially the extremes."

"It has nothing to do with me."

"That's *shit,*" Cale insisted. "You know that. And if you don't, if you really believe what you just said, then you're as inhuman as they are."

"You're young," Blackburn said, trying to control his anger. "When you're older, perhaps you will be wiser. Then you'll understand."

"I hope I don't gain that kind of wisdom."

Blackburn sighed heavily and nodded. "Then perhaps you will be wise enough to explain to me why I'm wrong." He got to his feet. "Stay here for a day or two, Cale. Don't follow us." He turned and walked back toward the smoldering village.

In the morning, Cale lay by the cold fire and listened to the sounds of the riders leaving. When the pounding of hooves faded away, he sat up in the gray light, listening to the murmur of the river, and gazed at the smoking ruins of the village. With the uneasy sensation of events strangely repeating themselves, he felt as if his encounter with Aliazar and Harlock *had* been a harbinger of this very similar morning.

The moving figures of the riders could be seen to the east, not too distant yet. Cale rode the pony back to the village, following the river until he saw the hoofprints in the mud marking where the riders had crossed—a wide, shallow stretch of water. He urged the pony forward, and they entered the river.

At midday the riders appeared to be nearer, and by midafternoon Cale was holding the pony back, afraid to get any closer. He could identify Blackburn, who stood out from the others because Morrigan was so much larger than the ponies. If they knew he was following, they gave no indication.

The land became uneven, pocked with burrow holes and covered by jagged pinnacles and cones of red stone. The riders entered this labyrinth of rock formations, and soon disappeared. Half an hour later, Cale followed them into the maze, moving slowly and cautiously, tracking the disturbed earth and catching an occasional glimpse of one of the riders ahead.

An hour or more passed, and he lost their trail as the ground became rocky. He moved even more deliberately, stopping often to listen; but the muted sounds of the riders echoed off the rocks so that gauging distance or direction was impossible. He was afraid they had seen him, afraid they were lying in ambush.

He entered a long, wide clearing that was empty and quiet. Across the way was a low ridge, and he could see pony tracks zigzagging up the slope. Cale crossed the clearing and dismounted, tying the pony's reins to a clump of thorny brush. He cautiously climbed the slope, dropped to his hands and knees, then came up slowly over the top of the ridge and stopped, awestruck.

Less than a hundred paces beyond the ridge, the land dropped away and the ground opened up as if some tremendous cataclysm had split the earth. Perhaps it had. The Divide was just what Blackburn had said it was—a great chasm—but far wider than Cale had ever been able to imagine, and from where he crouched no bottom could be seen. The walls were sheer rock spotted with clumps of vegetation and desiccated trees that grew at strange angles from the cliff face. Seeing it at last, he truly understood why Blackburn had said it was impossible to cross.

Only now did he notice the riders below him. They had dismounted, unsaddled the ponies, and now chased the animals away, driving them toward an open field to the north. Then the men gathered near the edge of the Divide and looked out across that yawning gulf, waiting. Blackburn and Morrigan were nowhere to be seen.

Nothing happened for fifteen, twenty minutes. Then a pod-shaped object rose into the air from behind a crag on the other side of the Divide, hovered for a few moments, then headed out across the chasm toward the waiting men. As the object approached, Cale could make out a kind of tail, and two angled blurs of motion atop the pod. A deep thrumming reached him, punctuated by rapid whistling sounds.

By the time the pod had crossed the Divide, Cale realized it was much larger than he had first thought. It landed on dangling runners, its side opened, and eight of the men climbed into the vehicle. It rose with a wailing not unlike the strange weapon the riders had used against the villagers, then headed back across the Divide.

Rock clattered behind him and Cale turned to see Blackburn riding Morrigan into the clearing. He tied Morrigan next to the pony, then climbed the slope to crouch beside Cale.

"You're stubborn, Cale. I told you not to follow us." He pulled Cale back down behind the crest. "If they see you . . ." Cale knocked his hand away, but did not stick his head back up above the ridge. "Forget you've seen this,"

Blackburn added. "Don't ever mention what you've seen, or you might just end up dead."

Cale stared hard at Blackburn. "You said the bridges were the only way across the Divide. That the Divide was patrolled so no one could fly across it."

"That's right. And what's happening out there right now *isn't* happening. You understand?"

Cale didn't reply. They sat crouched below the crest, silent and listening as the pod-shaped vehicle returned two more times. After the third trip, there was no sound of a return flight, and the day became uneasily quiet and still.

"That should take care of them," Blackburn eventually said.

"Why didn't you go with them?"

"I don't want to die."

"What do you mean?"

"Every one of them is dead right now, or soon will be."

"I don't understand," Cale said.

"And I'm not going to explain it to you. But you can take my word for it." He clambered down the slope. "Now it's time for us to head for the bridge, for the Northern Crossing." He stood beside Morrigan, looking up at Cale. "Let's go."

"I'll go alone," Cale said. He remained squatting on the ridge slope above Blackburn, arms resting on his knees.

Blackburn shook his head. "No, we're traveling together."

Cale remained motionless for a long time, but gradually realized he did not have a choice. Blackburn wasn't going to allow him one.

NINE

They rode south for six days, rarely speaking. The Divide was a constant presence on their left, usually in sight, and sensed even when not seen, as if it had its own special gravity that tugged and pulled at them. Cale still felt numbed by what had happened in the village, and disturbed by Blackburn's company; he rode on with his own thoughts, rarely saying a word to the man.

He caught his first glimpse of the bridge when they were still two days out from the crossing—a silvery, delicate network impossibly spanning the Divide. The western terminus was hidden, but he could see where the bridge met the far side, ending in a complex of variegated structures.

"Incredible, isn't it?" Blackburn said.

Two hours later, the bridge disappeared from view as a massive fog bank settled over the Divide, but that night, as they camped near the edge of the cliff, the fog dissipated and revealed crimson lights delineating the bridge's path across the abyss like some mysterious constellation of shimmering red stars. Despite his distress and his pessimism, Cale felt a surge of something like hope; the bridge and the lights seemed to hold a promise—the promise of better things to come.

Rain fell all morning. When they reached the outskirts of the settlement clustered around the bridge, the ground was muddy, and the gray light and dense drizzle cast a pall over the people and buildings. The huts and shacks were far more numerous here than anyplace Cale had ever seen on this world, but they were just as primitive, and the inhabitants looking out into the rain from doorways and windows appeared to be no better off than those he had encountered over the years.

"You won't be permitted to take the pony across," Blackburn said. "But I know where you can sell her."

"What about Morrigan?"

"I'm authorized to go anywhere with her." He confidently patted one of the saddle bags. "I've got the permit."

"And for that weapon you've got hidden away?"

Blackburn grinned and shook his head. "No one can get that kind of permit. And I don't have that weapon anymore."

Blackburn led the way to a sparsely patronized market area, the few customers slogging desultorily among the booths and storefronts. Blackburn and Cale rode to the far corner where two women kept a corral that held a decrepit pony, a pair of longhaired zebra goats, a tannagar wallowing in the mud, and a covey of bedraggled summerhens. Blackburn did the negotiating, and when they left, Cale rode behind him atop Morrigan, his rucksack heavier with a small bag of coins.

They attracted much attention as they headed for the official crossing complex—men and women called out offers to buy or sell as they passed, or invited them into houses or taverns. Blackburn ignored them all except for several child beggars who huddled together against the rain and silently held out plastic cups; he stopped, dropped a handful of coins into the cups, then pressed his knees into Morrigan's flanks and they rode on.

They emerged from the buildings and entered a wide strip of barren land that formed a buffer between the settlement and the fenced perimeter of the security complex, which was built near the edge of the Divide. Once they'd crossed the strip, Blackburn halted the drayver, who stamped her feet impatiently in the mud. On the other side of the fencing were several buildings constructed of metal, glass, and stone. For Cale they brought back pieces of childhood memories—fragmented images of buildings and vehicles and cities that carried with them a painful sense of loss. Rising out from the center of the complex was the bridge, still magnificent though dull and gray in the misting rain.

"If nothing else," Blackburn said, "you'll get a hot shower and your clothes washed. You don't pass, maybe you can buy back the pony." He turned around in the saddle and looked at Cale with narrowed eyes. "But you're going to pass, aren't you? I don't believe you have one solitary doubt."

Cale didn't reply. Blackburn nodded once, turned, and urged the drayver toward the first gate.

Blackburn seemed to be on friendly terms with most of the security personnel, so the searches and processing were perfunctory. Morrigan was led away, the saddlebags and Cale's rucksack were searched and scanned, then Blackburn and Cale were escorted into the first building and a room manned by five security officers. Several monitor panels glowed behind the low counter, and Cale became disoriented as more pieces of memory were resurrected—strapped into a couch, a woman beside him, screens such as this displaying text and images in the walls surrounding them; the same woman laughing, holding him on her lap as she squeezed a ball and changed pictures on a table screen. What was her name? San . . . Sind . . . ? No, something else.

Blackburn explained to the security officers that this was Cale's first time through, that he was an orphan, no idea who his parents were, but that there was a strong possibility he was second generation, or even further removed. The officers had obviously heard such stories before, but with Blackburn they seemed more willing to go along. The tests would make the final determination anyway, the senior officer commented. Even Blackburn, who had his permits and certifications, had to be retested.

They were separated, and Cale was led down a stark corridor to a series of rooms. He did everything he was asked. He stripped, and his clothes and rucksack were taken from him. Next came a burning shower with hot water and sprays of foaming soap, a thorough rinsing, then a second shower. Still naked, he was taken to a small cubicle where a man dressed all in silver scraped some skin from his ear canal, plucked several hairs from his head and several more from his crotch, then finally drew a narrow vial of blood from his arm. He had no idea what any of this was for, but he submitted without a word. After that, his freshly washed clothing and rucksack were returned to him; he dressed and was led to a windowless room furnished only with a chair and cot, and told he would have several hours to wait.

As he lay on the cot, he struggled with the resurfacing memories, images and feelings he had worked for so long to suppress, but which he could no longer keep locked away. What good were the memories? A life long gone, never to be regained. The memories brought only pain and loss, sharp reminders that he had been abandoned here by his father, his family. He did not know what had happened, or why, but that one feeling remained. And his father's last command, to never reveal the family name. Alexandros. What meaning did that name have here?

He had come from another world, he knew that, from a city perhaps like Morningstar; he had flown through deep space with his father and the woman who cared for him and taught him. *Sidonie.* Yes, that was her name. *Sidonie.* His father had sent him off with Sidonie, who had piloted a flying craft that had crashed. More images surfaced—men dragging Sidonie's body from the wreckage of the crash. Intentionally or not, his father had sent her to her death, and had abandoned him here to people like Petros and Mosca and Walker and Blackburn. Lying on the cot, he asked himself again: what good were any of those damned memories?

Cale slept fitfully. Dreams and memories broke apart and merged with one another, harsh and distressing. He felt relief when he was eventually awakened by a man gently shaking his arm.

"You're authorized to cross," the man said, handing him several plasticized documents.

Outside, darkness had fallen and the rain still fell, a heavy drizzle that produced a hissing sound. Blackburn waited for him with Morrigan. "Not a doubt," he said to Cale with a smile.

They mounted the drayver and rode through a gate, then set forth upon the bridge. The bridge was wide enough for five or six people to walk side-by-side, steep at first as it curved upward and across the dark chasm, but they were alone. The crimson lights were regularly spaced on both sides, glowing clusters of artificial lanterns mounted on metal posts. The surface was a hard gray material that absorbed Morrigan's steps with only dull, muted thumps, and despite the steepness and rain provided the great beast with enough traction so that her hooves never slipped.

"Three miles across," Blackburn said. "One of the narrowest points of the Divide. An engineering and construction marvel." As they rode on, he talked about materials and construction methods, deflector fields and wind harmonics, all of which meant nothing to Cale. Even if he could have understood it, he didn't care. It was beautiful, but it was just a bridge; more important was that it was a way across the Divide, a way to a new and better life.

Near the midpoint, they encountered two travelers headed west, an older man and woman pulling a wagon loaded with goods hidden and protected by a large tarp. The old woman grinned at them.

"Mister Blackburn," she said. "It's been a long time."

"Hello, Rosalie. Hello, Jack."

The old man sighed heavily. "Unfortunate," he said.

"What is?" Blackburn asked.

"That you are still alive."

Rosalie chuckled and patted Jack's arm with her gnarled fingers. "Don't mind Jack," she told Blackburn. "He holds grudges forever." Then, still grinning, she pointed a finger at Blackburn. "You'll get yours, you bastard. And you'll rot in hell with the rest of us." She chuckled again. The two of them hoisted the wagon handles and moved on.

As they descended the far slope of the bridge, the town surrounding the terminus became visible, artificial lights marking the streets and buildings, some flashing in bright colors through the rain. And yet, there was a seedy, rundown feel to the place that only increased as they rode nearer, caused not by the steady rain but by some other pervasive quality that seemed to emanate from the buildings, from the streets, from the shadowy figures Cale could now make out moving through the wet night.

As though reading his thoughts, Blackburn pulled Morrigan to a halt just before they reached the end of the bridge and the security gates.

"Civilization," he said, then snorted. "The town of Karadum. They've got power, heat, running water and sewers and working toilets, motor vehicles and computers, and who knows what else, but I have to tell you, Cale, Karadum is no better than what we've just come from. Not surprising, when you think about it. Morningstar is one thing. But what kind of people want to make their lives here, trading with the criminals banished to the other side of the Divide?

People like Jack and Rosalie, two poisoned and poisonous human beings."

"People like you?" Cale said.

Blackburn tensed briefly, then slowly relaxed. "Very clever, young Cale. Very clever." He said no more, and urged Morrigan forward.

Security passed them through after closely inspecting their documents. Most of the soldiers here, too, knew Blackburn, but they were not as friendly with him as those on the other side had been. Cale wondered why, but he was not going to ask.

They rode through one final gate, crossed another buffer zone, and entered the town. They were greeted by taverns and inns and other commercial establishments—Cale wasn't certain what they all were, since he couldn't read the signs. People hurried through the rain, crossing the streets, moving in and out of buildings. The roadways were paved, but the surface was cracked, broken by irregular holes filled with water and mud. A four-wheeled, motorized vehicle bounced past them, engine growling.

"Thanks," Cale said. "You can let me off here. I'll be fine on my own, now."

Blackburn shook his head. "You don't understand this place. It's not safe for someone like you, especially at night. You're . . ." He smiled, shaking his head. "You're an innocent. You'll be robbed and beaten, and count yourself lucky to be alive in the morning. At least for tonight, stick with me. I know a safe place to stay. Tomorrow, I'll help you make arrangements to get to Morningstar, assuming that's where you want to go. I'll help you get out of here, anyway."

Cale went along for now, afraid of what Blackburn might do if defied. One thing he was sure of, though—Blackburn was wrong about him. He had lost his innocence a long time ago.

They rode away from the bright colored lights, through streets that grew increasingly dark and quiet, and the rain fell harder. Then they entered another commercial area, the colored lights returning, but more subdued, flickering softly in windows and doorways. Blackburn pulled up in front of a small, two-story building with firelight warming its paned windows, and they dismounted. A young woman came out, greeted them, then took Morrigan's reins and led her around the corner of the building and toward the back.

"They'll take good care of her," Blackburn said. "They always do."

"What about your bags, all of your things? *My* bag?"

"They'll be in our rooms, untouched. Even here in Karadum there are people and places that can be trusted, and this is one of them."

Inside was warm and dry. Blackburn paid for two rooms, then took Cale into the tavern—ten tables, most of which were occupied. It was quiet, voices low and indistinct. Blackburn ordered the food, and they ate in silence, a meal of soup, bread, and thick slices of meat soaked in a heavy, bitter sauce. Afterward they went up the stairs to their rooms. With amusement, Blackburn showed Cale how the key and lock worked, and the light switch, then remained in the open doorway, watching him.

The room was small, furnished with a bed and nothing else. Cale's rucksack was on the floor at the foot of the bed. A window looked out onto the street below.

"Morningstar," Blackburn said. "Is that where you want to go?"

Cale shrugged, then said, "Yes." Better to give him an answer, he thought.

"In the morning we'll have breakfast, and then I'll help you make arrangements. I know some people who can take care of it."

"All right." He took hold of the door and stood looking at Blackburn until the big man nodded once and stepped back into the hall. "Thanks," Cale added, then closed the door, and locked it.

He turned off the light, then went to the window and opened it, letting in the cool fresh air of night and the steady clatter of rain on the streets and rooftops. Two people ran stumbling across the street, laughing and bumping into each other as they tried to avoid the deeper water-filled holes. But once on the other side, they became silent, and walked carefully to a shadowed doorway. One of them opened the door, allowing smoky light to spill out into the street, and they hurried inside, shutting the door quietly but firmly behind them.

He stood at the window for a long time and watched, studying the life of the streets below. People, wagons, carts, ponies, and a few motorized vehicles made their way through the rain; the smell of fish cooked over a fire, the aroma of burning incense very much like what the anchorite had used, and the dank odor of rotting garbage all rose to him from below. The rain let up, but never completely ceased.

He lay in the dark for an hour or more, listening to the sounds drifting in through the open window, then got up from the bed, put on his coat and poncho, picked up his rucksack, and left the room. He stood motionless in the dimly lit hall, afraid Blackburn would appear; when he didn't, Cale moved quietly down the hall and descended the stairs. The clerk asked for his room key. Cale gave it to him, then stepped out into the humid night.

It was still dark when he reached the outskirts of the town. Here there were no longer clearly marked streets, just well-worn pathways meandering among sparse and dilapidated dwellings that smelled of hopelessness and decay. He picked up his pace, marching through the mud and rain, and soon left even those ruins behind.

He had come all this way on foot—or at least most of the way; a few days on the pony hardly counted—and he saw no reason to stop now. He didn't need a pony, he didn't need Blackburn's "arrangements." It might take weeks, or months—he had no idea how far it was—but that didn't matter. There was no hurry. He would walk to Morningstar.

It was night the first time Cale saw the city. For more than an hour a distant glow had been visible in the sky, flickering slightly like some immense fire. When he eventually crested a rise, Morningstar came into full view before him and the glow blossomed, dazzling him with lights that seemed more numerous than the stars above. Crimson lights like those on the bridge across the Divide, but dozens of them moving in and out of darkness and other lights; green and blue lights flashing rhythmically to some unheard beat; stationary lights of gold pulsed in matching patterns; and thousands upon thousands of silver squares, shimmering lights that seemed to hang weightless above the ground, marking the tall, massive buildings at the heart of the city.

Excitement and wonder lifted his heart. Atop the rise he was exposed to a bitter wind, but he hardly noticed it. He was five weeks from Karadum, five weeks from the Divide, but it felt like five years and another world separated him from those places and those times. Smiling to himself for the first time in many, many days, Cale headed toward the city.

BOOK TWO

ONE

The moon came up off the slick surface of the canal in deep gold slices, reminding him of the night he'd met Aglaia at the lake shore. Cale stood on deck with both hands on the stern rail, watching the reflections flip and turn and slide in the boat's wake. They'd just come into the Grand Canal from the river, and when he lifted his gaze he could see the river's wide flowing current in the moonlight, slowly receding from them as they headed into Morningstar.

Terrel joined him at the stern and leaned against the rail. "You worried about something?" he asked.

Cale shook his head, keeping his eyes on the water and the city reflections that now joined the moon's in a sparkling kaleidoscope of colors. Then he looked up to see the now familiar lamps and signs and lighted windows lining the canal. He'd been in Morningstar for more than a year, but he still felt a sense of wonderment upon seeing the lights of the city at night. Near the river it was mostly residential, single homes with private docks, patrolled by security drones, shield-shimmers faintly visible in the darkness. As they neared the heart of the city, commercial establishments began to appear, restaurants and retail shops, and the homes gave way to apartment buildings and day roomers. Message streamers floated in the air, multicolored ribbons of neon text and images drifting from one street to the next, a few even gliding out over the canal before transmuting into different messages and reversing course.

A small motorized skiff, less than a third the size of the *Skyute* and manned by a solitary figure, slid past them on the left, headed out toward the river, breaking up the wake and shattering the patterned reflections. Cale watched the skiff recede from them, then turned to Terrel.

"You've seemed nervous all day about something," he said.

Terrel lowered his voice so that Cale could barely hear him. "I have something special going after we make our regular deliveries. Need your help—if you're willing."

Cale closed his eyes. Terrel's last "something special" got them beaten and robbed and pissed on before they managed to crawl through a window of the Serpent Club and get out onto the street. This time it almost certainly involved the layer of thermoplast crates hidden under the false floor of the cargo hold. He had no idea what was in them. But Terrel had done too much for him—gave him work, found a room for him, taught him how to make his way in this city, as much as Feegan had—so Cale couldn't refuse him. He opened his eyes and nodded in resignation.

Terrel grinned and wrapped an arm around Cale's shoulders. "Knew you would," he said. "I'm going to go check on Mikki, make sure she doesn't run us aground." He released Cale and started forward, then stopped and turned back. "Mikki says you were asking about the Resurrectionists."

Cale shrugged and nodded. "Someone's got to know how to find them."

Terrel shook his head. "You don't *want* to find them. They're crazy people, and you're crazy looking for them. Sometimes I don't understand you at all." Then he grinned again and said, "Well, I guess we all have our own kind of crazy." He turned and hurried forward, ducking into the tiny pilothouse.

As they pulled into Delany Wharf, the canal swarmed with boats of all sizes, the water illuminated by white and yellow running lights, the docks by silver-blue halo lamps, and the streets by long chains of red and green dragon-lanterns. Dock workers waited for them at Pier 18, and Mikki maneuvered the *Skyute* into the slip, reversed the engines, and cut back on the throttle, narrowly missing a water taxi and a mosquito boat. Cale and Terrel threw ropes onto the dock and the stevies quickly tied up the boat.

Mikki, Cale, and the three other crew members began unloading the star-labeled crates and bundles from the hold—boxes of cold-packed fish, fruits, and tubers from towns along the river; baskets of dried seed pods collected and transported on foot by recluses who lived deep in the jungle far upstream above a series of impassable cataracts; long garlands of shiny brown and orange riverweed especially prized by the Leungtchi communities in the southern districts of Morningstar; and carefully packed glass vessels of rare and highly desirable live mollusks some mad woman who lived in a hut by the sea always managed to supply Terrel.

A cargo jit waited at the end of the dock, its long wide bed now empty. The stevies set up a loading track between the deck and dock, started the motor, and the track began moving as Mikki swung the first crate onto it. As the packages reached the other end of the track, the stevies began carefully stacking them on the jit. Terrel jumped onto the dock and shook hands with his broker Manca, then the two of them huddled a few paces away. Terrel had a contract with the man—so many crates of fish, so many beds of riverweed, and so on—but the cargo hold was now filled with far more than the contract quantities, and he wanted to sell as much of the excess to Manca as he could; the prices would be better here than at most of the docks farther in.

A woman pedaling a cart-bike pulled up beside the *Skyute* and offered cold bottles of Monkeypaw beer for sale. Terrel broke off his conversation for a moment and bought beer for the crew and all the stevies, as well as one each for himself and Manca. The crew took a break long enough to pop open the bottles and take a long drink or two, then returned to work.

As he helped unload the cargo, Cale watched the negotiations and wondered if they were discussing the hidden cargo. Manca shook his head more than nodded, but Terrel kept at it, gesturing with his hands and laughing. Finally they reached agreement, shook hands, then walked over to the bursar's terminal, where they completed the transaction, the two of them punching codes and instructions into terminal panels. Part of the payment was apparently in cash, and Cale saw Manca pass a thick packet of currency to Terrel.

By the time Terrel had finished up and returned to the boat, all of the star-labeled cargo was packed onto the jit bed. Terrel pointed out the extra crates and packages that Manca was taking—the excess riverweed and live mollusks, as Cale had expected, as well as some of the fish and other foods—and helped them load it into the jit. The stevies broke down the loading track, swung it back into and under the dock, and untied the *Skyute.* Terrel waved to Manca, who was snapping instructions to the jit driver; Manca waved halfheartedly without pausing. Mikki started the engines, and they eased away from the docks.

Not long afterward they approached Belladonna Canal, which opened up to a clear and striking view of The Island. Ablaze with lights, the towering skyscrapers of The Island rose into the night sky like beacons of the world. Terrel maintained the *Skyute*'s speed as they passed the Belladonna's big commercial docks, and Cale looked at him.

"I won't deal with them anymore," Terrel said, answering Cale's unspoken question.

"You won't deal with them, or they won't deal with *you* anymore?" Cale asked.

Terrel grinned and shrugged. "Ah, it amounts to the same thing."

Cale nodded. "That's what I thought."

* * *

They left the Grand Canal and motored along Gibson Channel, a smaller waterway that was still bright and noisy, though it was nearing midnight. Cale recognized the lights of Cutter's Station, a small but busy commercial wharf that supplied a lot of smaller shops and restaurants and cafés in the Basilisk District. Cale lived just a few blocks away, and he thought he could see a corner window of Junko's building, where he rented a room. Mikki slowed the boat and angled in toward the main dock, which was crowded with people; a woman stood in the lamplight waving at Terrel, gesturing at a gap between boats.

"She'll take the rest," Terrel said. "Everything we've got left."

Not everything, Cale thought.

They tied up and went to work. There was no loading track here, and no stevies, so they did everything themselves, hauling the cargo across the gangway and loading it onto stationary pallets at the woman's direction. Terrel and the woman went into the pilothouse, and when they reemerged a few minutes later, Terrel's eyes were wide and bright, the pupils dilated so that he blinked spasmodically when he looked at the dock lights.

After offloading the last of the packed fish and leaving the cargo hold apparently empty, Terrel paid off Mikki and the others in cash, then went belowdecks once they'd disembarked. When he emerged ten minutes later, he was wearing his stasi boots and handed another pair to Cale; now Cale knew there would be trouble. The boots were calf-length and armor-plated, with a charged lava knife tucked into each, camouflaged but easily accessible.

"Don't worry," Terrel said. "I just want to be prepared. We motor in, make a nice, quick and quiet delivery, then leave. In and out in less than an hour. Ice." He patted Cale's shoulder, then helped untie the boat before he retreated into the pilothouse to guide the boat away from Cutter's Station.

By now it was well after midnight, and the *Skyute* motored slowly and almost silently along a dark narrow canal in the far western reaches of Morningstar. The moon had set, leaving behind an added shade of darkness. Cale had never been in this part of the city before, and everything about it was unfamiliar. Pale lights hung in loops from tall, flexible rods that dipped and swung about in some intermittent breeze or other mysterious force, radiating dark aquamarine hues that seemed somehow different from other lights in Morningstar. Buildings were low and sparse, most surrounded by dense vegetation, and from what little Cale could see of them appeared to have been designed and built by people from some other world, some other era—the walls and corners were all sharp, jagged edges of metal and glass webbed by sparkling sheets of wire mesh. Pained animal growls floated across the water, and the air felt and smelled heavy with the odor of smoke from distant or unseen fires.

Cale stood silently beside Terrel as he guided the *Skyute* into a channel so tight that there would be barely enough room to turn the boat around. On both sides, the banks were dark, with only an occasional lamp or sheltered fire casting faint illumination and shadows, just enough to hint at shanties and hulks of abandoned machinery, rotting personal docks and half-sunken boats; wavering lights flickered behind smoky windows. The air was still and quiet.

Ahead of them a stone quay had been built into the left bank. Two cool white lanterns burned at the end of the deserted quay. Cale turned to ask Terrel if that was their destination, but seeing the man's intense concentration, he remained silent. Terrel had one hand on the throttle, the other on the wheel, grip tense, muscles standing out on his forearms.

Terrel shifted the engines to idle, and the *Skyute* drifted slowly toward the quay. His skin was tight and shiny with sweat.

"Where is he?" Terrel whispered with clenched teeth. He glanced up at the ship's clock, nervously kicking one boot against the wheel housing.

Cale searched the shadows along the bank, but detected no figures, no signs of movement. The Island's lights in the distance seemed incredibly far away, hovering above solid blocks of darkness, so the buildings appeared to literally float in the sky.

"Shit," Terrel said. "Got to get out of here." He put the engines into reverse, increased the throttle, and began to turn the wheel.

The loud buzzing whine of motors exploded behind them, bursting in all directions as brilliant spotlights flooded the *Skyute* with painfully bright illumination. Cale spun around to see half a dozen small jetboats zigzagging around them, two or three crouching figures in each; the boats then slowed as they formed a ring around the bigger boat.

Terrel had already cut the throttle, idling the boat once again, but kept his hands on the wheel and throttle as he glanced anxiously in all directions, taking in the boats and lights that had so quickly appeared.

"Fucking pirates," he said, voice harsh and pissed. "Fucker sold me out, I'm gonna rip his hole wide open when I catch up to him, goddamn . . ." His cursing continued, but low and unintelligible.

A man's voice called out from one of the jetboats. "Don't need to see anyone hurt or killed. You let us take the stash, everyone leaves in one piece. All right in there?"

"Not a chance," Terrel muttered.

"Terrel . . ." Cale started.

Terrel snapped his head around and glared at Cale. "You don't know anything about this, so don't say a fucking word. Sorry, but it's too late now, so just shut it." He reached surreptitiously under the wheel housing, something snapped, then he pulled out two guns, Spitzer jim-jim automatics, and thrust one at Cale with a grin. Cale reluctantly took it from him, then Terrel stuck the other gun in his belt behind his back.

Terrel stepped to the side, where he stood in full illumination, and raised both hands. "All right!" he shouted, blinking against the glare. One of the jetboats moved forward and bumped against the stern of the *Skyute.* A man reached out to pull himself aboard, and Terrel made his move.

He stepped back to the wheel, jammed the engines into full reverse, and cranked the wheel hard to the right. The boat bucked and swerved with the sudden backward acceleration and Cale went sprawling across the deck, somehow hanging on to the Spitzer, then scrambled to his hands and knees. Glancing out through the cabin's open doorway, he could see the jetboat rising and twisting up out of the water as the *Skyute* overran it; there was no sign of the man who had been trying to board.

Engines revved up again, more lights appeared from somewhere, and gunshots cracked. Terrel crouched at the wheel, jerking it from side to side as they picked up speed. Cale stayed on his hands and knees, gripping the doorframe for support. The cabin windows cracked and splintered, projectiles ricocheted from the ship's hull, and a muffled explosion sounded from up near the bow. The boat shuddered as they scraped against the bank, and Terrel twisted the wheel once more, freeing them.

The jetboats were quicker than the *Skyute,* and Cale watched two of the boats pass them, swinging around to cut them off. Terrel stayed focused and kept the boat in full reverse, constantly zigzagging while trying to get out to the wider canal, where they might have a chance. Flashes and popping sounds came from the jetboats, followed by a couple of small explosions and splintering wood and plastic across the *Skyute* decks. A shattered piece of railing hit Cale in the head and he flattened himself out on the deck; when he touched his forehead, his fingers came away wet with blood.

He stayed down now, face pressed hard against the gritty surface of the deck, no longer trying to follow what was happening. The boat miraculously continued to swerve backward along the channel, occasionally scraping against the banks, or possibly into one or more of the jetboats—it was impossible to tell. The gunshots and cracks from other weapons increased, along with shouts and cries from the pirates. Cale turned his head and looked back at Terrel, who bobbed up and down trying to catch glimpses of their position, the throttle locked full, one hand on the wheel and jerking it back and forth, the other firing his Spitzer, swearing nonstop all the while.

Suddenly they were out of the narrow channel and in the canal. Terrel swung the boat in a wider, sweeping turn, overrunning another of the jetboats. He cut the throttle as he took the engines out of reverse, then engaged them full forward.

Cale rose to his hands and knees and nearly fell back again as the boat accelerated, then pulled himself up to his feet. He could see four or five jetboats still giving chase, two already pacing them. Then the boat surged forward, as if Terrel suddenly found more power in the engines, and they began to slowly pull away.

A flare of light appeared from the nearest jetboat, then another, and Cale heard bursts of shattering wood and glass, but couldn't see the hits. The *Skyute* continued to slowly but steadily put more distance between it and the jetboats. More shots, but no major hits.

For several long moments nothing changed. They appeared to be heading farther from the heart of the city, into a deeper darkness, when suddenly Terrel slowed the boat, swung the wheel hard right, and they veered into another channel. Cale watched the jetboats follow them, gaining ground for a few moments. Terrel accelerated once more as a series of brighter flares and screeching thumps burst around them.

The *Skyute* was rocked by a violent explosion that nearly knocked Cale from his feet once again. A terrible grinding roar erupted and the deck shuddered beneath them; then the boat slowed precipitously as the engines sputtered twice, caught twice, then died altogether.

"Fuck me!" Terrel shouted. He had his own gun in hand now and he turned to Cale, his face shiny with sweat and glowing with the flashing lights around them. "Shoot as many as you can," he told Cale.

"Just give it to them!" Cale shouted back. "They're going to get it anyway."

Terrel shook his head and gave him a crazed smile. "No, they won't. I'll burn the shit up first." Then he ducked out of the pilothouse, swung around, and dropped down into the cargo hold.

Everything became strangely quiet, no sounds other than the jetboat engines idling as they surrounded the now motionless *Skyute.* Cale saw figures standing along the banks on both sides of the canal, men and women holding wavering lanterns and watching the boats out on the water. The eyes of some animal glowed red in the reflected light. Then he looked at the pirates in the jetboats, most of them armed and wary now as their own craft idled and drifted slowly toward the *Skyute.* He dropped the gun and held out his arms, hands open and facing outward, and cautiously emerged from the pilothouse.

Surprisingly no one shot at him. The pirates seemed far more concerned with the figures on the banks than they were with him or Terrel. He took a few more steps, and still nothing happened; it was only just now sinking in that he had been, and might still be, in real danger of being killed.

No one moved, no one spoke. The idling jetboats rocked gently on the dark water, and the pirates paid Cale no attention. Instead, they warily eyed the figures on either bank, who in turn watched the pirates and the *Skyute.* Then the pirates slowly, carefully engaged their engines, turned the jetboats around, and headed away.

Terrel's face appeared at the entrance to the cargo hold, grinning. He started to pull himself up when a muffled explosion shook the deck. He lost his grip and fell back into the hold; a few moments later flames appeared from one of the vents. Cale ran to the cargo hold entrance and peered into the darkness now being sliced with wavering orange and red light. Heat rushed up into his face and he put up his hand in a futile gesture.

"Terrel!"

Another explosion knocked Cale onto his side. He tried to get to his feet, but slipped and fell to the deck. He heard a cry, and he sensed the heat in the deck, heat from a fire that must now be raging below.

Somehow mustering the necessary energy and will, Cale struggled to his feet once again, and searched for some means of escape. Flames licked up through all the vents as well as the main hold entrance. Cale heard a splash, then a scream and another splash, but the sounds told him nothing about what was really happening. All he knew was that he had to get off the boat.

He stumbled toward the stern; confused by the smoke in his eyes and lungs and the spitting and popping of burning wood, he somehow got turned around and found himself inside the pilothouse again. Reorienting himself, he pushed his way back out. *Get off the damn boat!* he shouted to himself.

The deck erupted before him in an explosion of flames and wood, oil splattering his face and blinding him. He screamed once, tried to cover his eyes with his hands, but it was too late. His eyes burned and watered and he staggered back, legs shaky and unsure beneath him. Suddenly he was falling and he threw out his hands. But he kept falling, for far longer than seemed possible.

He hit the surface of the canal, and the fetid water engulfed him. It cooled his burning face, but when he opened his eyes as he slowly sank, he couldn't see a thing. Remembering it was night didn't reassure him.

Cale stopped moving. He didn't try to swim, just drifted as he remembered that night all those years ago when he'd plunged into the freezing cold lake in his attempt to escape Petros and his clan, when he'd nearly let himself sink to the bottom, and he wondered if this was his time to do just that—if he was being offered another chance, another opportunity to leave this life behind, and perhaps find a semblance of peace.

He held his breath and remained motionless, undecided. He felt himself slowly floating toward the surface. Let someone else decide, he whispered silently to himself.

Someone did. When he finally floated to the surface, he felt hands grab him and turn him over, and he opened his mouth and choked and desperately sucked in the cool night air. But when he opened his eyes, he could not see his savior.

TWO

He lay sweating and feverish on a cot, not knowing whether it was day or night. The bandages and compresses on his eyes felt hot and sticky, as though fused to his skin.

His memories of that night were fragmented by pain. He remembered being dragged blind and burning from the foul canal waters, though it now seemed the burning had been his imagination—his skin appeared to be generally unharmed except for cuts and scrapes that were already scabbing over, itching wounds he fought against scratching. He remembered someone telling him that Terrel was dead, drowned. The boat had burned and sunk, and by now, he imagined, the pirates or someone else had sent divers to the bottom of the canal in an attempt to salvage what they could of cargo certainly not worth someone's life, though that was now the cost.

He had no idea how or when he'd ended up in this room. A physician had been brought to him, a woman with cool dry hands and a coarse but comforting voice. She'd cleansed his eyes and put a salve in them which eased the burning, applied compresses, and wrapped bandages around his head to hold the compresses in place. As she'd cleaned his eyes he had seen soft red flares of light and the shadows of her face, her fingers, so that he'd known he was not yet completely blind. Would he see again? he'd asked her. She couldn't say.

Couldn't say or wouldn't say, he wanted to know, but he didn't know if he'd asked that question aloud, or only in his thoughts. Either way, she was gone by then, and he was left alone with delirious visions and fevered dreams, wondering if he would ever see again.

Harlock stands swaying before the blazing tree, arms outstretched as if to take the flames into a final embrace.

"A screaming comes across the dark and starless sky!" he cries. "Artificial light . . . artificial darkness . . . artificial life."

Saliva rolls down his jaw, scatters as he resumes speaking.

"Jewel around a star . . . resurrect the dead . . . resurrect the living. . . ."

Then Harlock spins and stares at Cale with wild and glittering eyes seemingly devoid of intelligence, but filled with pain and rage and a window into the future . . . or the past. He reaches out to Cale, who pulls back, then the imbecile turns and leaps into the roaring flames.

* * *

The tree seemed to burn before him, hot and searing, then the tree transformed into the boat, and he thought for a moment that he was on the bank of the canal, watching Terrel's boat burn in the night, flames hissing in the water. Then he felt a warm, dry hand on his arm, and his whole body jerked, bringing him fully awake. Breathing hard, he realized where he was.

"Hush," a woman said softly to him, her voice soothing. Not the physician.

Why did she say that? he wondered. Had he cried out in his sleep? Or was it even sleep? Delirium, perhaps.

She laid a cool wet cloth on his forehead, another one across his chest and neck. "Nightmare," she said. "It's just a nightmare."

The wet cloths felt wonderful, soothing him. "Where am I?" he asked.

"Sit up," the woman ordered. "Eat."

"Who are you?"

She didn't answer him. She fed him bitter congee soup, spooning chunks of fish and roots and stringers into his mouth, wiping clean the broth that dripped down his chin.

"The demons won't find you here," she said. "We'll hide you."

"From who?"

"The demons who killed your friend and burned his boat."

"It was pirates. Just pirates, trying to steal our cargo."

"Demons," the woman insisted, then laughed deeply and

heartily, and he wondered if she was laughing at him or at some private joke. Maybe she was crazy. Crazy or not, she fed him the rest of the soup.

"You ever been with some kinda woman?" Feegan asks. Feegan is old and fat and stinks, but has taken a fatherly interest in Cale. On the outskirts of Morningstar, they sit huddled around a ceramic firepot, warming their hands and feet. Hail clatters on the shed roof.

It takes Cale a moment to realize what Feegan means, then he shakes his head.

"No?" Feegan says.

"No."

"Why not?"

Cale shrugs.

"You hank after a man instead?" Feegan asks.

"No."

"Shit, I can arrange it for you, you want. A woman, I mean."

"That's all right," Cale says. Then adds, "Thanks anyway."

Feegan sniffs and closes one eye. "A clean woman."

Cale shakes his head. Feegan sighs and says, "Suit yourself."

They sit in silence, both of them hungry and without any immediate prospects for food, but Cale feels strangely content.

"How old are you, kid?" the old man asks.

"Don't know," Cale answers. "Seventeen, eighteen. Maybe twenty?"

A snort and a nod. "Kid, your eyes look a lot older than the rest of you."

"My eyes?"

"They've seen some things."

Cale smiles faintly and sadly at that. "Yeah, they've seen some things."

He came alert with a sudden, almost painful inhalation of stifling air, and abruptly sat up in the darkness. Or was it truly darkness? He reached up and gingerly touched the bandages over his eyes.

Dream or memory or strange vision? Cale wasn't sure whether he'd been awake or asleep. *Yeah, they've seen some things.* He remembered saying that to Feegan. That fat old man who'd taken him in on his arrival to Morningstar and taught him how to live in the city and who'd fallen while drunk one rainy night, fallen and hit his head and gone into a seizure and died. Cale wondered now if his eyes would ever see anything again. Maybe he'd end up with mek eyes like the Sarakheen; a shudder rolled through him, a strange chill within the depths of his fever. He'd never see Feegan again, no matter what kind of eyes he had, and for some reason that saddened him more than it ever had in the months since the old man had died. A strange thing—he missed Feegan, and he only now realized that he always would.

Terrel stands shirtless and smiling on the riverbank, his dark, dark bronze skin shining with sweat. His hair hangs in knotted cords to his shoulders. Cale climbs the steep, muddy slope to stand beside him, and they look out over the dark green water, watching rings of flowers drift past from some funeral upstream.

"I should introduce you to my sister," Terrel says. "You could share your grief. Maybe eventually you could share more."

"Grief?" Cale asks. "Why grief?" Though he somehow understands.

Terrel doesn't reply. His smile widens and he spreads his arms and looks up at the hot sun above them and then he leans out over the edge of the riverbank and falls toward the water. . . .

The woman led him down a hallway to the toilet, then back to the stifling room and his damp cot.

"You stink," she told him. "I'll see if we can't arrange for a shower or bath for you."

"Do you know when the doctor's coming again?" Cale asked.

"Tomorrow." She handed him a cup of ice water. "Someone's been asking about you on the streets."

"Who?"

"Don't know. Beatt thinks the Rakasha. She thinks they want you dead, because of the boat and whatever it was went down to the bottom."

Cale lay back on the cot, resting the cup on his chest. "I don't think it was the Rakasha. Pirates were after the cargo."

"Ah, I know it's not the Rakasha. They probably don't give a shit about you. They don't give a shit about anyone who isn't in their way. Besides, it was a woman with a messed-up face asking about you. Didn't look much like Rakasha to me. More like one of their victims."

The Rakasha were the dominant bloc of organized criminals in Morningstar, and Cale had never had anything to do with them, so they shouldn't care what happened to him, let alone want him dead.

"Gotta go," the woman said.

"What's your name?" Cale asked for the third or fourth time.

There was a long silence, then the woman eventually said, "Karimah."

"I'm Cale," he said.

"I know," Karimah said. "You've told me more than once."

Cale nodded and said, "Thanks for everything." Karimah didn't reply, and he thought he could hear her get up and move away from the bed. When he heard the door close, he sat up, drank the rest of the cold water, and carefully set the empty cup by feel on the table beside the cot. He sat without moving for some time, listening to the quiet sounds in the building, people moving about, talking to each other, and wondered one more time if he would ever see again.

His right eye was healed, but the left would need more time. Now that he could see a little, he discovered that the doctor was taller than he'd imagined, and big-boned. She rebandaged the left eye, using a different salve and a smaller compress, her fingers firm but comforting on his forehead. His vision out of the right eye was almost normal except for a slight blur around the edges and a strange halo effect when he looked at the lamp. She gave him a tube of salve and a small bottle.

"Don't take off the bandage for three more days," she said. "Then use the salve the way I did, and five drops of this, three times a day. Keep the bandage on at all other times. Don't run." She smiled and said, "Don't let anyone hit you on the head, if possible. In a few days, ask for me, or another doctor, especially if you notice any pain or headaches developing."

"And it'll be okay?" Cale asked.

"Probably. If you're careful and take care of it." She stood and packed up her satchel.

"Thanks," he said. "I don't know how I can pay you. At least not for a while."

"You don't owe me anything. Terrel's my brother."

Cale regarded her silently with his one eye, now seeing the resemblance; more than that, though, he noted the tense she used.

"It's not your fault he's gone," she went on. "If anything, it's his fault *you* almost died. The least I can do is save your eyes."

"What do you mean by gone?" he asked.

She leaned forward and spoke quietly. "He's not dead, but it's better that everyone *thinks* he is. He made too many enemies this time, cost too many people too much money. He left Morningstar, and I don't know if he'll return. I doubt you'll ever see him again. I don't know if *I'll* ever see him again."

He didn't know what else to say, and neither, apparently, did she. She laid her hand briefly on his shoulder, then turned and left.

As soon as she was gone, another woman came into the room. She was short but sinewy, hair and eyes dark, black shirt and trousers nearly as dusty as her boots. The whites of her eyes were tinged with yellow, and Cale wondered if she was ill. She looked down at him, waiting for him to say something.

"Karimah?" he asked.

She nodded.

"Where am I?"

"You really don't know?" she said. "Terrell didn't tell you?"

Cale shook his head, confused. "I don't understand."

"He was bringing you to us."

"Us?"

She nodded. "The Resurrectionists."

THREE

He walked along the canal in the damp heat of early afternoon, waiting for a cooling breeze to wash up from the water. As usual, it didn't come. Market stalls lined both sides of the road, which was blocked off to vehicle traffic, but now, at the hottest time of the day, customers were few, and many of the vendors napped in the shade of their stalls or sipped at iced drinks, tiny solar fans directed at their faces. The sweet aroma of local spices and fermented brews hung in the air, laced with the occasional scent of harsh, inferior starweed smoke—most of the premium grade starweed was exported offworld. Cale wondered if *he* would ever go offworld. Everything seemed both possible and impossible to him right now; he could imagine himself aimlessly wandering the city streets for months, even leaving Morningstar and eventually ending up back at the Divide. Then . . . ? He might just cross back over and lose himself again. Despair welled up in him at the thought, at the recognition that it was even possible.

Karimah fell in beside him, on the side of his good eye, and matched his languid pace. They were a long way from the Resurrectionists' encampment, but this was where Karimah had told him to wait for her. She nodded toward a fishmonger's stall as they walked past. "Don't ever buy from him," she said. "That sign *always* says 'River Fish,' but he nets those stinkin' things from the canals." Then, glancing at Cale, she said, "You've been asking about us for some time now."

He nodded, mouth drying and pulse quickening. He knew that they had saved him from drowning, that they had saved his eyes and his life, but he had no idea what to expect from them or her.

"I'd guess we both have a lot of questions," she said to Cale. "Let's get something cold to drink."

They sat alone on the second-floor balcony of a café overlooking the road, shaded by a roof of cross-hatched strips of bark, and drank iced coffee sweetened with heavy cream. Below them a one-legged woman in filthy rags crouched against the wall, calling out to passersby, begging for coins and chits; the cloying smell of unwashed flesh and infection was intensified by the heat, and wafted up to the balcony.

Across the canal and a half-hour walk to the south rose the lofty towers of The Island, tall and elegant edifices he had yet to see up close, as inaccessible to him today as they had been all those years ago when the *Kestrel* had emerged from the clouds out of control and plummeted to earth on the other side of the Divide—he still had a vivid memory of the gleaming Morningstar towers receding from them as Sidonie had struggled to keep them aloft.

"How's the eye?" Karimah asked.

"Bandage comes off in a couple of days, it'll be fine."

"Why are you looking for us?" She sat back in her chair, her gaze steady on him.

"I thought I might want to join you," he said.

"Join us." And made a quiet sound that might have been a laugh. She produced a strip of pale green cigarettes, popped one off, and lit it without offering one to Cale. "What do you know about us?"

"Not a lot. Speculation and rumor." When she didn't respond, Cale went on. "I've heard that Morningstar was built on the ruins of an ancient alien city, and that you've been digging underneath Morningstar for years, trying to find alien artifacts. No one knows what you've found, and most people don't really seem to care. Word is all you've found, if you've found anything, are the ruins of an earlier human settlement."

"And what do *you* think?"

Cale hesitated, afraid to go on. The cigarette smoke made him queasy—or something did. He felt he was at a crucial juncture, that it was his last chance to back away and resume his own, normal way of life. Yet what was that? He *had* no normal way of life. No place to go. His pulse rate elevated, and he felt a strange pressure behind his eyes.

"I think you *have* found the remnants of an alien civilization," he finally said.

"What makes you think that?"

"Because I think I've seen alien artifacts myself."

Karimah slowly sat up, regarding him intently. "Where?"

"On the other side of the Divide."

A brief, intense silence followed. When Karimah spoke, her voice was quiet and steady. "Tell me what you saw."

Cale had gone too far now to hold back. He told Karimah about the deserted village he'd stumbled across, about the main building and the disturbing painting above the doorway, and finally about the strange glyphs on the wall behind the altar. He did not mention Sproul, nor the blue gemstones, nor the book now buried with Sproul's body. It seemed important to hold that secret, like the secret of his last name.

Karimah stubbed out her cigarette, took a pen from her shirt pocket, rummaged in other pockets until she found a blank scrap of paper, then handed both to Cale. "Draw what you saw on the wall," she said. "I know it won't be the same thing, but show me what the characters looked like."

Cale closed his eye for a moment, envisioning first the building interior, light slashing in through holes in the roof, the floor as he walked toward the altar, then finally, as he climbed the steps, the etched figures in the wall. Like patterned blades of grass, he remembered thinking. Then they were in his mind, solid and distinct, just as he had seen them that day. Once again, even over all that distance and time, he felt the power in the glyphs.

Shaken, he opened his eye and scratched out a few random groupings of the marks, deliberately *not* re-creating exactly what he remembered. He pushed the pen and paper back across the table and looked at Karimah, who was staring at Cale's drawing.

She nodded slowly, then with deliberate movements pocketed the paper and pen. "We've heard rumors of that place, just as you describe it. Over the years a few of us have gone across the Divide to try to find it. Always failed." She eyed Cale. "Would you be willing to guide one of us there?"

Cale shook his head. "I'm never going back across the Divide."

Karimah shrugged as if it was of no consequence. "Maybe you'll change your mind someday."

"So what is it?"

She finished her iced coffee and stared at him. "Come with me."

Two hours later they stood before a skin parlor in one of the busiest and most congested districts of Morningstar. The skin parlor was wedged between a bar and a stunner arcade, the trio of businesses in turn flanked by a music store and a shock shop. Above ground level, the concrete building rose another four stories with what appeared to be apartments.

Several blocks away, across the ring of canals that served as a kind of moat, rose the gleaming edifices of The Island. Up close, the buildings appeared to rise into and above the clouds.

"You seem confused," Karimah said.

Cale nodded, blinking at the glare of sunlight reflecting off the polished metal and glass, then turned back to the skin parlor. The door opened and a fleshy woman emerged, hardly able to walk. Her cheeks twitched spastically, and her lips trembled as if she were silently mumbling some prayer or other incantation. Long thin scars striped both of her arms. She eyed Cale, gave him a ghastly smile, then winked at him before turning and staggering down the street.

Cale turned to Karimah. "We're nowhere near where we've been staying, where you pulled me out of the canal."

"That's where we live," Karimah said. "We keep to ourselves, for lots of reasons. But the ruins are *here.* Beneath us. Morningstar was built right on top of them." She shrugged. "*This* is where we dig."

She led the way into the skin parlor, and Cale followed.

They began their descent from the third floor, in a wide central stairwell secured from the skin parlor and the building's other establishments by two doors and three key codes. The stairwell was bare and cool and quiet, the echoes of their footsteps strangely hushed and distant; the air smelled of damp clean earth. Three floors down they emerged into a vast concrete-walled chamber with a large freight lift, several loaders propped against the walls, and dozens of crates stacked or scattered about, some empty and some filled with chunks of stone or bits of metal or strips of ragged and rotted wood. An older woman squatted before a pile of rock and dirt that had been dumped from one of the crates, poking through it with long thin tweezers; she looked up and nodded at Cale and Karimah, then returned to her task without a word.

Karimah led the way to a narrow stairwell in one corner and they climbed down to the next level, which was unoccupied. Here the lights were dim and tinged blue, and the cooler air smelled of oil and rusted metal and a hint of scorched rubber. Cages marked the two shafts that led to the lower levels, and Karimah pointed out the emergency shaft across the room, the top of a metal ladder visible in its outlet. She opened one of the cages and they stepped inside, then she closed the interior gate, pressed a button, and they resumed their descent with a clunking jolt.

The cage elevator shuddered as it dropped, like some ancient mechanism kept functioning with makeshift parts and constant repairs. The shaft walls were shored with metal and wood scarred by the repeated passage of the cage, lit with moving patterns by the elevator's overhead lamp.

They hadn't descended more than thirty feet when the cage stopped before a wide opening in the dirt and rock; the gate opened and Karimah led the way into a long passage lit by strings of gold and silver angel lights. The air was warmer and drier than he expected, and a hot breeze moved past them carrying with it the smell of cinnamon.

The passage angled off to the right and pale light washed over them. They stepped into an antechamber carved out of the earth, the ceiling close to twenty feet above ground level. On the other side of the antechamber was a glass wall and a doorway twelve feet high and three or feet wide leading into a room with more glass walls. Cale and Karimah crossed the antechamber and entered.

Glass walls surrounded them, and a ceiling of paneled glass curved overhead. Floor lamps illuminated the large room, the soft white light penetrating the glass and revealing a sky of rock and earth only inches beyond the glass. Not a single pane of glass was cracked or otherwise marked.

Without a word Karimah led Cale to a spiral staircase

that wound down from the center of the room, and they continued their descent.

On the next level down they walked through a series of empty rooms faintly helical in appearance, as if upon completion the polished stone walls had been slightly twisted by the hand of some great beast. The high ceilings were faceted as though inlaid with enormous dark crystals, and an eerie glow reflected in bluish hues from the facets, the glow punctuated by tiny pockets of darkness. Their boots trod upon large tiles etched with diagrams of circles and arrowed lines linking one tile to another.

As they exited the last room, they emerged from the building and stood on a bridge of wooden planks laid across a deep fissure. Broken walls of stone and a large network of scaffolding were visible in the crevice below. The bridge led to an opening in another partially excavated building, its upper reaches disappearing into the earth above.

Cale followed her across the planks. He craned his neck and gazed up as he walked through the doorway, which was twelve or thirteen feet high like all the other doorways they'd passed through.

They entered a vast gallery lit by angel lamps, the golden lights mounted in the corners of the high ceiling, illuminating complex spirals carved into dozens of stone wall panels, lighting shiny maroon disks affixed to the floor.

"All this," Karimah said as they moved through the gallery, "and hardly anyone cares. An entire civilization—a civilization of intelligent aliens—extinct for reasons we'll probably never know. But there's so much they left behind, here and on other worlds, and most of it's like this, buried beneath our own cities, neglected, forgotten, dismissed." She shook her head in disgust. "Nobody gives a shit." She stopped and turned to him. "That's why we're here, to unearth as much as we can, save as much as we can, learn as much as we can. It probably sounds crazy, but some of us feel we owe it to them."

Cale shook his head. "It doesn't sound crazy."

Karimah snorted. "Then you're just as crazy as we are." She tilted her head and gazed up at the ceiling, which was painted a deep indigo so dark that gauging its height was impossible. "This is just the beginning."

He spent the next several hours in a state of overstimulation, at times hardly aware of himself. The Resurrectionists had strung all the rooms and chambers and passages with angel lamps, clusters of luminous gossamer that cast a clean warm light and diminished the shadows so that the details within were clear and visible if often incomprehensible. As they encountered people along the way, Karimah introduced Cale to them, and them to him, but their names slipped from his memory as soon as they moved on.

. . . Doorways and ceilings all so much higher than expected, and Cale became certain that the aliens must have been at least two or three feet taller than human beings . . .

. . . Channels that might once have carried water or other fluids along the floors of a series of interconnected dome-shaped rooms, the oxidized metal ceiling/walls etched with intricate depictions of lush plants and vague bipedal forms hidden behind the dense foliage . . .

. . . A vast network of severed pipe and cable that emerged

from walls and ceilings of a building that appeared to have had one side completely cut away so that its interior structure could be exhibited . . .

. . . Two women who carefully brushed and scraped away at a wall of dirt and rock in a room still partially buried; four shiny metal tubes lay in a basket behind them . . .

. . . A long wide hall with tables on one side and sinks on the other and pipes entering and exiting the walls, and racks of strangely shaped cutting instruments and gripping tools and implements whose functions were indecipherable, yet all organized and waiting to be put to use if their owners were ever to return . . .

"One more thing to show you," Karimah said to him. "For now, anyway."

By now Cale was truly captivated in some deep and terrible and wonderful way. He followed her along another high and wide passage, then through a doorway of dangling vines of delicately carved wood, and into an enormous vault lit by more angel lamps. He stopped, stunned and immobilized.

Hundreds or thousands of sheets of thin, coppery metal hung from wooden dowels suspended from the ceiling on nearly invisible wires, the sheets carved through and stenciled with markings like the tracks of terratorns and blades of grass. They angled in different directions, yet hung above their heads in a curving pattern so that Cale imagined that if he started here at the door and moved about the room, following them, reading them over the hours or days it would take, he would in the end achieve some special insight . . . or revelation.

"This is the writing you saw, isn't it?" Karimah said.

Cale nodded. More than she knew, he thought. He remained there a long time, staring at the metal sheets, the pages of alien text he hoped he might someday understand.

FOUR

Cale lay beside Karimah on the mat, his damp skin touching hers. Breathing hard, he lifted his hand and laid it gently across her belly, his fingers lightly brushing dark coarse hair. He felt her own fingers find his and weakly curl around them.

Light was a dim yellow glow here in their private cell some forty or fifty feet below street level, the glow produced by a phosphor globe suspended from the shored-up ceiling above them. Two metal sheets of the alien glyphs hung from copper wires and cast patterned shadows across the polished stone walls. Dark fabric draped across the doorway, muting the brighter lights of the adjacent passage as well as the sounds of those working in the chambers and passages around and below them. The air was warm and heavy despite the Underneath's ventilation systems. They usually slept back at the main Resurrectionist encampment, and occasionally in a cubicle two floors above the skin parlor, but Karimah insisted their lovemaking take place down here in the Underneath, surrounded by alien artifacts, lying amid the ruins of the Jaaprana's world. Sometimes the two of them stayed down here for days, working, sleeping, eating food brought down by others from above.

A bell chimed just beyond the curtain, and a woman spoke, voice hesitant. "Karimah? Cale?"

"Yes?" Karimah replied.

"Cicero's waiting. He said you were going to help him at the markets today."

She propped herself up on her elbows and looked at Cale. "Remember?"

Cale nodded, closing his eyes and wishing he didn't have to move.

"Tell Cicero we'll be up in a few minutes."

They climbed ladders and stairs, the air becoming steadily cooler as they came up into the building. Outside, it was winter, something it was easy to forget in the Underneath with its pockets of stifling air. They found Cicero sitting alone in the main basement, drinking coffee and reading a pocket folio.

Cicero was a small, wiry, and kindly old man with sparse silver hair that seemed to float about his head. He had been with the Resurrectionists for years, but he never did any of the excavation or exploration, never descended into the

Underneath. He helped out with whatever needed to be done above ground, and sometimes cooked huge meals for everyone back at the main encampment at the outer edge of Morningstar, serving large quantities of his foul-tasting home-distilled alcohol that made people quickly drunk and produced cramped bellies and painful hangovers. Cale didn't know much about the man, but he'd heard that Cicero had once lived on The Island; it seemed an unlikely story.

Cicero shook his head at them. "Put on some warmer clothes. There's snow out there."

"Snow?" Karimah said. "When did that happen?"

Cicero shook his head. "You people lose touch down there. It's been snowing for three days."

The snow was knee-deep, and there was a hushed feel to the city around them. This was Cale's second winter in Morningstar, but last year there had been no snow. The thinnest layer of gray cloud hung above them, and the mid-day sun burned a brighter gray disk through the clouds, bringing a glitter to the snow. A few vehicles skidded along the road, but most people were on foot. Businesses were open, and there were nearly as many people out as usual, but the pace was slower, as if everyone was taking advantage of the snow to relax and ease up on their frantic lives.

Cicero led the way along paths that had been dug out of the snow by others. The route to the markets brought them near The Island, within a hundred feet of its protective moat; its buildings appeared to grow and dwarf everything surrounding it, and the metal and glass gleamed more brightly than seemed possible from the clouded sun. Cale had been this close to The Island a few times before, but had never entered; it was more difficult to gain access to The Island than it was to cross the Divide. He felt the same way as he always did in its presence—that this place was mysterious and magnificent, intimidating and enticing . . . and malign.

They were still several blocks from the first market, walking along Gibson Channel toward a footbridge spanning the waterway, when a voice called out to them.

"Young Cale!"

Cale stopped abruptly, struck with fear at the familiar voice. He forced himself to turn and look across the road. Blackburn sat with another man at an outdoor café table, sheltered from the snow by an opaque canopy and surrounded by lush ferns and flowering plants. His shaved head was large and shiny in the light reflecting from dozens of faceted glass hangings. Cale couldn't see much of the other man, who was obscured by plants and shadows.

"Join us," Blackburn said with a sweep of his arm. "Bring your companions and join us." His smile did not provide Cale any comfort.

Cale looked hesitantly at Cicero and Karimah. Cicero nodded and said, "We should accept. The other man at the table is a Sarakheen." He turned to Cale. "You know who the Sarakheen are?"

"Not really. I've heard the name a few times, but I've never understood who they were."

"I don't like it," Karimah said with a frown.

"I don't either," Cicero said. "But it's impossible to know how the Sarakheen would react if we decline. And your friend Blackburn," he added, glancing at Cale, "he definitely doesn't take rejection well."

"You *know* him?" Cale asked.

"I know who he is. I saw him several times when I lived on The Island, but I never actually met him. It surprises me, I have to say, that *you* know him."

"The last time I saw him," Cale said, "we didn't part as friends."

Cicero nodded once. "*That* doesn't surprise me. We really should accept, anyway. We won't stay, we won't accept an offer of drink or food. We'll make polite conversation, then we can leave."

Cale looked at Karimah, who shrugged, then turned back to face Blackburn. "All right," he said.

They crossed the road, and when they entered the café the temperature immediately rose, became mild and pleasant as if they had passed through an invisible barrier. Seated upright and expressionless next to Blackburn, with a large smoke-colored drink before him, was the Sarakheen. He wore a black bodysuit, and his right hand and fingers were perfectly formed and articulated like a natural hand of flesh and blood, yet were constructed of metal and plasteel and glass.

Cale made the initial introductions, since he knew everyone except the Sarakheen. There was no real introduction of the Sarakheen; his name was a private matter, Blackburn explained. Although the Sarakheen didn't say a word, nor did his expression change, he shook each of their hands with his own, artificial hand.

Blackburn stood and put his hand on Cale's shoulder, as if they were good friends. "It's been a long time, young Cale." Cale just nodded without directly looking at him, and Blackburn turned to the Sarakheen. "This is the young man I was telling you about last year," he said. "The one I met on the other side of the Divide."

The Sarakheen leaned forward and studied Cale, his eyes widening slightly; yet his face remained unreadable, which Cale found intensely disturbing.

"Sit down," Blackburn said. "Have a drink with us."

Cale could not pull his gaze from the Sarakheen, could not manage to decline Blackburn's offer. Blackburn said something about getting extra chairs, Karimah responded, but their voices had become faint and distant. The Sarakheen's stare had shifted Cale into some other time or place.

"Cale?" Blackburn gripped his shoulder once more. "You'll join us."

Cicero took the opportunity to say, "We don't want to interrupt anything, and we need to go anyway."

"Underneath?" the Sarakheen said. His voice was surprisingly soothing, but that one word created an instant stillness and tension.

"No," Cicero answered calmly. "The markets."

At that, the Sarakheen smiled. Yet even the smile disturbed Cale, for it seemed not quite human; or if human then not quite normal. The Sarakheen turned to Cale, leaned forward, and shook his hand again, staring intently at him. Cale thought the Sarakheen was going to say something, but if he did intend to, he changed his mind and sat back without a word.

"Where can I get in touch with you?" Blackburn said.

"You can't," Cale replied, still frightened without quite knowing why. He turned from the table and walked quickly out of the café without waiting to see if the others followed.

* * *

Karimah and Cicero caught up to him on the other side of the Gibson Channel footbridge. Karimah took hold of Cale's arm and forced him to slow his pace. He stopped and leaned against a kiosk wall, breath ragged.

"What are they?" he asked.

"They're human beings," Cicero began, "though in some ways they seem hardly human at all. They live in an artificial world called Sarakh, which they built for themselves. Each of them has one mek arm, one mek leg, and one mek eye, and every one of them has their reproductive organs surgically removed immediately upon producing their second child." He shook his head. "I'm sure there are other things they do or don't do that I'm not aware of, but those are the most well-known. They come here to Conrad's World with some regularity," Cicero went on, "but they rarely leave The Island. I became acquainted with several when I lived there. I don't think anyone ever really gets to *know* any of them."

"They're freaks," Karimah said. "I've only seen one once before, but I tell you there's something very *in*human about them." She visibly shuddered. "I didn't like her at all, the one I saw. Didn't like this one, either. And they sure as hell don't like us."

"What?" Cale asked. "They don't like normal humans?"

Karimah uttered a harsh laugh. "What the hell are normal humans?" she said. Then she slowly shook her head. "If anything, they have disdain for humans as a whole. No, I mean Resurrectionists. They don't like *us.*"

"Why not?"

"We don't know," Cicero replied. "They've made indirect efforts over the years to shut us down. I always had the impression that they were behind Island Security's periodic harassment—Island Security would haul in one or more of us at a time with a charge of some political crime or other, and then ship them over the Divide. We were in different locations before, and even had our excavations sabotaged a few times, by people who had claimed to join us. We're a lot more careful about who we bring in, now." He looked at Cale. "You're the first new person in three years."

"And you think they don't know where you are now? You must have been there for years, as extensive as the Underneath is."

"They probably know," Karimah said. "Either they've decided we're not worth the trouble, or . . . or they're waiting for something."

"Waiting for what?"

"Waiting for us to find something," Cicero said. "Maybe something *they've* been searching for."

"I'll tell you what I think about those bastards," Karimah said. "I think they're searching for something very specific, and I think they've got their own excavations here on The Island, and they haven't found it yet. They think it's under The Island, but just in case it isn't, just in case it's where *we're* exploring . . . I think they're letting us go, and they figure if we do find whatever it is, they'll get the word, and come and take it from us." She gave Cale a wicked grin. "If that day ever comes, they're going to find that taking it will be a lot more difficult than they anticipate."

FIVE

In the spring, Cicero found Cale standing at one of the windows in the attic above the skin parlor, looking out across the adjacent buildings and up at the shining glass and polished stone towers of The Island. Cale heard the old man come up the stairs, and listened to his shuffling steps as he crossed the cracked wooden flooring, but didn't turn until Cicero was beside him.

"You think you want to live in there?" Cicero asked.

"I like it here just fine," Cale replied.

"Hmm." The old man sniffed. "I was not particularly powerful when I lived there, but I did have some influence. And a fair degree of wealth. Enough to live in one of the more exclusive residential complexes, in the upper levels. Enough to drink and eat well." He smiled wryly. "I'll be honest—I was wealthy enough to drink and eat to *excess.* To engage not in the highest, but at least in the high*er* circles of Island society. To be a regular attendee of certain expensive and vulgar entertainments. To pay for regular re-gen treatments." He turned to Cale. "I *am* over a hundred and thirty standard years old. Though I'm now aging more naturally once again."

"What happened?" Cale asked.

Cicero chuckled. "You might imagine some spectacular fall, a scandal, perhaps, or some disastrous business failure." When Cale shrugged, Cicero went on. "I gave it up, that's what happened. Quite voluntarily."

"Why?"

The old man waved expansively at the tall buildings. "All that comes with a price. A price I was one day no longer willing to pay."

"What price?" Cale asked.

Cicero shook his head. "That's not for me to say. The price is different for everyone. For some it's not much of a price at all. For others, the price is truly terrible. You will have to learn for yourself what kind of price you'd pay. And whether you can bear it."

"Only if I live there," Cale said. "And I doubt I ever will. I doubt that I can."

Cicero sighed. "You will live there someday, Cale. Or someplace like it. Someday you'll find a way. At least for a time. I sense an unstoppable drive in you, a drive to experience and understand all that this universe holds." He nodded more to himself than to Cale. "You'll go." Then he shrugged as if it was unimportant. "There's someone asking for you down by the canal. A woman."

"I don't understand. Who?"

"A woman. A woman with a damaged face. She waits in a canoe. She spoke to the guards and asked for you by name, and described you quite accurately. She said you would want to speak with her, although she would not give her name. Do you know this woman?"

Cale shook his head. He felt a growing apprehension, remembering Karimah's words all those months ago about "a woman with a messed-up face" looking for him. Who could this woman be, and what would she want with him?

"I think you should see her," Cicero advised him. "You should find out who she is and what she wants with you. Then send her away if you wish."

"I *don't* know who she is," Cale said. "But I know I don't want to see her."

"Yes," Cicero replied, "and that is why you should."

Cale emerged cautiously from the rear of the building, at the canal's edge; the two armed guards looked at him with recognition, but remained silent. Tico tipped his head toward the water below them where a woman sat alone in a finely crafted canoe. Her face was scarred and misshapen and her left eye was clouded and rheumy. A wide swath of silver cut through her otherwise dark auburn hair. Cale did not recognize her.

"You want to talk to me?" he asked.

The woman stood and regarded him, the canoe rocking slightly. "Privately," she replied.

Wary of her, he walked a ways along the canal, past the end of the building. The woman sat and paddled back to him and tied up to a gnarled root that broke through the concrete. Cale kept back, a strange distress rising inside him as she disembarked and clambered up the bank on her own. She stood before him, studying his face as he in turn studied hers, searching for some sense of the familiar. He put her age at around forty, though the damage to her face made it difficult to tell. The left side of her head appeared to have been violently crushed and then poorly rebuilt; it was striped with scar tissue, and her mouth was uneven, the corner pulled into a kind of permanent grimace; he wondered if she could see anything at all out of the clouded eye.

"It *is* you," she said quietly. He thought he could see tears welling in both eyes. "I've been looking for you for years, Cale . . . Cale Alexandros."

Cale's chest tightened sharply, and a numb sensation spread through his limbs, his knees nearly buckling. Not only from her words, but from her voice, some familiar and painful aspect of it.

"Who are you?" he asked.

"Sidonie."

He felt light-headed and paralyzed, unable to move or speak, as if something terrible would happen to him if he did—collapse, or disintegration. He had to will himself to breathe.

"Do you remember me, Cale?"

"Yes," he said, voice hoarse and barely audible. "I remember you."

Sidonie sat in the rear of the canoe and paddled while Cale sat in front, facing her. She was taking him to her home. There was only one paddle, but Sidonie's strokes were deep and smooth and propelled them steadily through the water. They quickly moved from Marlowe Canal to wider, cleaner channels, joining heavier boat traffic. Neither spoke, but Cale wondered if Sidonie's thoughts were as frantic and chaotic as his own.

Cale hardly noticed the city sliding past them; he was trying to hold himself together. Confusion and deep pools of emotion bubbled up in him, threatening to erupt and break him apart—rage and bitterness and an overwhelming despair that had been held down and hidden away for all these years. None of it directed at Sidonie—for her, he felt a painful affection and sorrow—but certainly released by her reappearance in his life.

An hour or so had passed when she pulled along a small dock southeast of The Island. From the dock it was only a short walk along an entertainment market to a four-story slagcrete building a few blocks off the canal. Sidonie led the way up to her apartment on the third floor.

The apartment was small, but had a large balcony filled with plants in pots of all sizes, long planters, hanging baskets. Two chairs were set amid the lush foliage, and she invited Cale to sit in one while she went back inside to make something for them to drink. Still distraught and confused, Cale settled into the chair and breathed in the damp and heavy aroma of the flowers, the pungent scent of herbs. The sun warmed the balcony, and the heat felt good on his skin, almost cleansing.

Sidonie brought out a pot of a hot, spiced beverage called kuma, and she gave him a cup and sat in the other chair, setting the pot on an overturned clay bowl. They sat in silence for a time, sipping at the kuma and occasionally looking at each other, but not speaking. Cale reflected on old man Feegan's words, telling him his eyes looked old. Yet right now, sitting with Sidonie, he felt at the same time much *younger* than his age, and he did not know how to reconcile those two things. She sat watching him, as if waiting for him to speak first, to ask the first questions.

"What happened to you?" he asked. As soon as he'd spoken he regretted asking the question, though unsure why.

"I don't really remember." She looked away from him, but there was something in her expression and in her voice that suggested to Cale that she remembered more than she was willing to say. It was then that his own memory returned, like a painful flash of light between his eyes: the men dropping the massive stone on her head. "I was unconscious for a long time, almost dead I guess, and when I came to, I was being cared for by an old couple who lived in the mountains. They'd found me near the wrecked flyer, and when they discovered I wasn't dead they took me in and nursed me. I stayed with them until I was recovered, then I made my way to the Divide, and eventually here to Morningstar." She turned back to him. "I was trying to find out what happened to your father."

She left it there, and he knew that she did not have good news about his father, yet he didn't know how he felt about that. "I hardly remember him," he said, a way of biding time to sort out his feelings, which he knew was an impossible task. "I remember my mother even less."

"I'm sorry, Cale. It took me a long time to find out what happened. The family ship, the *Exile Prince,* was destroyed, with no survivors."

"Except for us."

Sidonie nodded. She paused for a moment, then went on. "Your father told me that if anything should happen to him, I was to go to his brother here in Morningstar. Adanka Suttree. I tried, but I never did find him. I found where he'd lived, I found people who had heard of him, but he seemed to have disappeared around the same time your father was killed. Some of the people I talked to thought Adanka had died, but others thought he'd gone offworld. No one I talked to knew for sure."

"And you've been here ever since."

"Yes."

"Doing what?"

"Searching for you." She moved her mouth into a sad and distorted smile. "Waiting for you to return to life."

"All these years? Why?"

"I'm responsible for you."

Cale shook his head. "I'm responsible for myself."

"I *was* responsible for you. You were five years old, and you were my charge. I'd been responsible for you since you were born."

"More than my mother, I think," Cale said, a numbed anger and resentment tightening his neck and jaw.

"Maybe so," Sidonie replied. "But you *were* my responsibility, and you still are as far as the family is concerned."

"*What* family?" Cale asked, struggling to keep his rising anger under control.

"*Your* family. The Alexandros family. You may not know anything about them, but they *are* your family, and now that I've found you, it's time for you to return to them." She shifted her position, her attention fixed intently on him. "For several generations, your family was one of the most powerful on two worlds, Cale. Things changed. A series of misfortunes, deliberate or accidental, some poor business decisions. . . . The family was in decline at the time your father came here with us, and since your father's death that decline has steepened. They need you. Your mother needs you."

"Where were they when *I* needed *them*? When I was a child?"

She turned away from him, and he thought it was because she had no good answer. He was frustrated and angry and confused, and felt guilty because he knew he was hurting Sidonie, but he did not know what else to say or do.

"Why was the *Exile Prince* attacked?" Cale asked.

"I'm not sure," Sidonie said, still not looking at him. "Something to do with the family business. Competitors, probably. Trying to disrupt a special undertaking of your father's, a clandestine venture of his."

"Why was *I* on that ship?" he finally asked her. "And you? Why was a five-year-old boy put at risk like that? Why did I grow up on the other side of the Divide alone and abandoned? Why did *you* have to go through all this?"

"You weren't abandoned, Cale. Your father didn't plan that to happen. No one intended it."

"Explain that to a five- or six-year-old boy being beaten and raised as a slave for a bunch of criminals out in some godforsaken wasteland."

When Sidonie finally looked back at him, there were tears dripping down her face, streaming from the bad eye and rolling across the scar tissue to hang and then drop from her chin. He ached for her, knowing none of this was her fault.

"Because the family horoscoper told your father that your presence was required for his venture to succeed. A strange reason, maybe an insane reason, but that's what it was, that's why you were on the ship."

Cale felt bewildered. A horoscoper? He'd heard a bit about horoscopers since he'd been in Morningstar, and he didn't really know what they did or how, but they had sounded even less reliable than Harlock and his visions. He could hardly imagine a powerful family depending on one for advice. Had his life, all those years on the other side of the Divide, been the result of some charlatan's counsel?

Sidonie wiped the tears away, got up and poured them each fresh cups of the kuma, then sat back down. "All right, Cale. Tell me what happened to you over all these years."

Tell me. Cale sat motionless and silent, feeling paralyzed. He'd never spoken to anyone about his past, not even Karimah. But as he sat there with a strange electric buzz burning through him, he recognized a powerful urge to speak, and he realized that Sidonie was the only person he could ever imagine talking to about what had happened to him. He *needed* to talk to her.

He began with his earliest memories of life with Petros and the other villagers, and worked slowly and deliberately forward. He told her everything. The sun moved downward until it finally set and the stars began to appear in the sky above them along with the lights of Morningstar, holding back the night. Sidonie heated a stew, which they ate with fresh bread, then made another pot of kuma. They remained out on the balcony, Cale talking and Sidonie listening, until he reached the day of his life when, while living with the Resurrectionists, a woman with a scarred and misshapen face appeared, wanting to speak to him.

After a long silence, Sidonie began to talk, telling her own story. There wasn't much to it, she said. When she couldn't locate Adanka Suttree, she decided to make her home in Morningstar and wait. For the last two years she'd been working in a nursery, growing native plants to produce seeds for offworld shipment. Working and waiting and keeping her eye out for Cale. She'd thought she'd found him the previous summer, but he'd disappeared. Then several weeks ago, she'd picked up hints again of someone named Cale who was the right age. She followed up until she'd eventually found the Resurrectionists.

When she was done, Cale looked up at the stars gleaming weakly above them. "It's surprising we're both alive," he said. He turned back to her. Then, hesitant but unable to refrain from asking, he said, "Can . . . can surgery . . . ?" He couldn't finish the question.

She nodded. "Someday. But for now, I want the reminder."

He winced, feeling guilty, though not sure why.

She looked steadily at him and said, "It's time to go home, Cale. Now that you're found, it's time for both of us to go home."

"Where do you think home is?" he asked, the anger rising once again.

"The Alexandros Estates. On Lagrima."

Cale shook his head. "My home is *here.*"

"With the Resurrectionists?"

"Yes."

"That's not a home, Cale. They're not your family."

"They're more family to me than my own has ever been. Except for you," he added. Looking at Sidonie, his anger at his own family became washed away by the affection he felt for her, which arose from the scared five-year-old boy that still resided within him. "Why did you wait for me?" he asked. "Why did you keep looking for me? I could have been dead. I *should* have been dead."

"I knew you were still alive," she replied.

"How?"

She seemed embarrassed, and gave a slight shrug. "I found a horoscoper here. A genuine horoscoper."

"You believe in that nonsense?"

"It's not nonsense. *Astrology* is nonsense, and most horoscopers are frauds, astrologers trying to camouflage themselves with respect, but those few horoscopers who are genuine possess great insight into the directions of our lives."

"You believe they can tell the future?"

Sidonie shook her head. "No. But the authentic ones are great seers of the forces in our lives, the forces that act upon us, and those we produce."

"And you found an 'authentic' one."

"Yes, and he said you were still alive. Influencing the world around you, affecting all of us."

Which of course was just what she had wanted to hear. It was absurd. "And the family horoscoper who told my father that my presence was needed to ensure his success? What kind of success was that?"

"I don't know, Cale. Stygon was a good horoscoper. Your father had previously ignored his advice and paid a heavy price for it. He was determined not to make that mistake again." She breathed deeply once. "I don't know," she said again. "Perhaps Stygon was mistaken, or your father misunderstood him, or there was something else we just can't understand. I still have faith in the true horoscopers." She put her hand on his. "Come with me to see the horoscoper I found here in Morningstar. He can help you, help you decide what to do."

"I can make my own decisions."

"So you'll stay with the Resurrectionists."

"Yes."

"And your family? Your blood family?"

Cale looked away from her. "Go back to them without me," he said. "You've done more than they could ever have expected from you. Tell them I'm . . ." He didn't finish, but he turned back to her and shook his head. "Tell them whatever you want."

"I won't go back without you," she said, gazing intently at him. "*You* are my charge, Cale, no matter what your age, you are still my charge in some way, and I'll stay here in Morningstar until you decide to return."

"And if I never go back?"

She smiled gently at him. "Then I never will, either. I've made a good life here for myself. I can be content with that."

He stood up to leave. It was late. Or early. He could see the first pale light of dawn and he shivered, just now feeling the chill in the air.

"I hope you come to see me again, Cale."

"I will, Sidonie. Often. And you? Will you come see me?"

She shook her head. "No. I'll be here for you, but I won't go back to the Resurrectionists again."

* * *

Back to the Resurrectionists. Back to Karimah. Back to the Underneath. Back . . . home?

No, Cale admitted to himself. He was not deluded. This was not yet truly home, the Resurrectionists and Karimah were not yet truly family, but he believed that in time they could be, and that would do for now.

SIX

Cale rode in the front of the skiff, while Karimah operated the motor as they set off shortly after dawn. Over the first half hour, the skiff moved from Marlowe Canal out into larger channels until they reached the Grand Canal, then they reversed the process, transferring into smaller and narrower waterways as they moved farther and farther from the city center. Cale had no idea where they were going, and Karimah wouldn't tell him. As they reached the northern outskirts of Morningstar, the city rapidly deteriorated—people and buildings alike. The canals were lined with dwellings of broken concrete, cracked and rotting wood; shanties of metal and planks and brick held together by little more than hope; rusting wheeled carts, scoots, and planked wagons. An astonishing number of people moved among the ruins, sat by cookfires, or squatted hunched-over on mounds of garbage; a few half-naked children gazed listlessly at the skiff as it motored by. The stench and the misery were both undeniable and truly appalling.

Karimah turned into a narrow, deserted channel, and the skiff slowed, the motor idling quietly. The air seemed heavier, stagnant like the dark water which was scummed over with oil, gray clots of viscous matter, and beads of fluorescent yellow pollen. The bloated carcass of a small brown animal drifted past, the dead creature's head either submerged or missing altogether. Along the banks of the canal was a no-man's land, deserted and crumbling ruins choked and overgrown with diseased vegetation, cloying scented flowers open to the sky above—white and yellow engulfed by deep violets; yellows and oranges spotted with an iridescent brown; wide blue petals so dark they were almost black, spiraling around long creepers that trailed over the concrete banks and lay dying on the oily surface of the water.

Ahead, a wide stone bridge arched across the water. They passed into the shadow of stones, then emerged from under the bridge and into a large, artificial lagoon lined with tall, dark green spider trees; strung between the trees was a network of wire, reflectors, colored strips of fabric, and gruesome figurines, like some shaman's protective fetishes. Or something to scare off the birds and day-bats. At the far end of the lagoon, two canoes and a short, flat barge were moored to a rotting, partially sunken dock heavily canopied by the dense foliage of several trees that had been arched and tied together overhead. A pair of silver ducks waddled along the bank, but the dock was otherwise deserted. The water was surprisingly clean and clear, somehow kept separate and secured from the foul waters of the canal; it rolled away from them as they traversed the lagoon, reflecting the sun, the spider trees, and Cale's face in rippling patterns.

Karimah tied up the skiff, then led the way into the trees, raising a section of the wire network out of their path. In the shade of the trees, the air oppressed, warmer and heavier, and currents of heat swirled up from the earth, mixing with unexpected tendrils of cold that seemed to curl out from the trees' aboveground roots.

They emerged from the trees and stood before a large, ruined building, several stories of crumbling stonework overgrown with mosses and sprouting ferns. Music played somewhere nearby, quiet string jazz, and smoke rose from the far side of the building.

"Looks like Mom's firing," Karimah said. "She's got a wood-fired kiln as well as one that runs on fuel cells. She likes to use the wood-fired kiln when she can, even though it's a pain in the ass, because she says it's more basic and natural. Also produces more interesting colors and patterns." She looked at Cale and laughed. "You have no idea what I'm talking about, do you?"

"No."

"Mom's a potter. She makes just about anything you can imagine—bowls, plates, cups, vases, pots. Anything practical, and lots of just plain beautiful stuff for decoration. Whatever she and Dad don't need she gives away or trades at the markets. That's one of the reasons they live out here—they're within walking distance of a good source of clay." She gestured to the side of the building. "Let's go around. Day like today, Dad's probably in the garden."

When they came around to the south side of the building, Cale was taken aback at the size of the "garden." It was more like a small agricultural field, various shades of green running the length of the building and stretching several hundred paces to the south until it ran up against a dense stand of short, dark blue-violet trees. Rows of plants were divided by footpaths, and deep within the garden a tall, thin gray-bearded man with a wide-brimmed hat waved at them. He bent over to dig at something in the soil, then a few moments later walked toward them.

Her father's name was Rusk, and he shook Cale's hand with surprising vigor. He was bony and his skin was weathered and wrinkled; he smiled with genuine warmth and looked at Cale with blue eyes that shined.

"Pleased to meet you, Cale," Rusk said. "It's been years since Karimah's brought anyone to see the family."

Cale felt himself flush, and didn't quite understand why. The old man just patted him on the shoulder and said, "Let's go see Mama."

Karimah's mother appeared to be much younger than Rusk, though her long dark hair was heavily streaked with silver. Her name was Zaida and she was stoking the firebox of a brick kiln that had been built on the eastern side of the house. Smoke rose from a chimney that was close to two stories tall. A few paces away were several huge stacks of firewood, sorted by size. Zaida peered into a hole at the red crackling fire, then nodded once. She straightened, brushed her hands on her trousers, and shook Cale's hand.

"Should be okay for a while," she said. "You two are the first ones here. Let's have some tea, and you can show Cale around the place."

* * *

Karimah's parents made Cale feel welcome, an unfamiliar but pleasant sensation. From outside, the house appeared to be in ruins, but the walls were thick and solid, and the interior was well-maintained and secure from the weather—dry and cool and comfortable. The ground floor consisted entirely of one enormous room with a high ceiling, flooded with light from large windows. In addition to dozens of ceramic pieces placed throughout the room, a number of Rusk's watercolor paintings hung on the walls and post supports, realistic still lifes of garden foods, and impressionistic lagoon landscapes, reminding him of the anchorite's art books.

While Rusk made a pot of strong, smoke-scented tea, Karimah took Cale upstairs and showed him the rooms on the second floor, then led the way up a long and narrow flight of stairs to the vast open loft area where Rusk painted. From a small window in the south wall, Cale looked out over the enormous garden, then across the stand of trees and onto the outlying areas of Morningstar, a patchwork of multicolored flowers and greenery and blocks of buildings that gradually became more stone, brick, metal, and concrete, and less green, until the inner city was nothing but artificial structures, taller as they neared the center, broken only by roadways and canals. And at the center of it all, The Island, which from this far away looked much less impressive than it did from close-up.

"My brother and sister will be coming soon," Karimah said. She stood next to him, her shoulder gently pressing against his. "We try to get together like this every two or three weeks."

That explained the days she disappeared without saying anything to him. "You've never mentioned your family before," Cale said.

"Neither have you."

Cale nodded. He was reluctant to say anything at all to her. Too many years of keeping it to himself, not trusting anyone, not even Feegan or Junko or Terrel. Karimah, though. . . . Here she was bringing him into *her* family. He looked at her, and though he knew he could not tell her his family name, or how he had come to this world, he realized he could share at least some of his past with her.

"My father's dead," he told her. "He died when I was five. As far as I know, my mother, too."

"I'm sorry," Karimah said. "It's not much to say, but I am."

He shrugged and turned to her. "Let's go have tea with your parents."

They drank the tea outside, sitting beside a small pond shaded by a pair of fountainberry trees, near the kiln so Zaida could keep an eye on the temperature. She was glaze firing two different sets of bowls and cups, along with a number of vases, and explained the process to Cale. Karimah's brother Jemal arrived next, with his wife Katya and daughter Faith. Faith was fourteen years old, and stayed only long enough to give her grandparents and aunt a kiss, be introduced to Cale, then she was off to Zaida's studio to "throw pots," whatever that meant. Cale imagined her tossing pots across the room and shattering them against the walls, but he was sure the reality wasn't anything like that.

At midday, Karimah's sister Majidah arrived, with

her wife Toya and their thirteen-year-old son Max. Max spoke with a voice little more than a whisper, asked where Faith was, then, after wandering among the adults for a few minutes, said he was going to watch Faith.

The rest of the day passed slowly and enjoyably for Cale. He learned that Jemal was an analytics teacher at a small school near the river, that Katya worked as a med-tech in free clinics in the poorer areas of Morningstar, and that Majidah and Toya ran a barge café on the Grand Canal—they drifted up and down the canal, mooring in different districts each day, so that their customers were different every night, then cycled back to the same areas over time so that they got to know people in all parts of the city. Rusk talked about the garden, which provided much of their food, and Zaida talked about the orchids she was growing in a greenhouse sunroom on the second floor of the house—she pointed it out to Cale, at the southwestern corner of the building; through the steamy glass he could see dense patches of green and strings of brilliant colors. Gardening for pleasure was such a strange idea to him, but he thought he was beginning to understand it.

No one asked Cale about his past, or what he was doing now; no one asked Karimah what *she* was doing; no one ever mentioned the Resurrectionists, but Cale sensed that everyone knew. There seemed to be an understanding to avoid the topic.

As the sun set behind the buildings of The Island, Cale joined Rusk out in the garden while the others went inside to start dinner. Rusk opened a valve in a large pipe and water flowed through a system of hoses and pipes and sprayers, watering nearly the entire garden in a slow and controlled fashion. A few plants, however, needed hand-watering, and Cale helped carry watering cans out to a plot far from the building where several rows of tiny green plants were just beginning to emerge from the ground. Rusk showed him what to do, and they watered the seedlings together, carefully pouring water into the channels of each row, saturating the ground without harming any of the delicate plants. When they were done, they brought the cans back to the faucets and sat together on a bench with their backs against the building, taking in the last of the sun.

Rusk took a strip of cigarettes from his pocket, offered them to Cale, and nodded in approval when Cale shook his head. "It's a bad family trait," he told Cale. He popped one free from the strip and lit it. He smoked in silence for a time, eyes closed, face turned toward the setting sun. Finally he turned to Cale and spoke.

"We used to live near the center of Morningstar, not far from The Island. For years. Decades. Karimah grew up there, not here." He smiled. "She's an urban woman to her core. As we grew older, though, it was taking too damn much energy just to live, to get through each day. Too much noise, too many people, too much worrying about our own personal safety. We both realized we weren't appreciating life very much. Some do, in that environment, some people thrive in it." He shook his head. "Zaida and I don't. Lots of other people don't, either, but many of them can't ever get out. Some of those who *do,* well, they *really* get out, they retreat completely—into the jungles where they live like hermits, or other isolated places far from Morningstar. A few even freely choose to travel over the Divide and live there."

Cale nodded. "I met someone who did that. She was an anchorite, and she lived by herself in a cabin, and I don't think she's ever going to leave."

"Well, that's a little extreme for us. We like the comforts of electricity and running water." He chuckled. "Though I admit we had a hell of a time getting those two things in place here." He crushed out his cigarette stub in the dirt with his shoe. "And it's important to be near our children and grandchildren. This place has been perfect for us. A lot of work, but we've enjoyed almost every bit of that work, and we're both a lot happier." He lit another cigarette and looked askance at Cale. "So you've been on the other side of the Divide?" It was barely a question.

Cale nodded, realizing the slip he'd made. "Not by choice," he replied.

Rusk smiled, then said, "You don't talk much. I noticed that today. I like that in you, though I'm suspicious of it in most people."

Thinking of Blackburn, Cale said, "Someone else told me that, several years ago."

Rusk nodded, and went on. "Karimah's our youngest child. We still think of her as the baby of the family, even though she can probably take care of herself better than any of the rest of us. So we worry a little about her."

"Are you worried about me?"

Smiling, Rusk shook his head. "Not at all, Cale. She's a very good judge of character, and if she likes you and trusts you—which she does, or you wouldn't be here—then we do, too. But we worry about what you all are doing: The Island Security Forces and the Sarakheen and canal pirates and all the other crazy people who don't seem to like what you're trying to do, even if they don't really know what it is."

Cale didn't know how to respond, but finally said, "It's important to her."

"Yes, I know that. Is it important to you?"

"Yes, it is."

"Why?"

Cale thought about it for a while, and even though the only answer he had didn't seem satisfactory, he didn't have another. Besides, it was a true answer.

"I don't have anything else," he said.

Rusk nodded slowly, as if with a reluctant or sad understanding. "That's a shame, son. That's a damn shame."

Dinner was a long and extravagant event, with everyone seated at a table by a high window looking out onto the garden in the waning evening light. Food was plentiful, most of it provided by the garden, supplemented with fish and braised meats and bottles of homemade wine. By the time it was over, and Rusk was serving coffee and brandy and kuma and tea, darkness had fallen completely, and Cale realized they were expected to spend the night.

Soon the two youngsters, after cleaning up the dishes and kitchen, went off to bed—they were going to sleep on cots up in the attic rooms—but the adults remained at the table, drinking and talking for another two or three hours, until the moonlight began to glisten a silver green off the tops of the highest plants out in the garden. Karimah's brother and sister and their wives said their goodnights and went upstairs, then Cale thanked Rusk and Zaida for their hospitality, and Karimah led the way up to the second floor and a small room that looked out on the pond and the kiln.

While Karimah went down the hall to the bathroom, Cale went to the window and looked out at the quiet and peaceful night. After a time, Rusk appeared outside. Smoking a cigarette, he walked along the outer rows of the garden, then went over to the pond and sat. Zaida came out, walked over to Rusk, kissed him gently on the forehead, then went to the kiln and checked the temperature. She added more wood to the firebox, then stood and watched the glowing heat through the narrow vents, watched the smoke rise up from the chimney, a light gray cloud against the black evening sky.

Karimah returned and stood beside him, looking at his face. "What's wrong?"

He shook his head. "Nothing," he said, knowing that they both knew he was lying. He wiped the tears from his face, put his arms around her and pulled her to him, held her tightly, but it wasn't enough to ease the deep and painful ache that drove though him, and he wondered if it ever would be.

SEVEN

In the early autumn, Cale was returning from a visit to Sidonie in one of the Resurrectionists' skiffs when he found the way into Marlowe Canal blocked by a makeshift rigging of cables and ropes and patrolled by security launches. Cale pulled in toward the nearest launch and hailed the two-person crew.

"What's happening?" he asked.

The senior officer came to the aft railing and leaned toward Cale. "There's a breach in the canal," she said. "A big whirlpool's developed, sucking the water underground, and it's big enough to cause a problem for boats. You'd get pulled right in and end up drowned."

Cale stood up in the skiff and tried to see through the

ropes and cables, but all he could make out were crowds of people on the banks, watching the water near the Resurrectionists' building.

"Where's all the water going?" he asked. But even as he finished, a rush of panic flooded him as the obvious answer came to him silent and unwanted.

"Don't know," the officer said. "I've heard word of some kind of tunnels."

Cale felt momentarily paralyzed, then he quickly said, "Thanks," and pushed off from the launch, dropped to the bench seat, put the motor in gear, and jacked up the throttle. Moments later he pulled in to the nearest dock, squeezing in between two water taxis, banging and scraping both hulls; he locked the motor, tied up the boat, scrambled onto the dock, and ran.

As he neared the building, the canal bank was so crowded he had to cut over to the street for the final two blocks. He was just about to enter the skin parlor when he saw the Sarakheen standing at the curb. Despite the day's heat, he was wearing a full body-suit and thin gloves, which hid all evidence of his mek limbs.

Cale stopped a few paces away and stared at the Sarakheen, who gazed back at him with the same lack of expression his face had held that day he'd been with Blackburn. The silent tension between them seemed to extend for a long time, though Cale felt certain that only seconds passed. "No," he whispered to himself and broke his gaze from the Sarakheen and ran into the skin parlor.

Down the hall, barely able to punch the codes to unlock the door, then up the flights of stairs two and three steps at time, crashing out once as he caught a step and lost his footing, banging shins and knees and forearms; then back to his feet and on up to the third floor. One more corridor, then around the corner to the central stairwell. The door was propped open and he could hear shouting coming up from below. Breathing hard, he pulled himself through the door and started down the stairs.

He expected to meet people coming up, but didn't. When he reached the main entrance to the Underneath, he saw why—everyone was down here—those who had been above ground when the flooding had begun, and those muddy and wet or otherwise bedraggled who had obviously been below. There were people lying on the floor and others squatting against the walls, a few coughing violently, and still others standing around the main lift shaft. The lift to the level below was just coming up with Benka and Hamzaaz, who were both filthy with mud; Benka's trousers were split open and blood flowed from a long gash in his leg; Hamzaaz was bleeding from both arms, but she was able to help Benka limp off the lift as it stopped and other people moved forward to help.

Cicero spotted Cale and stepped in front of him, holding out his arms to block his way.

"Where is she?" Cale demanded, nearly screaming it.

"You can't go down there," Cicero told him. "All you'll do is get yourself killed. That place is a death trap right now."

"No! We can't just let them drown." He tried to shove Cicero aside, but the old man was stronger than he'd expected, and grabbed him by the shoulders, stopping him.

"Cale, just hold on and listen to me. *Listen* to me! You can go down to one of the next two levels and help, all right? Help the people coming up. The main lift is the only one working, and none of the rail systems, everything is ladders and steps down there now. Power's gone below the first level, which means the only lights are the emergency lanterns if anyone can find them. That breach is huge, it's a torrent pouring in there right now, coming in at the third level. We can't go below, or there'll just be more dead. You understand me? Cale? It's death down there. They're on their own, and we can't do anything else to help them. Cale? Cale . . . understand?"

Cale nodded, stupefied and suddenly weak, all energy leaking out of him, leaving him deadened and incapable of movement. He felt dizzy and dropped to one knee, head bent down. He understood, and he knew Cicero was right, and he was overwhelmed by despair. Breathing was suddenly difficult, as if his lungs had forgotten what to do. His eyes wanted to close, his entire body trying to shut down. Then he found a new reserve of strength somewhere and got back to his feet, looking directly at Cicero.

"Let me go help."

Cicero studied him, then nodded and said, "All right . . . all right. Be careful."

Cale hurried to the lift as it was headed back down and jumped onto the platform. It descended with intolerable slowness. When it finally reached the lower level and stopped, he hurried across the room to the nearest shaft and started down the ladder.

As he emerged from the dark vertical passage into the lamp-lit second level, he could hear the roar of the water below. Cicero was right. Loud and powerful like the cataracts upriver, where Terrel had taken him once. Five people sat on cots and stools near the two main shafts leading to the lower levels, watching the openings and waiting. They looked up as he crossed the chamber, and one of them, a woman named Jax, gestured for him to sit beside her on her cot.

He went first to the shafts and looked down into them. Bright lanterns had been lowered on ropes; they hung just above the streams of water that rushed out from the side passages and poured down the shafts to the lower levels. The lanterns were a hope, he thought, beacons guiding any survivors up to the top and safety.

He sat next to Jax and she handed him a water flask. Cale thanked her and drank, then handed the flask to the next person.

"Yes," Jax said, raising her voice to be heard above the water's roar. "She's down there. All we can do is wait."

Cale nodded, not quite knowing why, and turned to the nearest of the shafts, fixing his gaze on the light coming up from the lanterns, listening to the rushing flood. He waited.

Two hours later they heard a strangled, choking cry from one of the shafts. Cale and Jax hurried to it and looked down. Far below, partially lit by the lamps, a figure clung to the ladder, deluged by the torrent of water.

"We're right here!" Jax called down to the motionless figure. "You haven't got far!"

There was no reply from the person below, nor was there any movement. Arms and legs appeared to be wrapped tightly around the rungs, as though afraid to let go.

"Can you keep climbing?" Jax called.

Still no reply.

"Shit," Jax muttered. "Whoever it is probably can't make it any farther. We're going to have to go get them."

"I'll do it," Cale yelled.

Jax nodded once and didn't argue. She knew why he was volunteering.

First they tied a rope under Cale's arms so he wouldn't fall to his own death, then Jax gave him the end of another rope to tie around the person below. "Now go," she said. "I don't want to lose them. Not when they're so close."

Cale climbed onto the ladder and descended through the shaft. The light below hurt his eyes so he kept his focus on the rungs of the ladder before him. He passed through the collection of lamps and stepped down and into the torrent, clinging tightly to the ladder. The force of the water emerging from the side passage was stronger than he expected and nearly knocked him from the ladder, but he hung on and took it slowly and carefully, one hand at a time, one foot at a time.

As he went lower, the force of the water shifted direction and became all downward, pouring over him, making it difficult to see anything. He continued to descend, trying to keep the figure below him in sight. It was either taking longer than he'd thought to reach the person, or his sense of time was distorted.

Then suddenly he was there, his boots just two rungs above the person's head. He couldn't be sure, but he thought it was a woman. He took one more step down.

"I'm here!" he shouted over the rush of water.

The woman looked up, and Cale's heart collapsed. It wasn't Karimah.

Her name was Dirdre, and her face was overwhelmed

with exhaustion and panic as she managed to choke out, "Help me."

In despair, Cale worked his way down along the ladder until they were both clinging to the same rungs. The pouring water made everything slow and difficult, but he managed to loop the rope tightly around her, under her arms, then looped the extra length at the end down under her crotch and back up to the first loop. It took him another long minute to securely tie off the rope, then he tugged once at it. The rope became taut, but Dirdre wouldn't move; he pried her hand from the ladder and helped her make the first step. Finally she started to climb on her own. When she was several rungs above him, he tugged at his own rope, the slack was taken up, and he followed behind her.

The ascent seemed to take even longer than the climb down, and he could barely bring himself to follow Dirdre. He wanted to turn around and continue down to search for Karimah; but now that he was here with the water pouring over him and draining his strength, he understood with complete certainty that everything Cicero had said was true—descending any farther would be certain death. He hated himself for understanding that. Karimah, if by any chance she was still alive somewhere down below him, was on her own. That realization filled him with such despair that he could barely find the will to keep climbing.

But he did; they both kept climbing, and at some point Cale noticed that Dirdre was no longer on the ladder above him, and he realized they'd made it. Two more rungs, then he fell back into the chamber and lay on the floor, looking up at Jax, who crouched beside him.

"I'm sorry, Cale," she whispered. She took his hand in both of hers and squeezed. "You did good, and I'm sorry."

Some hours later he found he could no longer wait with the others, and on shaky legs slowly made his way up out of the Underneath. When he reached the main basement, Cicero convinced him to take a hot shower and get something to eat. Cale nodded, but he had something else to do first.

He emerged from the central stairwell on the third floor, then staggered down the two flights of stairs to the skin parlor and went straight for the front door. But when he stumbled out into the street, the Sarakheen was gone.

The whirlpool disappeared once the Underneath was completely flooded up to canal level and there was nowhere else for the water to go. Marlowe Canal was opened to boat traffic once more, and on the outside everything returned to normal.

Divers were hired to find and repair the breach, then pumping equipment was brought in, installed, and started. The water level in the Underneath began to slowly drop.

During the second day, Tico's body was found in the glass-paneled chamber, and later that night the body of a woman named Sarantina was discovered in one of the ladder shafts, trapped under a hatch blocked shut by a collapsed wall.

In the early morning of the third day, they brought Karimah's body up from one of the deepest accessible chambers. Hands shaking and legs so weak he could barely stay on his feet, Cale helped three others carry her body up the shafts, the lift, then up the central stairway. He repeatedly glanced away and then looked back at her, convinced each time that he would discover it was someone else they carried, which would leave him with some infinitely small and infinitely irrational hope that she was still alive. It was never anyone but Karimah, however; there was never any real hope. Finally they brought her to the third floor, where he laid her out on the sleeping mat in their room. The others withdrew, leaving him alone with her.

He sat hunched up beside her, helpless and numb. Coherent thought was impossible; random words and images, bits of recalled sound and odors, scattered around his seemingly hollow mind. With one ear turned toward her, he listened intently for a word from her purple-gray lips, a whisper, some hint of breath. Nothing. He stared at the bruised and bloated face, attempting to superimpose over the pale flesh an image of Karimah alive—her eyes open, her mouth turned up in a wry smile, her skin flushed with color as he lay with her on the pallet in their private cell in the Underneath. But he could not maintain that image, it kept breaking apart, and it was her inanimate and unchanging face that stared relentlessly back at him. He knew, finally, that she was dead, and that she would never speak to him again.

With Cicero's help, Cale placed her cloth-shrouded body in the bottom of the skiff, then started the motor and pushed away from the dock. Overhead, the sun was a hot, blurred disk of pale orange, smeared out and discolored by a thick haze. Staring at the obscured sun, Cale was overcome by a peculiar sensation that he was doing something wrong. He should be taking her body not in this motorized boat, but in a canoe, taking her home with his own physical efforts. Then, as he moved out into the Grand Canal, the feeling intensified, until it became an urgent demand. He swung the skiff around and headed back toward the south.

He tied up at the small dock near Sidonie's apartment, against the bank so Karimah's body could rest in the shade. Walking along the dock, he felt a sense of relief at seeing Sidonie's canoe. He hurried along the street and up the stairs of her building, and stood breathing hard before her door. He hesitated, afraid she wasn't in, not wanting to take the canoe without asking her, but knowing he would do it if he had to. Finally he knocked.

Sidonie came to the door and smiled when she saw him, but the smile transformed almost immediately as she looked into his eyes.

"What's happened, Cale?"

She tried to lead him inside, but he shook his head, opening and closing his mouth like a dying fish. Then, quite suddenly and almost peacefully, the tension in his throat disappeared, and he began to speak.

She put her hand to his cheek, gently brushed his skin, and listened.

Cale paddled the canoe through the midday heat, hardly aware of his surroundings, of the other boats in the water around him. The water's surface was shiny and choppy from the boat traffic, and the air smelled of oil and old fish, grilling meat and rotting vegetation. Someone called out to him from one of the large commercial cargo boats just before it nearly swamped him, and he heard the laughter of others who were watching from shore.

Once he left the Grand Canal, as each new channel became narrower and quieter than the previous, he felt a growing relief, along with a curious sense of peace. He never looked at the shrouded body laid out at his feet, but he was constantly aware of its presence, aware of where he was headed and why. His arms grew tired and he would occasionally rest, gliding slowly along the water, coasting to a stop, and he would sit motionless in the canoe, surveying the water and the banks on either side of him, searching for something he would know only if he saw it. But the sense of recognition never came, and he would dip the paddle into the water and resume his progress.

Sometime in the late afternoon he approached the stone bridge at the lagoon's entrance, and passed beneath it. After taking several strong, deep strokes, he let the canoe drift across the lagoon, now watching Karimah's shrouded body as if he expected to see some movement or other change as she neared her mother and father. The canoe slowed, until it was hardly moving forward at all. He sat with the paddle across his thighs, water dripping slowly from the blade, and listened to the quiet sounds around him—the flutter of wings; the gentle slap of webbed feet from a waddling duck; a high-pitched clicking within the trees; a faint splash from somewhere behind him.

The canoe bumped against the small barge, then gradually swung around. Cale grabbed the barge and pulled the canoe along it until he was up against the dock. He sat there for a long time without moving, then climbed out and tied up. He left her in the canoe and entered the trees.

When he came around the side of the building, he saw Rusk and Zaida in the garden harvesting long, green striped vegetables, picking them from the tall, gangly plants and placing them in a woven basket. Zaida looked up first, puzzled, then straightened and put her closed hand up to her mouth when she saw Cale's face and realized he was alone. Rusk looked at Zaida, then at Cale, then turned back to his wife and put his arms around her, pulling her tight against him.

In the morning, they buried her just beyond the far boundary of the garden, beneath a young spider tree. The whole family was there, the family Cale had met weeks earlier. Except for Cale, all of them wept at one time or another, hard or soft, but all strangely quiet. Cale waited for his own tears, but they never came.

When the last of the dirt was spread over her, Rusk and Zaida asked him to stay with them for the day, for the night if he wanted. They seemed to understand when he said he couldn't, or were so overwhelmed with their own grief that it didn't matter. He said goodbye to them and returned to the lagoon.

Cale sat in the empty canoe for a time, staring at the clean dark waters, studying the reflections of the hazy sky and the dark spider trees, and his own reflection rippling slightly as the canoe rocked gently beside the dock. He picked up the paddle, plunged it into the water, and pulled.

EIGHT

He spent the following days on the waterways of Morningstar, paddling the canoe from one canal to another, stepping on land only to relieve himself and refill his water flask. He bought cheap food from boat vendors, and large quantities of even cheaper beer; but he found that the alcoholic haze did nothing to ease the grief, and discovered he preferred the sober numbness that otherwise enveloped him.

In quieter waters he watched sleek brown stennets swimming beside the canoe in pairs, their tiny black eyes watching him with curiosity. Bulbous-eyed fish rose and splashed at dusk, sending out tiny wavelets in widening circles. In the mornings he watched the sun rise and light up the water with silver and gold reflections, and in the evenings he watched the sun set, coloring the water with darker hues, tinting the silver and gold with deep orange and red.

He visited familiar parts of Morningstar and areas he'd never seen before. One afternoon he paddled past the narrow channel where the *Skyute* had been attacked, and later, near the Resurrectionists' encampment, drifted over the spot where the boat had burned and gone down that night. He looked over the side of the canoe, hoping to see some sign of the sunken wreck. He saw nothing but black murky water, and eventually he dug the paddle into the water with long, deep strokes, making sure he would be nowhere near this part of the city when darkness fell.

At night he slept in the canoe, letting it drift on the water whenever the numbing weariness set in, ignoring the risk of collisions with other boats. One night, having drifted into the middle of one of the main canals, he was awakened by the blaring horn of a large cargo barge bearing down on him. Without panic, Cale calmly sat up, picked up the paddle, and pulled out of the barge's path just in time, the corner of the barge clipping the tail end of the canoe, the wake bobbing him up and down for a long time afterward.

After eight or nine or ten days he found himself paddling toward Sidonie's dock, and the day opened up to him as if he were emerging from a coma, some trancelike state. The setting sun seemed intense, colors became more vivid, the odors of fish and cooking fires and flowers intensified, and the sounds of people and music and engines and splashing water all grew louder, sharper, and clearer.

As he pulled in to the dock, he noticed that the Resurrectionists' skiff was gone, hopefully returned to them. He tied up and stepped onto the wooden planks, then stood there for a time, listening to the city, to the water, breathing in the scent of the deep orange lilies spilling over the banks. The dock moved under him from the wake of a passing boat, and he knew it was time to return to land, even if it was only to prepare to leave it once again.

He stood outside Sidonie's door, just as he had days before, once again hesitating, once again afraid she would not be in. He knocked, and when she opened the door she did not appear surprised to see him.

Cale walked out onto the balcony and looked out at the sun just disappearing behind the highest building miles to the west, a gleaming stone structure he remembered seeing several days earlier from much closer. Sidonie joined him on the balcony and gently put her hand on his shoulder.

"I've lost something," he said.

"I know . . . Karimah."

He nodded once, then shook his head. "More than that. Something that died with her. And not just because she died." He paused, struggling to find the words. "I'm not sure I completely understand. Because of *why* she died, I think." He turned to Sidonie. "It's gone, whatever it is."

She was silent for a time, studying him, then her own gaze lost its focus as if she were looking into some other place or time with sadness and utter certainty.

Cale turned and leaned against the balcony railing, then tilted his head back to look up and toward the east at the faint stars just now becoming visible in the darkening blue and purple sky. Sidonie stood next to him, her shoulder against his, watching the stars with him.

"Take me there," he finally said. "There's nothing left for me here."

"Maybe," she replied, sighing deeply. "I know I've encouraged you to go back, but I can't make any promises about what will be there for you. Nothing's certain."

He turned to her. "I learned that a long time ago," he told her, "but I didn't remember."

In the kitchen the kettle hissed and boiled and Sidonie went inside. Cale sat in one of the chairs and looked off into the west, at the remnants of bloodred sky and the lights coming on all over the city. Sidonie returned with the cups of hot steaming kuma, handed one to him, and sat in the other chair.

"I'm not ready," he said. "I have no education, there are too many times when I have no idea what people are doing or what they're talking about." He shook his head. "I can barely read. I can't go back to that kind of life like this. I'd be completely unprepared and overwhelmed."

"I understand," Sidonie replied. "I can find the places, the people who can teach you."

Neither of them spoke after that. They drank their kuma and watched night fully envelop the city, watched the stars glitter against the cobalt sky, and the red-white hazy tail of a spike ship rising from the port and heading toward the station, a starlike coin in geosynch orbit high above them.

He looked down and stared into his cup, at the sliver of reflected light on the surface of the hot kuma, and felt his hands begin to shake. A rushing sound filled his ears from within his own body and he set the cup on the floor, hands shaking even worse now. He couldn't look at Sidonie. He couldn't look at anything. Cale bent his head, pressed his palms against his eyes, and finally wept.

INTERLUDE

After four years he did not feel ready, but rather finally accepted that there was little else he could do to prepare for what lay ahead. Sidonie made arrangements for their passage to Lagrima, but it would be nearly a year before they could leave.

He had one final task, he told her, and she could go with him if she wished, but he would go alone if not. He had to go back across the Divide, to that part of the world that had wounded them both, and retrieve something he had left behind. Your innocence? she asked with a sad smile.

In early spring, after a week of preparations, they left Morningstar in the back compartment of a trader's van, and headed west.

* * *

They purchased two pack ponies and several weeks of provisions in Karadum, crossed the Divide, then headed north. He knew no other way back to Sproul's grave, so they retraced the route he had taken through this wasteland years before.

Eight days after the crossing, they rode into the ruins of the village by the river. Little had changed, except that the blood had long since been washed away and the corpses had become little more than bleached bones clothed in shreds of faded fabric. Cale led the way to the place on the river where he had last seen Lammia's dead body, but there was nothing there except for a thick patch of flowering plants that was just beginning to bloom.

In the next stretch of desert, he saw no sign of the burned tree that had induced the visions of Aliazar's imbecile brother, but the impassioned words and conjured images of that night filled Cale's thoughts as he and Sidonie rode across the parched and crackling earth.

Two days farther on, the vast, dark marsh appeared before them, gloomy and cold and somehow both dead and undead, as if it existed in some indefinable state between the two, and had so for uncounted centuries. They kept their distance from the marsh, using it only as a landmark. Cale occasionally glanced sideways at the mist-shrouded expanse, afraid a boat with two figures several years dead would appear drifting across the black waters, stark skeletons sitting upright on rotting wood with flaps of dried skin dangling from their bones. No boat appeared.

* * *

Sixteen days later they crested the low hillock and looked down at the ruined dwellings of the deserted hamlet. It was early afternoon, the day's heat at its peak—warm, but nothing like it was the first time he'd come here. The empty dwellings looked as if they had not been seen by human eyes since his own. The air was quiet and still and smelled faintly of the aromatic blossoms on the nearby plants.

"What is this place?" Sidonie asked.

"I don't know," Cale replied, searching the buildings for some sign of change and finding none, not even a further decay. As if the town had been in a state of suspended animation since he'd left it behind. "Something sacred," he said.

"Sacred to whom?"

Cale didn't answer. He looked behind them and saw nothing but dry low hills and sparse brush and a few spindly trees with budding leaves. For several days now he'd sensed they were being followed, though he had never seen or heard anything to confirm it, and had said nothing to Sidonie. He realized now that was part of why he'd decided to come here first before returning to Sproul's grave.

"What is it, Cale?"

"Nothing." He turned and kneed the pony and led the way down and into the deserted village.

They dismounted and tied up the ponies just outside the large central building. A heavy silence surrounded them, stifling somehow, the air stagnant. Inside the building, everything was unchanged—the pedestal still lying on its side; the metal bowl on the floor with the cold black and gray ashes of the fire he and Sproul had made; the rotting benches; the holes in the roof; the broken candles and shards of colored glass scattered on the floor.

"What's here?" Sidonie asked.

"Nothing," Cale replied. He moved forward, making his way toward the altar, and Sidonie followed.

The stone slab lay unmoved beside the altar, the wood splintered and crushed beneath it, and the altar itself was still empty, emitting not even a hint of the animate azure light that had flowed from it that night all those years ago.

Cale looked up at the high stone wall and stared at the alien glyphs, once more sensing the power in them. Or perhaps he was only sensing their utter strangeness. Sidonie stood beside him and together they studied the markings, neither speaking, until Cale felt entranced by them, as if he could almost understand their message on some deep and unconscious level.

Solid footsteps broke him out of his trance, and he turned to see Blackburn in the doorway, aiming a weapon at them. He wore a hat again, but no jacket, and the weapon he carried appeared to be a rifle of some kind. His face held little expression. He studied the two of them carefully, periodically glancing around the building, into the corners, never shifting his gaze from Cale and Sidonie for more than a moment, taking it all in until he was apparently satisfied.

"Don't move or say a word," he finally said. "I won't hesitate to shoot, not even you, young Cale."

Sidonie looked at Cale but didn't say anything. Blackburn came slowly forward, continuing to survey his surroundings as though afraid someone or something would leap out of the shadows and attack him. When he reached the altar, he looked down into the empty stone container.

"Are we *all* too late, then?" he said. He looked at Cale. "It was already empty?" he asked, intently observing Cale's face.

"Yes."

"You didn't find something that you've already stashed away somewhere?"

Cale shook his head. "Look around all you want," he replied.

Blackburn nodded. "Oh, I will. I believe you, but I'll search all the same." He sighed heavily, and something vital seemed to go out of him. "Do you know what *was* in there?"

"No. Do you?" Cale asked.

Blackburn didn't answer. His eyes seemed unfocused.

"Are you alone?" Cale asked, trying to distract Blackburn, afraid of where the big man's thoughts were going.

Blackburn's eyes came back into focus and he gave Cale a puzzled smile. "Of course. I'm always alone."

"I thought the Sarakheen might be with you. Aren't you working for him?"

Blackburn's expression hardened and his eyes narrowed, and he said, "I don't work for anyone except myself, young Cale." He cocked his head and regarded Sidonie for a time, as though just now noticing her. "Who are you?"

"Sidonie."

After looking back and forth between the two of them several times, Blackburn smiled with amusement. "Surely not lovers?"

Cale snapped out, "Why not?"

Blackburn was unfazed and his smile only widened. "No, I think not," he said. "More like surrogate mother and son,

I'd say." The smile quickly faded and Blackburn said to Cale, more seriously, "You've been here before, haven't you? That's why you're here now—you've come back."

Better to stay with the truth, Cale thought. "Yes," he admitted.

"But this wasn't empty then, was it?" Blackburn asked, nodding toward the altar.

"No." True enough—it wasn't empty until he'd left with Sproul. He pointed to the slab on the floor. "That was still on top of it." Finally, he gave Blackburn one last piece of truth. "It was too heavy for me to move."

"Why did you come back?" Blackburn asked. "If you don't know what was in there, why did you come all this way? Take all the risks?"

It was the question Cale had been afraid of, but now he'd had time to prepare an answer. "It had to be something valuable," he said. "Gemstones or precious metals, maybe some exotic drug, something. When I was on this side of the Divide before, I'd met people who were searching for some kind of incredible treasure, people who were willing to die trying to find it." Thinking of Sproul, he added, "People who *did* die trying to find it."

Still watching him steadily, Blackburn nodded—nodded in disappointed acceptance of some wonderful thing now lost. He turned to the wall of glyphs and appeared to be reading them. "I wonder who *did* find it. And I wonder . . ." He didn't finish. Still studying the glyphs, he resumed speaking in a thoughtful and puzzled tone. "I'll tell you a strange thing, Cale. I've traveled for years on this side of the Divide, I've spent much of that time searching for this place, but I've never found it before. I've been by that dry lake out there more than once, but I've never seen these buildings until today." He turned back to Cale. "What do you think? Does this place only appear on certain days? Is it only manifest when the moon and sun and planets move into some special alignment?"

Facing Blackburn's intense gaze, Cale did not have to pretend confusion, for he had no idea what Blackburn was talking about.

"You really don't know anything about that," Blackburn finally said, shaking his head in dismissal. "I thought you were going to lead me to it. Well, you did, but to no purpose."

"What *is* this place?" Cale asked, repeating Sidonie's question.

Blackburn smiled again and shook his head. He gestured with the weapon. "On the floor, facedown."

"Are you going to kill us?" Sidonie asked.

Blackburn laughed. "Don't be melodramatic." He pointed to the floor again.

Cale and Sidonie lay down beside the altar and Blackburn bound their ankles, then bound their wrists behind their backs. He left the building, and a short while later, through the open doorway, Cale saw Blackburn return atop Morrigan, the big animal shaking its head and kicking up dust and chunks of dried mud, as strong and feisty as ever. Cale watched Blackburn dismount, remove the bags from their ponies, and begin searching through them.

"Will he kill us?" Sidonie asked in a whisper.

"I don't think so."

Over the next hour Blackburn went through all of their bags, then undertook a thorough search of the building, finding nothing. He squatted beside Cale, the rifle resting across his knees, and sighed heavily.

"It really was empty."

Cale didn't bother to respond. Blackburn rocked slightly on his haunches, looking past him at the wall of markings once again. "Would've changed my life," he said. "Might have changed all our lives."

That's what Sproul believed, too, Cale thought, and he supposed that in a way it was true.

Blackburn got to his feet, then turned and started to walk away.

"Aren't you going to untie us?" Cale asked.

Blackburn stopped and turned. "Can't do that. I don't want you coming after me. Morrigan can outpace those pathetic pack ponies of yours, but I don't want the trouble. You and your surrogate mother or lover or whatever she is, you'll free yourselves eventually. Be thankful I'm leaving you the ponies." He raised and tipped his hat to them, and the sun coming in through the hole in the room gleamed brightly off the shaved head. Blackburn replaced the hat, turned, and left. Outside, he mounted Morrigan, and galloped away.

In the cool and cloudy early morning hours three days later, after taking a circuitous route, Cale and Sidonie approached the tall, solitary stone and Sproul's grave. The terrain was unbroken for great distances all around them, and Cale was certain they had not been followed.

They hobbled the ponies on the other side of the stone, then set to work together to open up the grave. The clouds thickened, and a cold and damp breeze kicked up, but no rain fell. As they scraped and dug away the earth, exposing Sproul's remains, Cale was surprised that there was only a dry, musty odor. The fleshless ribcage and skull appeared; nothing remained but the dirt-covered skeleton and clumps of hair, the bones stripped clean by whatever subterranean creatures or microorganisms dwelled in the ground.

The alien book was tilted and wedged between the pelvic bones, while glimpses of the blue stones could be seen among the scraps of stained cloth that were all that remained of Sproul's vest. Cale lifted the volume out of the grave and set it on the ground before Sidonie. He raised the cover and turned it over, then very carefully lifted one of the metal pages so she could see the markings etched through it.

He went to the ponies, and from his personal rucksack he removed a bag of thick heavy leather. He returned to the grave, knelt beside it, and as he dug out the blue stones and placed them in the bag, he explained his plan to Sidonie.

"I'm going to pack the book uncovered in among all my other supplies," he told her. "I'm not going to try to disguise it or hide it. But I want to bring these with us, because I want the guards at the Divide crossing to think that the *stones* are what we're trying to get across. I think they'll react just as Sproul did—fixate on the stones and ignore the book."

"But if the stones killed Sproul, aren't you risking the same thing?"

Cale shook his head. "I'm going to keep them in this bag and let it drag a ways behind us. That should be safe enough. I was with Sproul for several days, usually close to him, and I never got sick."

"And when we get to the Divide?"

"I'll have to keep them in the rucksack for a short time, but I'm willing to take that risk. The guards will focus on the stones, I think. My guess is they'll take some of them as 'payment.' And I hope they won't even notice the book."

When the bag was three-quarters full, he stood, leaving the rest of the stones with Sproul's remains, then he and Sidonie refilled the grave. He packed the book in his rucksack, tied a long cord to the bag of stones, tossed the bag to the ground, then tied the other end of the cord to the back of his pony's packsaddle.

"Let's go," he said. "I want to be as far from here as possible before we make camp for the night."

Sidonie nodded her agreement. They unhobbled the ponies, mounted, and rode away from the grave as the first drops of rain fell.

Several days later, just after midday, they arrived once again at the burned village. Despite the painful images and memories the place conjured up for Cale, they decided to spend the night near the river in the only hut that was reasonably intact. They were both exhausted from the days of travel and welcomed the chance to rest, grateful for shelter from the damp night air.

After helping Sidonie clean the hut, Cale went out to wander about the ruins. He walked among the charred remains of the huts and other buildings that had once comprised this village, deliberately studying the skulls of the dead and reminding himself that these skeletons of bleached and scorched bones had once been living men and women.

The evidence was there even amid all the devastation: a smoke-stained necklace of polished stones; a charred boot; a gold ring around the stripped finger bone of a detached hand.

Eventually he made his way upstream to where he'd made camp that night. Someone else had made use of the site since then, for there were far more half-burned branches, dead coals, and ash in the makeshift fire pit than he had produced that one night. He poked through the ashes with a stick; they were clumped with moisture, and patches of black moss grew beneath them.

He followed the river back downstream until he reached the flat patch of grass that had once held Lammia's dead body. Nothing at all remained; perhaps if he were to walk out into the water and wade downstream and search among the rocks and the riverbed, he would find her bones. Cale knelt on the grass and watched the water rushing past, rippling over stones and dead branches. He had known her for only a few hours, but the ache of her loss still resided within him, adding itself to the much larger ache of Karimah, so that both were linked in death.

The scent of the flowers blooming around the edges of the grass was strong and comforting. Cale lay on his back, breathing deeply, and watched the high scattered clouds drift by above him.

The sun was setting when he returned to the hut, and Sidonie was seated at a table with the alien book before her. Two thin wooden sticks protruded from it, like page markers. The coppery covers reflected a swimming, burnished light from the oil lamp she'd found somewhere.

"You never looked closely at this, did you? Looked *through* it, page by page?"

"No. I didn't have it long. I didn't think there was any point. I couldn't read back then, but even if I could have, I couldn't have read *that.*" He pointed at the book and sat across from her.

Sidonie nodded once and said, "Yeah, it's Jaaprana writing. But you *could* have read it. Or a part of it. You didn't realize it, but it's not *all* in the Jaaprana's language." She opened the book, carefully turning the metal leaves a few at a time until it lay open where it was marked by the first stick. There, the page was no longer like a stencil; etched onto the metal leaf in black were rows of figures, ideographs he couldn't read but which he'd seen in some of the anchorite's books and on signs in several districts around Morningstar.

"I think that's Chinese," she said. "We can find out for sure later." She turned another batch of pages until she came to the second marker, where the figures changed once again—this time to the Roman alphabet. "Reform English, more or less," she said.

Cale sat stunned, confused about what to think, with no idea where to begin, no idea what it might mean. "Have you read it?" he asked.

"No, only the first page. I wanted to wait for you." She got up and knelt by the camp stove, where a pot of kuma steamed and brewed with a gentle hiss. "I thought we should read it together."

Cale nodded absently, staring at the words on the page upside down before him. He was both excited and afraid. Excited about the possibilities, and afraid that the text would turn out to be mundane and pointless, making this entire excursion a waste of time.

Sidonie brought the pot and cups to the table. Cale slid his chair around so that they sat side by side, and they began to read. . . .

I was already a revenant when you arrived. A ghost from your future and our past.

Also from your past and our future.

I have been waiting for years, for decades, and now for centuries.

Here.

Now.

The initial waiting ended decades ago with your arrival on this world. I watched you build a city, the one you call Morningstar, watched you build it atop the rubble which in turn lay atop the ruins of our own ghost cities, which in our deaths we had deliberately sunk into the earth where they lay in hiding, waiting as I waited. And where they still lie, hiding and waiting.

Waiting for you, and for us. For our return.

* * *

Waiting for you.

Who are we? You name us the Jaaprana, from the city where some of your people first discovered remnants of our lives. What we name ourselves cannot be translated into any of your languages without confusion and misunderstanding, so I refer to us as the Jaaprana even though that is not who we are.

We are a people in a way similar to the way in which you are a people.

I lived among you, invisible, though sensed by a few who had no notion of who or what I was. I learned your ways, your languages, until I could create this manuscript, which holds the keys to our return.

Not my return, however, for I sacrificed my life to become the revenant for this world, the keeper and the maker of this manuscript.

There followed many pages providing a broad overview of the history of the Jaaprana, from their earliest appearance in cities on their home world, to their first ventures into space, and to their subsequent colonization over many decades of fourteen other worlds. References were made to conflicts, to wars, to catastrophes natural and self-inflicted, to great technological advancements and social achievements, to scientific successes and failures.

Not so different from human history, Cale thought. This entire section had the feel of an obligatory recounting of the Jaaprana's story as a civilization, and perhaps that was just what it was. But he and Sidonie kept on, and soon the tone changed again, intriguing him once more. . . .

Then came the time of our death.

But not our end.

We were dying as a people. No new generations arose, and no understanding or solution despite the greatest of efforts.

Extinction loomed.

Re-genesis became the only option.

Willing our deaths, willing the destruction of our cities, willing our entombment in the Graveyard of Saints.

Centuries will be needed for our re-genesis, and now you are needed to initiate the final steps, to revive the Emissary and release us.

You are the one who can bring us back, the one who can unite your past and ours, your future and ours.

We have much to offer you, as you have much to offer us. The wisdom of lives that can only come from those who have lived them.

We learned a great lesson from our coming deaths. A value to life that cannot be understood unless lost and regained.

A lesson your people have not yet learned.

There is a gate to where we lie entombed, to the Graveyard of Saints. A gate to a place out of time, a gate to a place that is not a place. You must take this manuscript through that gate and to the shrine in the Graveyard.

The gate will be found near a star of solitude, an inner world that is not a world but a portal where no other worlds exist. The star's own special satellite.

This volume contains within it the map to the star of solitude, and the gate. When it is opened to the end page, you will find a tab laid into the binding. Press the tab and a chart will manifest to guide you. This is your destination.

The gate lies near the star, fixed in its position. You enter the gate by a straight path, the path through the gate and toward the star, the two aligned before you. The gate will take you not to the star, but to the place that is not a place, which is named Graveyard of Saints.

Our mausoleum and our home.

* * *

In the Graveyard of Saints you will find a shrine: the processor of this manuscript.

Lay this manuscript in its place atop the shrine, and revive the Emissary. When the process has begun, take it back and keep it with you. For if the Emissary does not awaken or does not function, you must find the next and you must have the manuscript with you to begin again.

When the Emissary awakens, you will pass on this manuscript when requested.

This will be your final task, for it shall be the Emissary who will set in motion our re-genesis.

And our return.

Those were the final words. Cale looked up at Sidonie.

"What do you think?" he asked.

"It would be incredible if it's true." She breathed in deeply, then slowly let it out. "What I can understand of it. I don't know, Cale, it *sounds* true to me. It *feels* true."

Cale nodded in agreement. There was something about the words, a feeling of power to them that was much like the power he'd felt in the village when he'd first seen the alien markings on the wall behind the altar. He could not have explained what that power was, or what produced it, but he felt certain of its presence.

"Try it," Sidonie said. "Activate the star chart the way it says. If nothing happens . . ." She shrugged.

Cale opened the book to the last page, a metal sheet blank and thicker than the others, then held the page straight up and looked at the binding. He saw a dull black tab at the edge of the binding, laid the final page atop the others, and slid the tab to one side.

Panels folded out from the spine, hinged to the book and angled slightly up and toward each other. A faint whirring sounded, then crimson glowing matrices appeared in the air before them. The red lines glistened, then brightened and expanded until they filled all the shadowed reaches of the hut. The matrices faded, replaced by gold and silver stars, a night sky surrounding them, shining brightly so that it seemed that he and Sidonie had become suspended in space. Near the center, a single star appeared as a larger pulsing green light.

"Cale?"

"Yes?" he said quietly, regarding the shining stars, the pulsing green star at their center.

"Are we going there?" Sidonie asked.

Cale looked at her and nodded. "Oh yes. Someday. We'll find a way, Sidonie. We'll find it." He reached toward the oil lamp and turned down the wick until the flame went out, and they sat in the darkness, surrounded by stars.

Eleven days later, skies clear and bright and hot above them, Cale and Sidonie rode into the dusty settlement of the Northern Crossing. They sold the ponies and whatever provisions they couldn't carry, then approached the border station on foot, the bag of blue stones now tucked into Cale's rucksack. Several hours later, when Cale had been cleansed and tested and was dressed once again, one of the security officers handed his rucksack to him with a poorly hidden smirk. Cale knelt and glanced through his belongings; the bag of stones was definitely smaller, and the senior officer stood to the side, watching Cale with a steady gaze as though daring him to complain. But Cale had seen the corner of the strange book, and that was all that mattered. He opened his mouth as if to protest, then closed it without a word. It was understood by all—the missing stones were the price for passage, and Cale felt only a twinge of guilt that the security officers might soon be paying their own far higher price.

When Sidonie emerged from the building a few minutes later and joined him, Cale said nothing, and they set out together across the bridge.

They lost half of the remaining stones to the security officers on the other side of the bridge, but entered Karadum with the alien book intact. As soon as they were out of sight of the station, Cale pulled the bag of stones from his rucksack and tossed it into a pile of trash on a side street behind a gambling house. They walked on.

The next morning they bought a ride in a trader's van not unlike the one in which they'd come to Karadum. They would be in Morningstar in a few more days, and then after that they would soon be leaving—leaving Morningstar, Conrad's World, this star system. They were returning home, Sidonie said. Cale wasn't so sure. But now, at last, he was willing to see if it was possibly true.

BOOK THREE

ONE

Lagrima.
Home?

They began their descent in artificial twilight, then emerged from the orbital station and into the unexpected blinding glare of the sun. Cale shaded his eyes, blinking, just as the steelglass before him polarized and eased the glare. Seated beside him, Sidonie put a hand on his arm. "Sorry, I forgot to warn you about that."

The passenger ring continued its drop down the outer rim of the space elevator's cargo shaft, rotating slowly, while the sun appeared to be setting in fast-motion, the sky's colors transitioning from lighter hues to darker, from the palest turquoise blue to wide swaths of deep yellow and fiery orange. Then, as the sun disappeared and their view slowly spiraled toward the south, the sky became a dark rose that blossomed into a rich bloodred. Disoriented, feeling as if they were descending through time as well as space, Cale watched the final transitions through darkening violet and then cobalt and indigo until, as they entered complete night, stars appeared both above and below them.

The thousands of shining points below and steadily approaching were not stars at all but the lights of Lagrima. The city lay spread out beneath them for miles in all directions, its boundaries delineated by a band of darkness blacker than shadow.

The sea came into view, strangely lit from beneath the water near the shore, the shallows a bright aqua that darkened toward slate as the water deepened, and eventually became nearly black. Several thin appendages of the city's eastern perimeter extended out over the surface of the water, buildings and avenues gleaming with light and movement. Tiny sparkling shapes rose and fell with gentle swells out on the deeper darker waters. Translucent cloud-like forms drifted above the sea, trailing gold streamers.

Their rotation and descent continued, revealing a ragged, sparsely lit coastline that stretched far away from Lagrima, somehow separate and independent of the city, and which then disappeared into darkness and heavy mists. Then the main city reappeared, vaster and nearer now, brighter and more alive though they were still miles above it. Multicolored lights of flying vehicles wove chaotic patterns above the city.

Sidonie pointed to a glistening structure of gold and crimson lights near the distant edge of the city, the lights forming the three-dimensional shape of a glowing-eyed falcon with talons outstretched as though reaching for its prey. The image was familiar to Cale in a vague and unsettling way, so that he wanted to turn away from it and yet stare harder at it at the same time.

"Home," she said. "The Alexandros Family Estates." She shook her head. "It used to be more than three times that size, before you were born. The largest on this world, the largest on *two* worlds. It was still nearly twice that size when we left, and much nearer to the core of the city. Things change so fast here."

She gestured at a vast and sparkling emerald enclave shaped like a pyramid, and an enormous tower of silver and blue lattices rising two or more miles above the city. Both were significantly larger than the Alexandros Estates, denser and higher, as well as covering far more territory, and both gave off a blazing luminescence that pulsed into the night like the beating of gigantic and primeval hearts.

"The Saar Family Consortium, and the Titan Consortium," Sidonie explained. "They used to be weak competitors, much smaller than what you see. Now they're leaving you far behind, and mostly warring with each other. Before long they'll try to completely eliminate you."

"That might be a good thing," Cale said.

"Cale," she said, looking sternly at him. "The Consortium is your inheritance. Your heritage."

Cale didn't reply, and soon they were again facing the sea. Shadowy forms looped through the water, thin white lines of waves sluiced up the long expansive slopes, never quite reaching the clusters of people and shelters scattered along the beaches. Smoke rose from dozens of outdoor fires; a scattering of black disks shot out over the water; an elongated balloon drifted above the docks.

When they came around to face the city once more, farther down the shaft, Cale finally began to appreciate how extensive Lagrima was. Structures that were clearly several hundred stories high still seemed quite small, and he now realized that the city boundaries were sixty or seventy or more miles distant. Lagrima would completely dwarf Morningstar if they were to be set side by side.

One final slow rotation and he could make out swimmers in the sea and diners at outdoor tables on long floating docks, distinct roadways and smaller individual buildings, and the throngs of people in the streets around the port facilities.

The passenger ring slowed, and eventually came to a stop far above the street, at a featureless platform that extended several hundred feet from the elevator and hid the streets below. Several hovering vehicles waited at the edge of the platform, sleek and expensive in appearance.

The seat restraints remained in place, and Cale glanced at Sidonie. "Not for us," she said with her amused and crooked smile. "We get off at street level. This is for the elites. Would have been us, I suppose, if we weren't coming in unannounced and under different names."

Two women and a man emerged first from the inner elevator compartments and stepped out onto the platform. Bodies enclosed in elaborate coppery exoskeletons, they walked leisurely across the platform toward the waiting vehicles. They were followed by a family of two adults and several children all dressed in simple hooded brown robes;

behind them trailed three self-propelled carts stacked with crates and metal tubes and elaborate yellow baskets, guided by an old man with two tufts of white hair sprouting just above his ears. Last to emerge were four masked and helmeted figures wearing what appeared to be military uniforms, dark green shock suits with insignia on their upper arms.

As the first three slid their exoskeletoned forms into the rear compartment of a long blue and silver vehicle with blacked-out windows, the elevator resumed its descent. It dropped into a dark shaft, then emerged with a burst of light into a vast terminal swarming with people and vendor carts and jinrickshas.

The seat restraints unlatched and retracted. Cale and Sidonie stood and retrieved their bags from the locked cubicles behind their seats—rucksack and duffel bag for Cale, two duffels for Sidonie. Everything they owned. "Hang on tight to your bags," Sidonie warned him. "What security they've got down here is just about worthless." They stood in front of their seats, and after an unintelligible digitized voice sounded, the steelglass before them rolled up into the ceiling, letting in an incredible rush of noise. They stepped out into the terminal.

The heat washed over him, heavy and damp and enervating, and he stopped and swayed, momentarily dizzy. "Wait until midday," Sidonie said. "You'll see why so much of the city is climate controlled."

"Where to now?" Cale asked.

"We'll walk. It isn't far." She pushed her way into the crowd and Cale followed.

Sidonie had decided not to go to the Alexandros Estates

right away, to wait until daylight when people were more likely to be awake. She knew of an inn that at one time had been run by one of her cousins, and they would stay there if it still existed. If not, there was no shortage of places to stay here in the port sector.

Cale felt overwhelmed by the unfamiliar smells and sounds and lights of the streets. Music and barked orders and the aroma of cooking foods and sputtering signs and a blaring klaxon and squawking animals and the stench of burning plastic all became mingled so that he could barely distinguish one from another. He tightly gripped his bags and tried to stay focused on Sidonie as they walked past jinku parlors and taverns and stunner arcades and day spas and neural hook-ups, soup sellers and street preachers and ratpacks and pedalcart cabbies and two barking dogboys crawling past them on all fours.

Fifteen minutes later they discovered that the inn had changed names and ownership several times in recent years. Now it was a stunner arcade. They stood for a while and watched the jerking forms in the stunner booths through the front window, then turned away. They'd have to find some other place to stay.

A straw hat bobbing in the mass of people across the roadway caught his eye. Something very familiar about that hat . . . not just the hat but the way it moved, something about the gait it implied.

"What is it?" Sidonie asked.

"Don't know," Cale replied. "That hat. I thought it . . ." He pushed forward through the crowd and stepped into the street, weaving his way through the vehicles and pedestrians, trying to keep the straw hat in sight. He followed it around a corner and across another street, steadily gaining on it.

As Cale got closer, he could make out the figure beneath the hat. In one hand the man held a string sack filled with two bottles and several paper-wrapped parcels. As Cale saw the skinny bare arms and legs and the ragged shorts, memory rushed through him and he thought he knew who it was, even though the old man was by himself. Cale pressed forward, squeezed his way between two people, and put his hand on the man's arm.

The old man cried out and spun, holding his free hand up as if to defend himself or deflect a blow. It *was* the face Cale remembered.

"Aliazar," he said.

Aliazar lowered his hand and looked up at him with squinting eyes. He straightened a bit and the tension in his face eased. He regarded Cale intently, then slowly nodded once.

"Ah, young sire. I know you. From another time and another world, yes?"

"Yes," Cale answered.

"You've grown up. A young man now. But . . . I don't remember your name."

"Cale."

"Ah, yes. Cale. I remember now." He leaned to the side, looking behind Cale. "And who's this with you?"

Cale turned, then stepped to the side, introducing Aliazar and Sidonie to each other. "We met on the other side of the Divide," Cale explained to her.

The old man laughed, gesturing at the crowd and the buildings around them. "A little different, this place, don't you think? Where we first met was a little quieter." He sighed. "A lot more peaceful."

"What about your brother?" Cale asked. "Is he still with you?"

"Harlock? Of course. Until one of us dies." He held up the string sack. "I was getting supper for us. He's with the menagerie."

"Menagerie?"

"Only a manner of speaking. My idiot brother and I signed on with a traveling festival of sorts a few years ago. We're staying on the beach for two or three weeks, performing. Why don't you join us for supper? There's plenty here. And if you need a place to sleep, our tent's big enough, easy."

Cale looked at Sidonie, who shrugged in reply. He turned back to Aliazar. He was drawn to the old man, even though he suspected Aliazar had drugged him that night all those years ago. Something to do with Harlock and his visions. Still, Aliazar hadn't taken anything from him, hadn't done anything but leave without a word in the morning.

"Okay," Cale said. "Thanks."

The beach was less crowded than the streets, but not by much. Few people were in the water, but hundreds wandered among the fires and booths and distilleries, or strolled out onto the floating docks lined with bars and restaurants and dance pavilions.

The traveling festival was set up far back from the water, a roped-off encampment of fifty or sixty tents of various sizes and shapes, though all were made of the same green and red wave-patterned fabric. Aliazar's tent stood on the perimeter, the smallest in sight, its open flap facing the sea. Aliazar asked Cale and Sidonie to wait, then ducked under the rope and clambered through the tent opening. He emerged a few moments later, cursing.

"I told him to stay here," Aliazar said. "He doesn't realize how easy it is for him to get lost. Half the time he doesn't even realize he *is* lost. The hours I spend looking for him . . ."

They stood together and surveyed the beach, the festival grounds, the streets behind them, searching for some sign of Harlock.

Cale saw him first. Harlock stood hunched and misshapen out near the end of the closest floating dock, staring intently at something in the sea. The dragonlights from the restaurant behind him gave his face a strange flaming glow and cast a long shadow across the water. His clothes were drab rags and his feet were bare.

Aliazar shook his head. "He better be careful not to fall in. He can't swim, he knows that. Hah. Neither of us can." He turned to Cale and Sidonie. "I almost drowned once, fell off my boat into a swimming hole. Harlock stood on the shore and bawled. Didn't have enough sense to go get someone. I was lucky enough to get hold of the boat and hang on until someone found us." He started across the sand toward the dock.

Cale and Sidonie followed the old man. They hadn't quite reached the dock when Harlock lifted his head, stepped forward, and dropped into the water. He sank quickly with no sign of struggle.

"Harlock!" Aliazar cried.

Without thinking, Cale shucked his bags at Sidonie's feet, then broke into a run, taking the last few steps across the sand, up the stone ramp, and onto the floating dock. He ran along the edge of the dock, a mostly clear path ahead of him, jumping over a series of planters, a springboard, and a purging trough, hardly breaking stride.

When he reached the end of the dock he looked down through the clear water and saw Harlock on the bottom, his body upright, feet and hands and arms drifting like thick pale kelp. The water wasn't very deep, less than fifteen feet and illuminated by drifting underwater lamps. Cale kicked off his boots, took a long deep breath, and dove.

The water was warm, and so clear and well-lit it seemed he was looking through hazy air. A flat orange creature with two bulbous eyes swam toward him, only veering away at the last second so that Cale felt the tickle of its tails on his ankle.

Cale swam down at an angle to come around in front of Harlock, kicked and stroked twice more as he reached the big man, and drifted down to the bottom, looking into Harlock's open eyes.

Harlock's eyes widened briefly, then softened, remaining open. Cale was certain those eyes implored him to leave, to swim back to the surface alone and leave Harlock to his newfound peace.

For a moment Cale thought about granting Harlock's wish, but he just couldn't do it. He swam behind Harlock and wrapped one arm around his chest, crouched, then kicked off the sandy bottom. Harlock didn't resist, didn't struggle, but didn't help. Cale pulled with his one free arm, kicking fiercely, legs whipping the water again and again, thrusting them slowly but steadily upward.

They broke the surface and hands grabbed them, dragging

them up and onto the dock. Cale crouched on his knees, coughing, and watched as two med-techs carried Harlock away from the edge, laid him out on a pad, then bent over him as they pulled out their rescue equipment. Aliazar hopped from one foot to the other, gazing down at his brother and moaning.

A short time later Sidonie arrived, struggling with all the bags. She dropped them onto the wooden planks and sat beside Cale, putting her arm around him.

"You all right?"

He nodded. His thighs shook, even though he was warm, and his breath still came hard and fast. He felt incredibly tired; not all of it was physical. "I don't know about Harlock, though."

"I heard one of the med-techs say he was going to be fine."

Cale looked at her and said, "He might live, but Harlock will never be fine."

Harlock slept inside the tent, snoring. Cale, Sidonie, and Aliazar sat at a table near the tent flap, drinking spiced wine from stone cups and listening to the snores and the hushed sounds of the beach at night.

"He wanted to die, didn't he?" Aliazar said. "He . . ." His voice trailed away. He looked out at the dark waters decorated with the shape-shifting jewelry of reflected lights.

After a while Cale answered. "I can't really know."

"I think he's wanted to stop living for a long time." He breathed in deeply, then released it with a quiet moan. "The visions . . . they're hard on him, they take everything from him, but they're all he has."

"He has you," Sidonie put in.

Aliazar looked at her. "I'm his brother, and I'm to take care of him, but I don't know what that means anymore." He turned to Cale. "Maybe that means you should have let him die."

"I couldn't," Cale said.

Aliazar nodded. "And I can't, either."

TWO

Cale hardly noticed the city moving silently past the hired air sedan's windows as they traversed Lagrima, and only a few specific images registered: a transparent fountain that floated thirty feet above the ground, two spouts of fluorescent green water arcing out and down and then flowing back into the central core of the fountain; the road's surface liquefying and bubbling as two conversing men sank into the street, then smoothing out as they disappeared; a building shaped like an upside-down teardrop with solid walls in which windows and doors materialized and dematerialized with astounding frequency. He was conscious only of a vague impression of traveling through a technological wonderland, a city and people of a distant future that existed only in the imagination of some mad visionary like Harlock. None of it was familiar, nothing evoked even a fleeting pull or twist of emotion. Sidonie felt much the same.

"Lagrima is in constant flux," she said. "Buildings and neighborhoods change, they grow and shrink, new ones sprout into existence while others disappear. Even the streets and walkways sometimes change direction or level. Only the port and the sea remain relatively constant." She sighed heavily. "It's been more than twenty years, Cale."

The sedan glided into view of the main entrance to the Alexandros Estates, though it remained some distance away. Those who had business with the Family, or hoped to, waited on floating platforms before metal and glass latticed gates. Crystalline walls rose and curved above the platforms toward a massive falcon's head that stared down at them with open beak and glowing black and red eyes.

A panel in one of the gates became transparent, and an armored and helmeted figure stood in the opening, behind the faint shimmer of an active Metzen Field. A floating platform with two women drifted toward the open panel, and the women bowed.

Sidonie tapped codes onto the guide screen and the sedan veered away from the entrance and dipped toward ground level. They skirted the perimeter of the Estate: the lower walls formed of featureless black stone, the upper walls a dense network of beautiful figures carved in dark red woods, shining webs of coppery cable, and waterfalls emerging from unseen sources and pouring over massive clumps of giant ferns.

The boundary of the Estate stretched on and on, and it was hard for Cale to imagine that the Estate had once been two or three times larger. As they came around to the rear of the Estate several miles from the main entrance, the black stone gave way to stretches of rough-hewn dark wood and light brown rock broken by black metal gates, the walls thirty feet high and all giving off the pale yellow glow of Metzen Fields.

The air sedan set down in a clearing surrounded by bronze trees, and Cale and Sidonie disembarked. The vehicle rose into the air behind them and flared away, headed back to its station.

The heat was oppressive, without a breath or hint of a breeze. Sidonie led the way through the bronze trees, the metal leaves chiming gently when touched, across a stretch of broken ground, then along a gravel path to one of the metal gates. Stone falcon heads with open beaks flanked the gate. Sidonie approached the one on their right, leaned forward, and whispered into its beak. A few moments later the Metzen Field faded and the gate swung open.

They entered and walked along a winding, high-walled passage that took them deeper into the Estate. Eventually they reached another gate, another set of falcon heads, and once more Sidonie whispered into an open beak. A heavy contented sigh whispered around them, Sidonie pushed the gate and went through, and Cale followed.

They entered a courtyard overgrown with flowering stalks and shrubs and dense hedges choked with creepers awash in beautiful pale violet and white blossoms. A sweet, cool perfume hung in the air. Grasses hid the legs of three benches and a wooden table. Pieces of flagstones were visible, enough to hint at a meandering path that eventually led to a massive wooden door that glowed with its own Metzen Field. The door led into an immense building that rose in terraced fashion and extended as far as he could see to both sides.

"We'll wait here," Sidonie said. "After all this time, the House won't let us inside. Into my courtyard, yes, but no farther. It can't be sure we're actually still alive. Meyta will come if she's here."

"Meyta?"

"The Keeper of the House."

They sat on one of the benches, the rotting wood giving under their weight. Sidonie turned her head slowly, surveying the courtyard.

"This was my place," she said. "I loved it here, when it was cared for. It was my place to be alone, even from you. I only brought you here once, when you were a tiny baby."

Nothing was familiar. He felt strangely empty . . . numb.

A long time passed, an hour, maybe more, the heat growing. The city noises did not penetrate here, but the courtyard had its own quiet sounds: the rustling and clicks and whirring of unseen creatures moving through the dense foliage, and the dripping of water from several different directions, the water as hidden as the creatures.

The large wooden door slowly and haltingly opened with cracking sounds and a brief squeal. The aroma of sweet cooking spices emerged from the doorway along with two armed soldiers, weapons held at ready. The soldiers were followed by a bent old woman leaning on a cane as she stepped into the deep grasses, her head tipped to one side as she stared at Sidonie. She stopped a few feet away from the bench, but remained silent.

"Meyta," Sidonie said.

The old woman closed one eye and her cheek twitched. "Is it really you?"

Sidonie nodded, and Cale could see tears forming in her eyes. "Yes, Meyta."

Meyta's lips trembled and she straightened slightly, then came forward and brushed a dark and gnarled finger lightly along Sidonie's ruined face. When she spoke, her voice was choked and quiet. "Yes, Sidonie, it *is* you." She turned to Cale. "And . . ." She halted, swallowed visibly. "And who is this?"

"Cale," Sidonie said.

"I thought you might say that." She appeared to shiver. "Let's go inside." She gestured dismissively at the two soldiers, then turned back to Cale. "Welcome home."

They moved through a series of windowless corridors, ceiling lights brightening as they approached and dimming as they passed, then entered a long wide hall with glass walls that echoed their footsteps and looked out onto more gardens.

"Do you remember me?" Meyta asked.

"No," Cale answered. "I'm sorry."

Meyta coughed out a harsh laugh. "Don't apologize, young man. You'll have plenty of other things to be sorry for."

"Where are we going?" he asked.

"You'll want to see your mother." When Cale didn't reply, Meyta turned to him and said, "Yes?"

Unnerved, he glanced at Sidonie, but there was no help from her. He breathed deeply and said, "Yes."

She nodded once. "I don't blame you for being unsure."

"Should we wait?" Sidonie asked. "Should we prepare Elizabeth?"

"No," Meyta replied firmly, turning back and continuing. "You'll see, it doesn't matter. The shock might even be good for her."

Sometime later they passed through a wide doorway and a vast atrium opened before them, bright with sunlight and awash in brightly colored plants. Birds flew high above, moving among the upper branches of trees that pressed against the glass panels. Water flowed over rocks in a dozen small brooks and pools, dripped from wide-leafed plants and down slopes of stone and moss. Paths of white crushed shell wound among the plants and waterways, leading to a kind of island near the center of the atrium.

Atop a rise on the island, a white-robed woman sat in a wide-backed wicker chair, looking out onto the largest of the atrium's pools where two bright green serpents carved their way across the surface of the water in complicated patterns around one another. The woman's hair was quite long and straight and very dark but for several wide streaks of silver. On the table beside her was a black teapot and cup, and a plate with pastries. As Cale and Sidonie and Meyta approached on one of the paths, the woman turned and faced them.

Cale's breath and forward motion ceased abruptly and all sound became a rushing in his ears. He knew that face. It was the first truly familiar sight on this world and it made him dizzy and weak, and he wondered if he could remain standing. Breath returned and he tried to take a step forward, but his legs wouldn't move.

He hadn't expected this. He didn't know what he *had* expected . . . perhaps nothing.

Meyta and Sidonie had stopped a few feet ahead and looked back at him. Meyta's expression had softened. "Cale," she said quietly yet firmly. Hearing his name, he was able to move again and they resumed walking toward the island and his mother.

They crossed a thick wooden plank that spanned a tiny stream, then continued up a set of shallow stone steps.

"Good morning, Meyta," Cale's mother said as they approached.

"Elizabeth."

"Who have you brought to me today?" She glanced briefly at Sidonie, then regarded Cale with a steady gaze. "Who is this person?"

"Your son, Elizabeth."

She smiled. "Which son is it this time?"

"Cale."

His mother's smile faltered for a moment, then returned. She sipped from her cup, then gestured to him with her hand. "Come closer."

Cale came forward until she could have touched him had she chosen. She stared at his face, into his eyes, and nodded once.

"Yes, you could be Cale grown into a young man. But you're still dead."

"No, Elizabeth," Meyta said. "Not dead. This *is* Cale. He's survived."

She turned to Meyta. "I appreciate your efforts, Meyta, but it's no use. All of my children are dead."

"No, Elizabeth," Sidonie repeated, stepping forward. "We escaped from the *Exile Prince.* We survived. He's your son, and he's alive."

Elizabeth looked at her with disdain. "Who are you?"

"Sidonie."

"Sidonie." She tipped her head from one side to the other. "What happened to your face? You should get it reconstructed. Yes, I can see it could be you. It's a shame you're dead, too."

"Elizabeth!" Meyta's voice was sharp and loud. "They are not dead. Elizabeth, listen to me. This is your son Cale, and he's alive!"

Elizabeth's face tightened, she glared at Meyta, then violently swept the pot and cup and plate from the table and across the rocks, where they shattered. She stood abruptly. "Never do this to me again, Meyta." Without looking at either Cale or Sidonie, she turned and walked off the island, striding quickly along one of the paths, not slowing until she reached the far end of the atrium and disappeared through a doorway.

Cale stared after her, at the empty doorway, once again unable to move, unable to speak. To his great surprise, he felt his heart breaking.

THREE

Cale spent the following days in exploration, sometimes with Sidonie but more often alone. An air of dissolution permeated the House and Estate, becoming outright decay in some of the less-frequented rooms and tracts.

The House itself was larger than any of the villages he'd grown up in on the other side of the Divide, a sprawling web of single- or multileveled wings and individual rooms, passages and stairways, bright open sunrooms and windowless underground chambers. One hundred thirty-seven rooms, Meyta told him. At one time there had been over three hundred.

. . . A cavernous room filled with rotting wood furniture

so heavily coated with dust and mildew that Cale hardly dared to breathe.

. . . Two narrow adjoining rooms with tiled floors in mosaic patterns depicting fanged creatures engaged in combat. Five floor drains in each room, but no fixtures of any kind, no clue to what the rooms had been used for—nothing but blank windowless walls and shining metal doors.

. . . Facing north, a small worship kiosk constructed of pale wood with windows open to the outside, where several of the House staff came to pray or meditate every morning before sunrise.

. . . An entire wing of steelglass walls with a southern exposure, ceilings filled with skylights, but every room empty and silent and still, the walls absorbing any hint of echo, abandoned sunrooms waiting futilely to be revived.

Outside of the House, the Estate itself seemed to have no organization, no coherence.

. . . On the eastern perimeter, a large tract of overgrown forest that Sidonie said had once been the site of weeklong treasure hunts organized by the Alexandros Family and attended by hundreds of Lagrima's elite. Now Cale would have needed defoliants to penetrate more than ten feet into those woods.

. . . A vineyard that was still well-tended and grew imported grapes and sarlets that were harvested and made into wines for the House.

. . . Two crystal quarries long abandoned, one half-filled with water that had become the home of floating plants and nests of bright yellow birds, the other dry and dusty yet sparkling with thousands of tiny dots of color.

. . . Stables for llamas and poylets and musk goats, all of

which were meticulously groomed and cared for, ridden by the children of the servants.

And finally, at the main entrance to the Estate, the Consortium's offices, a high narrow building of polarized glass where more than a hundred people worked daily running the Family enterprises, executing the trades and investments and daily business dealings that kept the Alexandros Consortium from going under. Barely.

Then, too, there were the encounters with his mother. . . .

In the main kitchens one morning, the air filled with the warmth and aroma of the yeasty spice bread that was baked fresh every day for the House, his mother stood by a window, drinking tea. Cale approached her.

"Mother . . ."

She glared at him and raised her hand, saying, "Don't dare say that to me again. I'll speak to Meyta, and you will be dismissed from service immediately. Do you understand?" When he didn't respond, she repeated herself, louder and with a harsher edge. *"Do you understand?"*

"Yes," he replied.

Her expression softened. "I know you're new here, so I'll let it go. Still . . . Mother?" A faint smile of amusement. "An odd salutation, don't you think?"

"Yes," Cale said again.

She turned from him and left the room, shaking her head.

* * *

"Who are you?" she asked him. They stood in one of the House's glass corridors, looking into an abandoned greenhouse. Through the cracked and dirty glass panes they could see networks of pipes and hoses dangling from the ceiling, dirt and rock scattered about the floor, and dusty tables and shelves and the desiccated remnants of once-flowering plants and shrubs.

"Cale."

"That was my son's name. Did you know that?"

"I *am* your son."

"You look very much as I imagine he would have looked had he lived to be your age. Has anyone told you that?"

"Yes."

"He died when he was quite young," she went on. "A child." Her gaze was far away now, looking past him and into the greenhouse. "All of my children are dead, all eleven of them." She paused, as though recounting all those deaths in her mind. "This family is cursed."

"Cursed, maybe," Cale said. "I won't disagree. But your children are not all dead. *I* am still alive, Mother. I'm *alive*."

"All dead." Her voice was quiet, and she didn't look at him. "Like the gardens. Our family, barren. When I die, it ends."

"Mother," he said firmly. "I am your son, and I am alive."

"I tried." She went to the glass door and opened it. "I gave him six daughters and five sons, and they all died." She stepped out onto the cracked earth. "Every one . . . every . . ." Her voice faded as she wound her way among empty pots and planter boxes, dry and leafless branches, upturned roots, brown clumps of dead grass. Cale stood in the doorway, watching her. Beside a dry pond was a plant with one flowering stem. She knelt before it and plucked the stem. The dried petals fell away and dropped silently to the brown earth.

His mother sat in the shade by an artificial waterfall that emerged from the wall of the House and fell in three stages over rocks and into a pool at her feet. A dense cluster of tiny yellow flowers floated atop the water, encircling a spray of bright green stalks topped by buds that were just about to bloom.

Cale sat in a wooden chair a few feet away so that, while he was not directly in front of her, he was sure he was in her field of vision. The day was hot, but the waterfall's fine mist helped cool the air, especially in the shade.

"Mother."

She didn't respond. She continued to watch the water moving in ripples across the pond, her hands folded in her lap.

"I know you've been through a lot, the deaths of all of my brothers and sisters—your children. The death of your husband. My father. I guess you're afraid, afraid of believing, maybe, and then finding out it isn't true. Or maybe afraid of having to grieve again, I don't know.

"But I'm not dead, Mother. I'm your son. Cale. Sidonie and I survived the attack on the *Exile Prince,* we survived a crash on Conrad's World, we survived years of . . . of. . . . We survived, Mother. We are alive, both of us. *I'm* alive. Your son."

She stood, took a couple of steps, then knelt at the edge of the pond and dipped her hand into it. When she raised her hand she kept her fingers cupped, holding a little of the water, then brought it to her forehead and let the water drip down her face.

"Mother . . ."

She set her hands in the thick moss on either side of her legs and leaned forward, staring into the pond.

Cale couldn't stand it anymore. He got up from the chair and cried out, *"Mother!"* When she still did not respond, he closed his eyes for a few moments and breathed deeply, trying to hold himself together, then opened them, took one last look at her, and walked back into the House.

Cale's mother had requested snow, and snow had fallen over the House and much of the Estate all day. The snow continued to fall into the evening, a light emerald green in the bioluminescent lights that hung about the House.

She sat in the library before a fire that burned in a fireplace of transparent bricks set in the corner where two glass walls met, topped by a half-domed glass ceiling. The snow fell onto the dome, melted, ran along the curved surface, then dripped to the ground. Cale sat in the back of the room by the two high walls of ancient bound books that had not been opened or read in centuries, and watched his mother watch the snow and fire.

With both hands she pulled her long hair together at the nape of her neck and held it there. Cale thought her hands were shaking, but he couldn't be sure. Gradually uncurling her fingers, she released her hair so that it draped across the back of the chair. She tilted her head back and watched the snow falling directly toward her.

After a seemingly interminable silence, her head tilted

forward so that she was once again looking into the fire, into red and orange and blue flames that waved listlessly above glowing lengths of scaled wood, at embers that pulsed with some great creature's hibernating heartbeat.

Then, so quietly he was certain she could not hear him, Cale whispered, "Mother."

He sat silent and still, and watched.

At sunrise Cale sat in a rooftop garden atop the highest level of the House, ten floors up and atop a tower that rose from the kitchens. From this vantage he could look out over the entire Alexandros Estate and discern all the perimeter walls that surrounded it. The rising sun was hidden behind one of the taller city buildings to the east, and long shadows lay across the Estate.

This was all *his* now. That's what everyone kept telling him. Sidonie, Meyta, the managers who had been running the Family business as his mother had retreated from active participation. They all waited for him to take control, give them direction. It was absurd.

Sidonie came up the stairway in the center of the roof and joined him. "I've been looking for you since last night." She stood at his side, looking out over the Estate. "Surveying your domain?"

"I don't want it."

"I know," she said, "but that doesn't matter. It's yours. Still, you *can* just walk away from it, if you want. It will go on as before."

"A slow and steady decline until the whole thing completely collapses. My mother might be right."

"About what?"

"This family is cursed."

The edge of the sun came out from behind a tall building near the heart of Lagrima, forcing them to squint and turn so that they were facing south toward a copse of diseased spine trees set back a hundred feet from the House.

"She still doesn't acknowledge me," he said.

Sidonie nodded. "It's possible she never will."

Cale closed his eyes, focusing on the warmth of the sun and the morning aromas: the fresh spiced bread, incense from the worship kiosk, the perfume of starflowers opening up on the roof around them.

"Why were you looking for me?" he asked.

"Do you want to know what your father was doing? Why we were going to Conrad's World?"

Cale opened his eyes and turned to her. "Of course I do."

"I've found the person who knows."

"Who?"

"The Family horoscoper."

"Oh, yes, the Family horoscoper. No wonder we're dying."

"Cale, all of the consortiums use horoscopers. I tried to explain to you before, the real ones, they're not the charlatans you think they are."

Cale shook his head. "All right, where is this horoscoper?"

"Stygon's in exile. He's living in West RiverRun, on the Tze Kang River."

"Why exile?"

"Your mother exiled him when she heard that our ship had been destroyed."

Cale smiled. That might have been the last rational decision his mother had made.

"We can go today," Sidonie said. "He's expecting us."

Cale hesitated, suddenly fearful. He breathed deeply and looked out over the Estate, his domain. "Let's go."

FOUR

Prolastaya piloted them to the edge of Lagrima and set the sedan down at the perimeter wall, where he would wait for their return. Cale and Sidonie disembarked and passed through one of the city's gates, entering West RiverRun on foot.

The air was hot and sticky and reeked of garbage and stagnant water and rotting meat. Lining the dirt roads and the river were shacks and lean-tos on the verge of collapse. Crowds of people milled listlessly in the streets, making their way among food and merchandise vendors, among diseased beggars so weak they could barely sit upright, among smoking coals and chanting monks and screeching birds perched atop ten-foot-high wooden poles. A few children with bloated stomachs ran squealing through the crowds, but most were as lethargic as the adults. The thick muddy river flowed sluggishly toward the city, its surface mottled with filthy yellow foam. Cale had seen the Tze Kang within the walls of Lagrima—clean and clear and alive with colorful fish as it meandered through the city and eventually flowed into the sea. People swam in the river inside Lagrima; the closest anyone came to that here was two men on the bank pissing into the water.

After weeks of Lagrima with all its wealth and sophistication and seemingly endless wonders, Cale felt as if he'd been suddenly transported to some other place—back to Conrad's World and the other side of the Divide.

Sidonie led the way off the main streets, across a barren field and through clusters of thorny brush, then up a gentle rise away from the river. A small but clean and well-maintained house sat at the edge of a lush stand of trees. A tall graying man stood in the open doorway, wearing sandals and a loose tan shirt and trousers. The man's face tightened as Cale and Sidonie approached, his attention on Sidonie. He said nothing, just bowed slightly and shook her hand. Then he bowed toward Cale and took his hand as well. "I'm Stygon. You probably don't remember me, Cale."

His face *was* familiar, though, and his smell, and those two things made his legs weak and his stomach turn. "I think I do," he managed to say.

"Good," Stygon said with a smile. "Please, come in."

They sat in cane chairs in the tiny garden behind the house, under the shade of trees with intertwining branches and enormous leaves broader than Cale was tall, and lush blue and white flowers that wafted their heavy scent upon them. A small oasis that denied the poverty and decay all around them. The clouds had burned away here, and the air was hot and damp, even in the shade, but Cale could hear the rush of a nearby stream, and a faint breeze made its way through the trees like the hushed breath of some water deity, hinting at the possibility of cooling comfort withheld.

A young man served them iced fruit tea and thin crackers, then returned to the house. Stygon got up from his chair, lit a joss stick, then knelt and placed it in a holder before a stone figure of a squat animal with a human face. Silent and motionless for a time, he eventually rose with a creaking of joints and returned to the chair; his gaze moved back and forth between Sidonie and Cale.

"I did not believe I would ever see either of you again. I had some small hopes when you first left all those years ago, but when we learned of the *Exile Prince*'s destruction—"

"Why did he take me?" Cale asked, cutting him off. "I was just a child. A *young* child."

Stygon paused and breathed in very deeply before answering.

"As part of his preparations he asked me for a reading, of course. We discussed it at length, as we always did, and I told your father that your presence was required for his venture's success." He paused, looked away. "I also told him that the venture would likely result in his death."

"He would die, but the venture would be a success?"

"Yes."

"How could that be?"

"I don't know. The readings don't explain, they don't interpret. They reveal influences and directions and probable outcomes. Your father chose to go despite knowing he would probably die."

Cale shook his head. "He died, and yet it wasn't a success, was it?"

"I could not say," Stygon replied with a shrug. "It may well be that the venture *was* a success." He looked at Cale as if Cale himself might know how that could be.

"What was the goal of this venture?"

Stygon hesitated, as though afraid to reveal something he had kept secret for decades, which he almost certainly had. He studied the back of his hand, as if it could tell him what to say. "He was attempting to acquire the Rosetta Codex."

Cale's chest and stomach tightened. "What's the Rosetta Codex?"

"A book of sorts. An old manuscript whose existence has been claimed some small number of times over the years, but never reliably confirmed. Reported more than once as found, but always lost. A manuscript in the language of the Jaaprana aliens, yet also in several human languages. All the same text, so that it would provide a means of deciphering the alien language. It would give us a way to translate all those alien texts and documents that have been discovered over the decades."

"Why is it called the Rosetta Codex?" Cale asked.

"After an ancient artifact called the Rosetta Stone, from Earth at a time long before spaceflight. It was a stone tablet with the same text in three or four different languages, one of which had never before been deciphered. It provided the necessary clues for deciphering a written language that had long been dead." Then quietly, more to himself than to Cale and Sidonie, he muttered, "Coptic? Or Egyptian hieroglyphics?"

Cale nodded his understanding. "Why did he want the codex?" he asked. "What did he plan to do with it?"

"I don't know," Stygon replied. "He wouldn't tell me. I assumed he would sell it, which would have turned the Family's fortunes around. The Sarakheen would have paid a vast fortune for it."

"The Sarakheen?" Cale's voice was strained and hoarse.

"Yes. They believe in its existence more than anyone. Your father and I conducted a great deal of research on the codex, or rather on the stories surrounding the codex. The Sarakheen kept coming up. Do you know anything about them?"

"A little."

"Most people will never see a Sarakheen in their lifetimes. They are forbidden from entering any star system with their own ships, and the Aligned Worlds have been diligent about enforcing that ban. Now they are only allowed in human star systems individually, in ones and twos as paying passengers on human ships."

"The Sarakheen are human," Cale said.

"Perhaps," Stygon said with a shrug. "They have no regard for the lives of those who aren't Sarakheen. Or regard them as little more than animals."

Cale wasn't sure that was so different from most other human beings, but he kept that thought to himself. "And their interest in the codex?" he asked.

"They apparently have quite a number of Jaaprana manuscripts," Stygon said, "and have been attempting for decades to decipher them. They believe the Jaaprana held some secret for the integration of mind and machine—the ultimate goal of the Sarakheen."

The Rosetta Codex and the Sarakheen. Could that really be what his father had planned to do with the codex? Sell it to the Sarakheen? Somehow Cale doubted it. It didn't matter. *He* had it now, and he would not sell it to the Sarakheen. He would not sell it to anyone. No one else might know it, but the codex was more than just a means to translate other texts, and he had his own ideas about what to do with it. It was time.

"Cale." Stygon gazed steadily at him. "Can you tell me, then?" he asked.

"Tell you what?" Cale asked in return.

"Was your father's venture a success?"

Cale didn't answer. He kept his gaze steady on Stygon, and the silence carried a sense of gravity.

Stygon nodded. "I always trust the readings."

They left Stygon's house and walked along the river once more, returning to Lagrima.

"Now what?" Sidonie asked.

"Find out what the codex really is," Cale said. "Find a way to go to the gate." He turned to her. "I have control of the Family resources, right?"

"What's left of them, yes."

"We'll outfit a starship and find the gate."

"Sounds simple."

"No, it won't be simple, but that's what we're going to do. Are you with me?"

"You should know the answer without asking, Cale."

He looked at her with both affection and appreciation. "Yes, I do."

FIVE

Cale walked with Sidonie among the phosphor-lit trees and the pulsing lights of bioluminescent nightflies as the building's interior and exterior switched places and melded with each other, confusing him. He half expected night to become day with a similar caprice, but night remained night whether viewed directly in the open sky above him with its stars and the occasional cloud infused with the lights of Lagrima, or viewed through the high and wide windows of the Titan Consortium Garden Pavilion. The ceiling with its faint halo lamps seemed to appear and disappear at random, much like the people who stepped out from the trees and greeted them in passing, many of whom were complete strangers but some of whom had over time become familiar and, with each event like this, more friendly and open . . . and willing to do business. Which was, Sidonie continually reminded him, the purpose of being invited to and attending these affairs.

As though sensing his discomfort, Sidonie put a reassuring hand on his shoulder. When he turned to look at her, he was again taken aback by the transformation of her face: a complete reconstruction, with rebuilt bone structure, newly grown skin, even a prosthetic eye, though it functioned only marginally better than the damaged eye had. The only remaining evidence of the old injuries was the inch-wide band of white hair on the opposite side of her head, and a tiny crooked scar on her upper cheek that she'd insisted be retained—she wanted a reminder every time she looked in the mirror, she'd told him.

"You're doing just fine," she said.

He didn't feel fine, but kept on as if he did. An androgynous figure in a black body suit approached and wordlessly held out a tray of drinks in variously shaped glasses. Cale had learned enough by now to know what most of them were, and he picked up a tall fluted glass filled with dark brown ale while Sidonie took a glass of golden wine.

A slight change in the Family's status had occurred almost immediately upon Cale's assumption of the Consortium leadership and role of primary decision-maker for all commercial and financial matters. In the months since, the actuality of a Family member in charge after so many years of his mother's indifference and neglect changed Lagrima's perception of the Alexandros Family, and the Family was taken at least *somewhat* seriously again. Profitable business transactions were once again possible, agreements and contracts could be made, and invitations to some of the more prestigious social occasions, like tonight's *SolsticeEve Fete,* began to materialize.

Of course, Cale depended heavily on the advice and counsel of the Family brokers and managers, comptrollers and financiers, all the other professionals on retainer. But he also discovered that his own intuition and common sense, along with Sidonie's, were more valuable than anyone expected. He was a fast learner, yet unafraid to admit his ignorance. Little by little, the Family was slowing its financial slide.

An elderly gray-haired woman in a long simple black robe approached them and put out her hand, eyes on Cale. Her face was heavily wrinkled, either from extreme age or because she'd chosen not to have standard re-gen treatments.

"We haven't met," she said, "but I've wanted to for some time, Cale Alexandros. I'm Indira Youssaf."

Cale took her hand in his; it was warm and dry, and though her grip was strong he felt as if her bones would snap if he twisted her hand with any force. "I'm glad to meet you," he said. "I know of you, I think."

"I'm the Jericho Family matriarch," she said with a wry smile. "I knew your father quite well. Our families executed innumerable mutually beneficial commercial transactions over the years, although they unfortunately came to a halt some time ago. I think a resumption of that relationship might now be quite workable. Perhaps we can discuss the possibilities."

"Of course," Cale said uncertainly. "Maybe in the next few days we can get together . . ."

"I was thinking of *now,*" she said, and with that she

moved to his side and turned and hooked her arm through his. "There's a privacy grove not far from here," she added. She stepped toward a shadowed path leading into the trees, gently but firmly pulling him.

Cale held back and looked around for Sidonie, but she was nowhere in sight. He imagined her voice whispering in his ear, saying *"Go with her . . . this is an opportunity not to be missed."* He turned back to Indira Youssaf, and let her guide him forward.

A year later, when the personal invitations began to come to Cale from the daughters and younger widows or divorcees of some of the more prominent families and consortiums, Sidonie knew they had begun to turn things around, at least in the eyes of Lagrima's upper echelons. Cale, however, turned them all down as politely as possible, and Sidonie suggested he accept at least some of them.

"I'm not interested," he told her.

"Not in any of them?" she asked. "You're not making any commitments by accepting, Cale. You're just opening doors. You must find some of them attractive. Enjoy yourself. It's expected. You might even be able to conduct business with one or two of them, put together a more profitable transaction. That's the way it works here."

Cale shook his head. "That's not me," he said, then repeated, "I'm just not interested."

"I know," she said. "That's why you worry me, sometimes, Cale."

"There's no reason to worry, Sidonie."

"There are always plenty of reasons for me to worry." She

hesitated, then asked, "Is it Karimah?" When he didn't answer, she said, "That was a long time ago, Cale. You need to—"

"You don't know," he said sharply, cutting her off. He regarded her with defiance, daring her to contradict him.

She returned his gaze, unwavering, then nodded once. "You're right, Cale. I don't know. I'm sorry." She sighed deeply, turned, and walked away, leaving him alone with his enduring pain.

Cale hired Donello Brazzi, the premiere transport broker on Lagrima, to find a ship for them, but even after months of inquiries and offers and bribes, none of the working interstellar ships were available for purchase. He hadn't given up, however, and now Cale and Sidonie were with Brazzi in orbit around Lagrima's moon Santa Maria, approaching a starship freighter that had been out of service for several decades and orbiting Santa Maria ever since. Brazzi piloted the shuttle, and he pointed at a small dot of light on the view screen.

"There she is," Brazzi said. "We're lucky this ship even exists. Lucky twice that it's *here,* in this system. I don't know if they're being built anywhere right now." Brazzi shrugged. "A hundred years ago, a manufacturing combine on Thrax built them, putting out one every six or seven years, and another combine back on Earth did the same. What I know, they've both been shut down for decades."

He made a slight adjustment to the shuttle controls, then resumed speaking. "You know the Huckel Family?" He went on without waiting for a response. "Loanda Huckel's the head of the Family, near to a hundred years old and looks every bit of it. Small Family, big ambitions. They bought this ship to go into the interstellar transport business, hoping to get very rich very quickly." Brazzi laughed unpleasantly. "They got very *broke* very quickly. Loanda Huckel made some lousy decisions on what to buy and sell. Didn't quite bankrupt the Family, but close enough. They still own this thing, hoping for who knows what, but I think they've about given up."

"And you've inspected it?" Cale said.

Brazzi nodded. "Inside and out, one end to the other. Spent several days with a team of engineers going over every bit of it."

"Will it serve?" Cale asked.

Brazzi gave a sort of swaying half-nod, turning down his mouth. "Not like she is right now. She's structurally sound, but near to half obsolete. With the time and money, though, you can make her right. Maybe two years to retrofit her. Expensive, but a lot cheaper and faster than going to Thrax or wherever and ordering up a new one."

They talked finances for the next several minutes—estimates on the cost of retrofitting the ship and hiring a crew, and what it would take to convince the Huckels to sell. Brazzi grinned. "That's what negotiating's all about, isn't it?" Then he gave a confident nod. "We'll be able to work something out." Then he cocked his head at them. "But I hope you make better decisions than Huckel made." He made another minor course adjustment, and they closed in on the derelict ship.

Three months later, the Alexandros Family Consortium took ownership of an obsolete but "structurally sound" interstellar freighter. It had been previously, and pretentiously, christened the *Star of Destiny*, but Cale and Sidonie renamed it, and had decided on the *Night Traveler*. It seemed a neutral enough name to Cale, which was important. He wanted nothing to do with signs or omens, portentous names, horoscopers, or discussions of fate or predictions of the future.

Tugs moved the ship into orbit around Lagrima, and the long months of work began.

Cale sat with Sidonie in the abandoned greenhouse, drinking coffee and listening to the morning rain on the recently repaired glass roof. He gazed out into the gray gardens, almost afraid to look at her. "This is going to be hard, but it's important."

There must have been something in his voice—how could there not be, he had to admit—because he sensed her stiffen beside him, sensed held breath and suspended movement. He finally turned to her, and it was obvious she was not going to ask him, she was going to wait in silence. She still looked strange to him when they were alone together, like someone else, or as if she were wearing a mask. He'd become accustomed to her reconstructed face when they were among others, but when they were alone he forgot, or somehow expected her face to revert to what he had known since their reunion in Morningstar.

"I want you to go back to Conrad's World," he told her. "I can't go myself, or I would. I've got to stay here and continue rebuilding our business assets. I can't stop now."

"Agreed," Sidonie said. "You can't." She sighed heavily. "What do you need me to do?"

"Find the Resurrectionists, those still remaining, and bring them here."

"All of them?"

"No. There's a man named Cicero. Tell him what we're doing, and he'll know who to bring."

"And if Cicero's dead?"

Cale shook his head. "He's not. Or at least he wasn't a few months ago—I got a message cube from him. But if something happens to him before you get there, then you'll find a woman named Beatt. If not Beatt, then a woman called Springer."

"They're going with us?" Sidonie asked.

"Yes."

"When do you want me to go?"

"As soon as we can arrange passage."

"I'll be gone a long time," she said.

"Yes," he replied. "Probably more than a year. I think I can do okay with the social events on my own now."

A subtle smile appeared. "Yes, Cale, you can." Then the smile was gone. "Why?"

"Why the Resurrectionists, you mean?"

"Yes."

"I owe it to them."

She nodded as though she understood, or at least understood its importance to him.

"I'll go," she said.

The only sounds were the rustle of creatures crawling among the dead plants and the clatter of rain on glass.

SIX

A river in midair carved its way around the corner of a green obelisk-shaped building of glass and flowed past high above Cale, several meters deep and twice as wide, nearly as wide as the thoroughfare he strode along. He slowed and stopped to stare at the clean flowing river overhead. Vague shapes undulated within the dark blue water, aquatic creatures, perhaps, or shadows of flying animals above. Two women sat drinking on a balcony ten or twelve stories above the street with fishing rods, and cast baited lines into the water; a chain dangled from the balcony rail, and hooked by the mouth at the end of the chain was a mottled, shiny-skinned four-legged creature with limp fins and a stubby mass of a vestigial tail.

After nearly three years here, Cale was still struck with wonder at seemingly impossible phenomena like a river appearing in the air above him, unlike the people around him who continued on their way hardly noticing this manifestation, or not noticing it at all. Cale still felt that wonder . . . but also unease and unreality and a sense of displacement.

Cale left the main thoroughfare, crossed a cluster of bubbling hot springs, then climbed a low grass rise. He descended the slope on the other side and stopped at the edge of an animal park, leaning against the vine-covered railing. Horned marboks sprinted past him in both directions across the rocky trails, as if they were fleeing from some unseen or imagined predators.

Someone to his right leaned against the rail, a large and dynamic presence, and a familiar voice said, "Hello, young Cale."

Cale didn't turn, but he stared at Blackburn's shadow stretching out before them, at the familiar outline of the hat he'd worn on Conrad's World.

"You never told me you came from a famous family," Blackburn said.

Still not looking at him, Cale said, "You never asked," trying to keep his voice under control. His stomach and chest and throat strained with the tension.

"Not true, Cale. When we met, I asked if you had a last name, and you told me you couldn't remember."

Cale nodded deliberately, recalling the first time he'd seen Blackburn: a powerful figure riding into the village atop Morrigan in the pouring rain, tipping his hat to Cale in greeting. Then Cale recalled the last time he'd seen Blackburn, the big man walking out of the building in the abandoned town at the edge of the dry lake bed while Cale and Sidonie remained bound and helpless inside.

"You also never told me you'd found the codex."

Cale slowly turned to him, furrowing his brow. "Codex?"

Blackburn smiled. He wore black and gray clothes, and heavy black boots, dressed more for Conrad's World than for Lagrima. "No, I don't imagine you'll admit to that, will you?"

"What are you talking about?"

He put his hand on Cale's shoulder. "You've been struggling to keep the Family Consortium solvent. You've done well to prevent a complete collapse, but it's always going to be a struggle, and you may still lose it all in the end. I have an offer for you. The *Sarakheen* have an offer for you. For the codex. Enough wealth to guarantee the Alexandros Family will never worry about its finances again."

"I still don't know what you're talking about," Cale said. "There's nothing the Family has that you or the Sarakheen would want that much."

"You've acquired an interstellar freighter," Blackburn said.

Cale kept his expression fixed, surprised once again at what Blackburn knew and afraid of what Blackburn might guess. What was he getting at? Cale was almost afraid to speak, but with steady voice he replied, "Yes, we have."

"Expensive," Blackburn said, releasing Cale's shoulder and taking a step back. "A small fortune to acquire, months and another small fortune to retrofit, and a third small fortune to stock it with worthwhile cargo. Three small fortunes, only one of which you have—or I should say *had,* since you've spent it to acquire the ship. You've been doing better with the Family's commerce, but you're overleveraging it and you're in the process of mortgaging most or all of the Family's assets to finance this venture. An enormous risk."

Cale felt a calm spreading through him, relief that Blackburn misunderstood. "With enormous potential rewards," Cale answered. "We used to own and operate interstellar freighters directly, several generations back. That's how the Family originally built up its wealth and power. But you know that, since you seem to know so damn much about my family."

"Yes, I know that, and I know they divested the line once they'd acquired the bulk of their wealth so they wouldn't have to take those risks."

"Now we have to again," Cale said with a shrug.

Blackburn shook his head. "But you don't, young Cale." He stepped toward Cale and gripped his shoulder once more. "Sell the codex to the Sarakheen, and you won't have to take the risk. You won't have to risk everything, which is what you're doing now."

"I don't have a choice," Cale told him firmly. "I don't have this codex you keep talking about."

A smile slowly worked its way onto Blackburn's face, but there was no smile in his eyes, no friendliness in the way his fingers gripped Cale's shoulder.

"All right," Blackburn said. "I hope you don't have any plans for the next few hours, because I'm going to take you with me. We're going to see a performance of sorts."

Cale pushed back from the railing. "I'm not going anywhere with you."

"Yes," Blackburn insisted.

Cale heard someone approach from his left and turned to

see the nameless Sarakheen he'd met on Conrad's World, the Sarakheen he'd last seen standing on the street as the Resurrectionists' tunnels flooded and Karimah drowned. The Sarakheen's face held no expression, but his eyes radiated a disturbing intensity in their hard shine. He wore a black single-piece, and gloves that hid his mek arm and hand.

"No." Cale stared at the Sarakheen. A cold and hard anger knotted up inside him, seared through with a pain he had thought long forgotten.

"Yes," Blackburn said once more, pressing something warm and metallic against Cale's neck. Cale felt an electric jolt arcing into his skull, his vision became a wash of silver, and he collapsed.

When he came to, he found himself strapped into a seat inside a dragoncub, the engine thrumming. Blackburn sat relaxed in the seat beside him, while the Sarakheen piloted the craft, his metal hand and arm embedded in the control console. Cale sat up, the seat restraints flexing to allow the movement. Blackburn glanced at him, said, "Awake, are you?"

Cale's neck was stiff and painful, and he rubbed it, tried to stretch it out. "What *was* that?"

"Neural disruptor." Blackburn paused. "Multiple charges can cause permanent damage, so I'd rather not have to use it on you again."

Cale shook his head. "You won't have to." He looked out through the dragoncub's window and saw they were above the northern edge of Lagrima, where the industrial and warehouse district began. Rectangular buildings of all sizes spread out below them, set within a grid of transport lines that eventually curved and converged as they headed toward the ports. Steam rose in columns from some of the buildings, dark smoke from others, while still others seemed abandoned.

The dragoncub slowed, then dropped toward one of the taller buildings that appeared deserted: rusting metal stairways clung to its outer walls, windows had been boarded over, pieces of twisted metal and broken machinery lay scattered about the roof. They veered toward a clearing amid the debris and settled to the rough surface with surprising gentleness.

Cale was still shaky as he stepped down from the dragoncub and onto the rooftop. They were outside Lagrima's climate-controlled zone and the heat was intense. Blackburn led the way to a rooftop shed and pulled the door open, revealing a shadowed stairway descending into the building. He started down first, followed by Cale, then the Sarakheen.

They descended two long flights in near total darkness, more by feel than by sight, then emerged onto a landing about thirty feet above the floor. A warehouse, Cale thought, nearly empty and dimly lit by a few lights that hung from crossbeams several feet below them. The lights were shielded and directed toward the ground so that Cale and the others remained in darkness. Any windows or other openings were boarded over or covered so no light entered from the outside. The air was hot and stifling and smelled of dust and stale smoke.

They stood at the landing rail and looked down on a circular section of the dirt floor that Cale now realized was the focus of the lights. This circular area was swept smooth and surrounded by piles of sawdust. Farther back were two sets of raised seats, five on one side of the circle and six on the other. Like the rest of the warehouse, the seats were empty.

"The audience will arrive shortly," Blackburn said.

A few minutes later a man in dark coveralls appeared and walked about the cleared circle, looking at the sawdust piles, counting the seats. Apparently satisfied, he left.

Finally a few people began to silently appear, escorted by the man in the coveralls who directed them toward the seats. Cale recognized one of the men—Enol Darfunslaar, one of the top executives of the Saar Family Consortium—and the woman—Kati Shinchosha, an independent trade broker he'd negotiated several deals with during the past two years.

Over the next few minutes the rest of the "audience" came in and took their seats. Cale recognized more than half of them, all top executives or other elites in Lagrima's business and social circles.

"Friends of yours," Blackburn said. "Some of them."

Cale shook his head and whispered, afraid to be heard by those below. "I just know a few, that's all."

"They can't hear us," Blackburn assured him. He gestured vaguely below them. "One-way sound baffles. They won't have any idea we're up here watching."

When everyone was seated, the coveralled man left again, then returned shortly carrying a large coil of rope and a bundle of metal blades, followed by three men barefoot and otherwise dressed only in calf-length trousers. One of the men was tall and bulky with weathered skin, while the other two were thinner, lanky, both with much darker skin. All three were already sweating.

The coveralled man pointed, positioning the three men around the circle's perimeter, then dropped the blades to the ground and uncoiled the rope. It was actually three lengths joined so they looked like the arms of a sea-creature, with leather bands at their free ends. He strapped one band around the right wrist of each man so that all three were now connected to each other by the rope. Then he picked up the long and heavy knives like miniature swords, and placed one each into the men's left hands.

"What the hell is this?" Cale finally asked, turning to Blackburn.

The big man gave him a grim smile. "A competition. The winner's prize is a huge amount of money, a home in Lagrima, and a job."

"The *winner*?"

"The one who can walk out of that circle alive."

"I'm not watching this," Cale said, and stepped back from the railing.

Blackburn grabbed his arm and squeezed, then pulled him back, forcing his chest painfully against the railing. "You are."

Cale turned his gaze back to the scene below. The three men were now on their own in the circle, eyeing each other, taking cautious sliding steps, pulling tentatively at the rope, testing the strength of their opponents. Their awkward left-handed swings and jabs with the knives confirmed that all three were probably right-handed, which somehow added to the horror in Cale's mind.

For the first couple of minutes there was mostly tugging and feinting and sidestepping, and an occasional all-out lunge that caught empty air. Shallow slices appeared on all three men, seeping blood, but no one appeared seriously wounded yet. The bigger man began to yank and tug more forcefully at the rope, using his bulk and strength, twice nearly pulling one of the other men off his feet. He stepped up his efforts, gaining confidence.

Too much confidence, perhaps, for he took to swinging his right arm back and forth as he leaned back, trying to jerk one or both of the other men off their feet. He lost his own balance, tried to adjust, then his left foot slipped on the dirt and he fell onto his side with a pained grunt. His fall pulled the other men toward him, and they each swung their blades as they stumbled closer, one nearly severing the large man's arm at the shoulder, the other slicing across the man's thigh.

The large man howled and twisted on the ground, driving his face into the dirt as if that might take away the pain. The two smaller men eyed each other in a brief but silent communication. At nearly the same time they launched themselves at the fallen man and began hacking and slashing away at him with their knives. Blood spattered and sprayed with each stroke and poured onto the dirt, pooling and thickening. The larger man lay still, dark gashes bleeding heavily, pieces of flesh and guts scattered about.

The other two men staggered to their feet, panting heavily and bleeding from their own fresh wounds—they'd each taken a few swings at each other while slaughtering the man who now lay at their feet. They tried to step back, but both were brought up short after only a couple of steps by the rope still strapped to the dead man's wrist; the wrist and fingers now flapped grotesquely a few inches above the blood-soaked earth as the two men pulled at their own ropes, trying to maintain a safe distance from one another.

"Look at your friends," Blackburn said. "The watchers."

Cale did, and though the light was dim, there was enough to make out their faces. He was nearly as sickened by their expressions as by the violence they so eagerly watched. One or two seemed genuinely appalled by what they witnessed, though why they chose to be here was an unanswered question. The others, however, appeared engrossed, even fascinated, and two—Kati Shinchosha and a man who was only vaguely familiar—seemed to actually relish the carnage, leaning forward with eyes wide and mouths slightly open. There was something carnal in their faces.

Blackburn chuckled beside him and Cale pulled his attention away from the "watchers" and returned it to the two men still on their feet. Both men panted heavily, weaving and staggering, their bodies practically painted with blood and dirt and bits of flesh. Cale was certain it wouldn't last much longer.

One of the men pulled back, not tugging, simply stretching the rope, and while keeping his gaze on the other began to saw at the rope with his knife. When the second man saw what the first was doing, he heaved himself forward to attack. As he did, the first man switched the knife from his left hand to his right and swung it with rope still trailing up and across, slicing a deep gash across the other man's face, slicing through his nose and one eye. The other man howled, dropped his knife as he instinctively covered his face, and the first man lunged forward, knocking the other onto his back across the already dead man. Chest heaving, the first man straddled the second and drove his knife into the man's throat.

Cale finally turned away as he saw the man pull the knife

out, releasing a pulsing stream of blood, and bring it back down to strike again. Cale stepped back and pressed himself against the wall, eyes closed but unable to shut out the warm odor of blood cut through with some acrid stink that burned his nose.

Blackburn offered a quiet commentary, as if certain Cale wanted to be kept informed of everything that transpired below them. "The winner can barely stand," Blackburn said. "Not surprising. He's being released from the rope, after dropping the knife, of course . . . and . . . he's being led away." He paused. "Now we've got a couple of extra aides to help with the bodies. And a wheeled cart, so no one has to work *too* hard." Another pause, longer. "Now the bodies are gone, the ropes and knives and the scattered body parts all cleared away. The ringmaster is spreading a nice thick layer of fresh sawdust to soak up the blood, so we can be ready for the next one."

Cale opened his eyes and stared at Blackburn. "The *next* one?"

Blackburn nodded. "There will probably be two more bouts, maybe three. Likely only two contestants in each, but you never . . ."

Cale turned and shoved Blackburn aside to get to the stairwell doorway, then started up, half running and half stumbling, scrabbling with hands and feet up the two long flights.

He emerged from the warehouse and sucked in the outside air which, though hot, seemed cool and fresh. The dragoncub was gone, the roof deserted. He staggered to the edge and knelt, looking down at the transport tracks below. An old man crouched before a brazier beside the tracks and fanned a small clump of smoking coals. Footsteps sounded behind Cale, but he didn't turn around even when Blackburn and the Sarakheen had flanked him at the roof's edge.

"What was that supposed to be?" Cale asked. "A threat of some kind?"

"A threat? In what way?"

"I sell you this codex thing, whatever it is, or I'll end up in there fighting to survive."

Blackburn laughed. "You think the victors actually survive?" he said. "You think they're allowed to live? Not for more than a few hours, anyway." He paused. "No, that wasn't a threat. I was trying to show you something about the people you do business with. Something about those at the apex of 'civilized society.'"

Cale shook his head. "You think you're showing me something I'm not already aware of?"

"Maybe not." With a shrug he said, "Then think of it as a reminder. More evidence to help you understand why you should help the Sarakheen, why you should sell them the codex."

Cale glanced at the Sarakheen, then looked at Blackburn. "You don't make any damn sense," he said.

Blackburn turned toward the city, toward the rising towers and tree-covered floating archipelagoes and the drifting airborne fountains and the rivers that flowed in midair. "Progress," he said. "We can create wonders and marvels of all sorts, we can do almost anything we can imagine. We were able to leave Earth and spread out among the stars." He slowly nodded. "Lagrima is a good representative of all that, a center of commerce and technology."

He lowered his gaze, brought his head around to look at Cale. "Socially, however, *psychologically,* we've been stagnant since we walked out of the African savannas and began to build our cities." He pointed a finger at the rooftop under their feet. "We just witnessed that. As human beings interacting with one another, we're no better than we were ten thousand years ago." He paused. "On its most important level, humankind is an evolutionary dead end."

Cale pushed himself up from his knees and stood between the two men. He looked out at Lagrima, the warm coppery smell of blood and waste still lingering in his nose. "What does that have to do with the Sarakheen?" he said, not looking at either one of them.

"Everything," Blackburn said. "The Sarakheen *are* the next evolutionary step."

Cale resisted the urge to make a snide remark. "In what way?"

"They are moving toward the full and complete integration of man and machine. Intellect without the contamination of hormones or chemical imbalances or genetic modification."

"Why doesn't the Sarakheen tell me all this?" Cale asked, turning from Blackburn to the blank-faced figure on his right.

The Sarakheen's mouth moved into what might have been a touch of amusement. "Blackburn does an exemplary job of speaking for us," he said. "If he says something I don't agree with, or that might give rise to misapprehension, I'll let you know."

"Do you understand?" Blackburn said. "The desire to

become machines. Machines guided by individuals, individual personalities, individual and undying minds. Close to immortality, I imagine." He cocked his head at Cale. "Do you understand?" Blackburn repeated.

"Maybe. What I don't understand, though, is what any of that has to do with this codex you keep referring to."

"All right," Blackburn said. "I'll pretend you really don't know what the Rosetta Codex is, I'll pretend—for the moment—that you don't have it."

He then proceeded to explain, and though his description was brief, it matched most of what Stygon had said about it.

Blackburn glanced at the Sarakheen, then continued. "The Sarakheen have an extensive collection of Jaaprana manuscripts, texts that have been recovered from the seven worlds where archeological sites have been discovered. I don't understand it all—something to do with Jaaprana illustrations, the remains of machinery, the design and proximity of certain equipment—they have determined that the Jaaprana had in fact acquired the knowledge that the Sarakheen themselves seek. They believe the Jaaprana had the knowledge and the means to carry out the complete integration of the organic mind and inorganic machines. They believe the Jaaprana carried out this integration, this *transformation,* and in doing so left this galaxy or even this universe, or in some other way vanished, abandoning their now irrelevant cities. And finally the Sarakheen believe the texts and manuscripts they have, once deciphered and translated, will provide them with that same knowledge. I don't know how they've reached this conclusion, but they are certain of its validity."

The Sarakheen leaned toward Cale and broke in for the first time. "*Very* certain," he said.

"And the Rosetta Codex will make the translations possible," Cale said.

"Yes," answered the Sarakheen.

Cale turned away and looked down at the old man below. The old man squatted beside the brazier and drank from a dark red bottle. Cale could not help but think of thick warm blood sliding down his own throat, sickening him. He pushed back from the edge of the roof and turned toward the Sarakheen, staring at him.

"Why did you flood the tunnels?" Cale asked.

"What tunnels?" Blackburn asked.

Cale ignored Blackburn and repeated his question. "Why?"

"We reached the conclusion that it was unlikely that the Resurrectionists would find the codex, extremely unlikely that the codex had ever been in those ruins. We salvaged those Jaaprana texts they *had* recovered, then flooded the tunnels. The Resurrectionists . . ." He made a sound that had a strange rasp. "They had served their purpose, and they were troublesome. We'd had enough of them."

Cale tilted his head, stunned and shaken. "You don't care what I think about that, do you?"

The Sarakheen shook his head. "No, it's of no concern to me."

"But you think I have this Rosetta Codex, whatever it is, and you want me to sell it to you."

"It's a commercial transaction," the Sarakheen replied. "We are offering you enough wealth to become the dominant consortium in this system, dominant once again over both worlds."

Cale slowly nodded. *The next step in human evolution.* We need to find a different next step, he thought.

"I don't have the codex," he said, looking directly and steadily at the Sarakheen.

Blackburn snorted and started to speak, but the Sarakheen held up a hand, cutting him off. He studied Cale's face, and the two men regarded one another.

"I'm leaving," Cale said, and only then did he look away from the Sarakheen.

As he started toward the outer staircase, Blackburn grabbed his shoulder.

"Let him go," the Sarakheen told Blackburn. "He said he doesn't have the codex."

"*I* don't believe him."

"Let him go."

Blackburn momentarily tightened his grip, then released Cale and stepped back. Cale almost felt sorry for the big man, for the sense of powerlessness he must feel right now. But he was far more concerned about the Sarakheen. Cale was certain that the Sarakheen did not believe him about the codex, which meant he would be seeing the Sarakheen—and Blackburn—again.

"Cale," the Sarakheen called. Cale looked at him. "When we first met, Blackburn told you my name was a private matter. Do you remember?"

"Yes."

"I reveal it to you now. You've earned it." He bowed his head slightly. "My name is Justinian."

Cale didn't respond. What did it matter? It was just a name, Sarakheen or not. He turned away from the two men, walked to the edge of the roof, stepped over and onto the metal framework of stairs, and started down.

SEVEN

Cale was awakened in the crystal garden just off the northeastern corner of the House, near the abandoned quarry. He'd spent the night on a bed of dead mosses beside a brook that wandered through the garden, and had watched the faint and flickering stars above him until, long after midnight, he drifted off to sleep. Now, lying in the shade of a hedge wall, with the rising sun lighting up the crystalline leaves and flowers around him, he came awake to the gentle touch of Losatto, one of the House retainers, who tugged at Cale's bare left foot.

"I'm sorry to wake you, sire," Losatto said.

Cale sat up and brushed dead plants from his clothes. "What is it, Losatto?"

"A summons put out by Con Dotzick from the front gates." Con Dotzick was the master gatekeeper and interviewed everyone who came to the front gates requesting an audience with any of the Consortium's commercial representatives or Family members. He was skilled at discriminating between those petitioners who should be granted access and those who shouldn't. "Two men wishing to see you, sire. They claim to know you, and said you would want to see them." Losatto smiled. "The guards wanted to turn them away, but Con Dotzick insisted on hearing them out."

"Who are they?" Cale asked.

"They're called Aliazar and Harlock," Losatto replied. "Brothers."

Cale nodded. "Con Dotzick was right, as usual." He stood, brushed at his clothes again. "How did you find me?"

"Meyta, sire. She inquired of the House. It told her where you were." He hesitated. "Do you want me to request a transport?"

"No, I'll walk. It will help me wake up. Thank you, Losatto."

Losatto nodded slightly once, and retreated.

An hour later Cale arrived at the Estate entrance and was led by Con Dotzick to an antechamber where Harlock and Aliazar sat on a cushioned bench against the far wall. The walls were bare dull stone, devoid of windows, and no door other than the one Cale came through—it occurred to him that the antechamber was as much a cell as it was a waiting room.

Harlock raised his head and vaguely acknowledged Cale's

entrance, eyes not quite focused on him. Aliazar stood and shifted his weight from one leg to the other, pressing his hands together.

"We have to go with you," Aliazar said. There was desperation and fear in his voice.

"Go with me where?"

"To the star."

"What?"

"That's what Harlock said," Aliazar replied. "Not 'stars.' He said you were going to the 'star.'" He looked at his brother, whose face held no expression at all. Harlock's mouth hung open and slack, eyes void of affect. Aliazar then turned back to Cale. "He said if we didn't go, there would be disaster. Death and disaster. I believe him, I believe there will be someone's death, someone's disaster, if we don't go with you." He paused and tipped his head to the side. "You are going to this *star* Harlock referred to, aren't you?"

"When did he tell you this?" Cale asked.

"Last night. His vision . . . a vision that woke him up out of his sleep . . . never before . . . I couldn't quiet him, I couldn't calm him. . . ."

Cale looked at Harlock, but there was no indication that he understood what was being said. "Yes," Cale finally said, "I'm going to that star."

"And you'll take us with you?"

He turned back to Aliazar, searching for any sign of betrayal in the old man's eyes, wondering if he could even recognize such a sign. Was there a connection to Blackburn, to the Sarakheen? He returned his attention to Harlock, who rocked and hummed while he listlessly scratched behind his ear.

"Yes," Cale said without looking at Aliazar. "I'll take you both with me."

Three weeks later, when next he went into orbit to check on the *Night Traveler*'s progress, it had the look of a vehicle that could one day actually take them to the stars, no longer a useless agglomeration of metal lost and adrift in an orbit that would soon decay and send it to a fiery death. Sections of the ship were laid open or stripped bare, sheets and beams of metal and parts of machines strung together with cable hung motionless about the ship, but it all looked to be in the service of restoration and repair, preparation for flight.

Overshadowing the sense of progress, however, were several things that continued to bother him: Sidonie's ongoing absence; his encounter with Blackburn and the Sarakheen; and Aliazar's distress and fear of his brother's visions.

Press on, he told himself, move forward. There was no other choice.

Another seven months passed. Cale stood outside, shivering in the snow that fell heavily on the House and Estate, observing the sunlit buildings and flying vehicles of Lagrima in the distance. His mother had been requesting snow more often lately, and he wondered if that was evidence of her further dissipation.

A door opened, clattering. Cale turned and saw Cicero standing in the doorway looking out at him with a touch of a smile. Behind him stood Sidonie.

"Come in, Cale," the old man said. "It's too cold out there for me."

Cale remained motionless, paralyzed by the unexpected pain that poured forth upon seeing Cicero, the pain of memory and grief he was still unable to put to rest, the pain of carrying Karimah's cold and lifeless body up from the Underneath. The pain of irretrievable loss.

"Cale?"

Was that Cicero's voice, or Sidonie's? He couldn't tell, his hearing had become suddenly hazy, all sounds faint and distorted.

"Cale?"

He nodded, but didn't otherwise move. The snow was wet and the chill froze all feeling for a moment, and he at last understood why his mother called for it so often.

Outside the snow continued to fall, but inside a fire warmed him. Cale was relieved to see Sidonie again after all this time, and heartened to see Cicero, but he was extremely disappointed that none of the other Resurrectionists had come, and stated so.

"It's different there now," Cicero said. "The *Resurrectionists* are different. Most of those you knew are gone, moved on to different lives. Those that remain . . ." He sighed. "We cleaned out the Underneath, and we've continued to excavate over the years, but progress is slow and for many . . . their hearts are no longer in it. It feels like an obligation they'll never be free from." He paused. "And to be honest, I didn't trust that many of them, not even to discuss this. Of the few I *did* trust, none were willing to . . ." He smiled. "I don't even know what we'll be doing, or where we'll be going, only that it has something to do with the Jaaprana, and that it will probably be dangerous."

"That's still all we can tell you," Cale said.

"It's enough," Cicero said. "It was enough to get *me* here."

Cale regarded Cicero with appreciation, and affection. "I'm glad you are."

Later, when she and Cale were alone, Sidonie spoke with him, uncertain and upset. "Blackburn's here. I saw him at the port."

Cale nodded. "Did he see you and Cicero?"

"I don't know, maybe, but it wouldn't matter. I'm pretty sure he wouldn't recognize me now."

"Yeah, that's true." He smiled at her, thinking he sometimes hardly recognized her himself.

"You don't seem surprised," she said. "Have *you* seen him?"

"We've seen each other. And a Sarakheen. The same one I'd met on Conrad's World."

"You talked to him? To Blackburn?"

"Once."

He hesitated at first, steeling himself, then finally told her about his encounter with Blackburn and the Sarakheen. Every detail still etched in his memories, the images that sometimes brought him instantly awake and sweating in the middle of the night. He told her about the final conversation on the rooftop.

"You don't think Blackburn believed you about the codex."

Cale laughed nervously. "No. The Sarakheen didn't, either." He sighed. "He's just waiting. Watching and waiting. One day he's going to come after me . . . after the codex." He nodded. "So I guess we're waiting, too."

EIGHT

The *Night Traveler* hung against the star-filled sky, alive and alight and a real ship at last: a long and silver cylinder that sent out a dozen shining threads and pods as the various crews finished up the last of the work, preparing the ship for its new "maiden" voyage.

Cale watched the ship grow larger as Sidonie piloted the shuttle toward its forward docking station. They were to meet Captain Bol-Terra and Myrok, the navigator. They had not yet told Bol-Terra and Myrok about the codex, the star chart it contained, or their ultimate destination. Only now, with their scheduled departure just eight days away, did Cale and Sidonie feel they could risk the secret accidentally or purposefully being revealed to someone else; now, they had no choice.

"No one following us?" Cale asked.

"Not that I can tell," Sidonie replied, studying the readouts and data feeds. "Normal station traffic, no one in the vicinity other than the authorized work crews, no one headed in this direction. All clear for now."

"For now," Cale repeated.

"For now will do," Sidonie told him with a smile.

They met on the bridge, the main view screens displaying a dense splash of stars across the blue-black sky. Bol-Terra and Myrok expected a routine meeting: a review of the manifests and travel itineraries and supply logistics, discussion of details and any last-minute changes. Cale looked at the two men. They wouldn't have imagined the kind of last-minute changes they were about to receive.

Captain Bol-Terra, stocky and bearded, wore faded blue coveralls that vaguely resembled an outdated uniform: frayed gold stripes cut at an angle across his upper arms, a tarnished metal star dangled from one cuff, and the Alexandros Family crest had been sewn to his breast pocket. Myrok was probably the same height as Bol-Terra, but so thin and gaunt he looked taller, and wore similar coveralls but without the stripes or star.

They all pulled themselves into chairs around a circular table and strapped in, each with their own data terminals embedded in the beveled surface before them. Bol-Terra's eyelids lowered to give an appearance of boredom, while Myrok looked at Cale and Sidonie with no expression at all.

"This trip is going to be more than just a mundane trade run," Cale told them. When neither Bol-Terra nor Myrok showed any reaction, he went on. "In fact, after the first leg to Winter's Eye, we're going to have a change of destination." There was still no reaction, and Cale said, "You don't seem surprised."

Bol-Terra shrugged, picking at his ear, but remained silent. Myrok nodded and said, "We never did think it was what you told us. Well, at first, maybe, but not for long."

"Why not?" Sidonie asked.

"Nothing obvious," Myrok replied. He grimaced slightly. "I don't know . . . a little too well-planned, maybe. Never second guessing the cargo, never any substitutes, never any changes. Just too damn quiet and tidy."

Bol-Terra nodded, still picking at his ear. He rubbed his fingers on his trousers. "That's about right."

"Why didn't you say anything?" Cale asked. "Ask us about it?"

Now it was Myrok's turn to shrug. "We figured you'd tell us when you wanted, when we needed to know. Which I guess is now."

"Did you ever consider pulling out because we hadn't told you everything?"

"Not really. Our job is to get this ship where you want it to go, and to get it there in one piece. I don't think either of us cares *where* that is. And I don't know about Oswell, but I figured it would be a lot more interesting than a conventional trade run."

Bol-Terra leaned back in his seat. "True for me, too."

Cale breathed in and looked at both of them. "I don't think you'll be disappointed."

He took the codex out of his bag, set the volume on the table, and held it in place with one hand. Sidonie fingered her terminal and dimmed the bridge lights. Cale opened the codex to the back, letting Bol-Terra and Myrok watch the metal pages as they fell from one side to the other. Once past the last of the pages, he unlatched and unfolded the shimmering metal panels, then activated them.

The glowing matrices manifested in the air before them and the stars came to life in gold and silver above the table in their dense and complex pattern. As before, on Conrad's World, in the village where Lammia and her family and friends had been slaughtered, one star near the center pulsed green and bright. Cale pointed.

"*That's* where we're going," he said.

Myrok had taken the codex into the next cabin to attempt synchronizing the chart with the ship's navigational systems in the hope of identifying the star. He'd been in there for more than four hours, and still there was no luck. Captain Bol-Terra had gone to meet another loading crew checking in, leaving Cale and Sidonie alone in the bridge to wait.

Now Bol-Terra returned and sat at the table, strapping into the seat and glancing toward the cabin door. "Nothing from Myrok?"

"Not yet."

Bol-Terra nodded. "I have a few more questions."

"Go ahead," Cale replied.

"What about all the cargo?" He picked at his ear again, over and over, a habit that had become irritating to Cale.

"It's real freight, and there's a lot of it. I oversaw some of the loading myself."

"We'll be making the first leg," Cale told him. "We don't want people here to think it's anything but a normal freight run."

The captain reflected on that, then asked, "Are you coming with us?"

"Yes," Sidonie answered. "We both are."

"Will you tell me why we're going to this as yet unidentified star?"

Cale shook his head. "Not yet. Not until we get there."

Bol-Terra's mouth moved briefly down and up in a kind of facial shrug, then moved into the suggestion of a smile. "Will there be extra pay?"

"Yes. For everyone. Will the crew be okay with the changes?"

The captain nodded. "We're a small crew, and a *good* crew. We've worked together for years. Treat them right, pay them fairly, and they'll do everything you ask." He tipped his head forward, half closing his eyes. "And they'll keep it to themselves."

"Thank you, Captain," Sidonie said.

"What happens if Myrok can't ID the star?" Bol-Terra asked.

"Don't know," Cale replied. "I'll take it somewhere that has greater resources."

"Like Lagrima's Academy of Astronomy?"

"Yes, someplace like that."

"Which would be the end of any secrecy. Word would get out, not just about that 'star chart,' but about the book as well."

"You know what it is?" Cale asked.

"I can guess," Bol-Terra replied. "I've heard the stories. Never believed them before." He tugged at his ear. "I guess I do now."

Myrok came in then, face flushed with relief and excitement.

"Got it," he said.

Before they returned to Lagrima, Cale and Sidonie took the codex with them to one of the loaded cargo holds. Just inside one of the inspection hatches, a series of cubicles had been built into the bulkhead for the storage of smaller delicate or valuable items. All of the cubicles in this hold were empty. Cale placed the codex into one of them, programmed and locked it with a code he and Sidonie had agreed on earlier, and activated the gel-foam that would surround and protect it.

He turned to Sidonie. "Something happens to either one of us, the other will go on, bring the codex through the gate. No turning back. Agreed?"

"Agreed," she replied.

Cale felt suddenly exhausted. His eyes wanted to close, his whole body wanted to shut down.

"Sometimes it's hard to believe it's finally happening," he said. "All these years . . ."

Sidonie nodded. "Somehow it feels more unreal to me now than it did two or three years ago, or even ten years ago. Yet we're only a few days away from heading out."

"You've stuck with me all this time. Even when you didn't like or agree with what I was doing."

"That's how it is with us, Cale. That's how it always will be."

They regarded one another silently, then started back to the shuttle.

Cale found his mother at the Family cemetery, which until today he had not even known existed. Wearing a loose and flowing robe of pale green decorated with sprays of golden leaves, she knelt before a polished black stone marker. Stripes of shade and evening sun lay across her, bronzing her skin.

The cemetery was situated in a small grove of low, scraggy trees, a carpet of thick mosses dotted with black or white or gray stone markers of various shapes and sizes, some newer, but many worn and aged. The only sounds within the grove were the dry rustle of leaves and the gurgle of water tumbling over rocks from somewhere nearby.

Cale approached his mother, then stopped and stood a few feet behind her and to one side. He could read his father's name on the marker before her—Faulkner Alexandros—but he couldn't make out the smaller inscription and dates.

"It's just a cenotaph," she said. "His body was never recovered." She took a single, long-stemmed violet flower from within the folds of her robe and laid it before the marker. She bowed her head and closed her eyes, perhaps in silent prayer.

The stripes of sun narrowed while those of shadow widened, the sun now touching only the top of her hair. Cale watched his mother and wondered if he would see her again, and wondered whether it mattered to either of them.

But as soon as he asked that of himself, he realized that it *did* matter to him, even if it held no meaning for her.

She raised her head, glanced briefly at him, then gestured toward another black stone marker to her left. "That one is yours," she said. "It, too, is a cenotaph . . . for the same reason."

"You know me, then."

His mother slowly shook her head from side to side. "I only know the dead." Then, not looking at him, she added, "You're leaving."

"Yes," he replied. "I don't know when I'll be back."

"No one ever knows . . . and too many never come back at all."

"I'll be back if I can," he told her.

She smiled faintly. "At least you said 'if.' None of the others ever did."

She rose to her feet, took a few steps toward the left and forward, then knelt before Cale's cenotaph. She laid another violet flower gently before the polished black stone with Cale's name carved across its face.

"Goodbye, Mother," he said.

When he was certain she would not respond, he turned away and left her there with her memories and her grief.

Cale and Sidonie rose into the shadow of Lagrima's night, slowly spiraling upward in the space elevator toward the docking station. They carried even less than they had brought with them when they had first arrived nearly five years ago. Cale shouldered the rucksack he'd kept since his days on the other side of the Divide, and Sidonie held only a small satchel. A few personal items. Everything else had been loaded aboard the *Night Traveler* days or weeks ago. The crew, too, had been aboard for days, along with Cicero, Aliazar, and Harlock.

Below them, the lights of Lagrima glistened within an uncomfortable silence, the gold and crimson falcon near the outer edge slowly diminishing. The hovering and flying multicolored lights above the city looked like bits of shining color unattached to anything substantial, blown about by chaotic breezes.

Home?

It was still a question for Cale. He had never felt at home anywhere, and didn't really know what that felt like. He turned and looked down once more at the receding lights, at the city and world that fell slowly and steadily away from them. They continued their ascent in silence, each alone with their thoughts as they headed toward a place and a time unknown, toward a future that still hid from them all its infinite and unknowable self.

BOOK FOUR

ONE

The *Night Traveler* [jumped] . . .

. . . and remerged into the universe.

Adrift, the stars innumerable, the night sky thick with them, like blackcloth sprinkled with the dust of gemstones.

Cale lay back in an observation lounge seat, the steelglass dome's metal canopy fully retracted to reveal the deep skies of space. He sensed movement, like gentle rocking on the water, though he knew he was stable and motionless. He recalled that night nearly twenty years past (or was it even longer?) when he'd been pulled out of the freezing lake and lay shivering on the floor of the boat, looking up at a clear night sky. So many stars, he'd thought at the time, but it was nothing like this.

He could lose himself in this vast and empty expanse, and he thought it might not be so bad to remain lost.

A slight vibration alerted him, and the floor hatch opened. Myrok pulled himself up and into the lounge, sealed the hatch, then settled into the control seat as Cale sat up. Myrok nodded in greeting.

"We've got what we hoped for," he said. "Hold on." He manipulated the seat controls and the lounge began to slowly rotate around the circumference of the ship.

Cale fought the vertigo that washed over him as the stars trailed silver arcs overhead; he clutched the seat arms and closed his eyes until the lounge smoothly came to rest.

"Sorry," Myrok said. "I forget not everybody's used to this."

Cale opened his eyes when he felt relatively steady. "I'm all right."

Two sets of glowing crosshairs appeared on the clear glass dome, one green and one red. They moved in tandem, just centimeters apart.

"Yours is the green," Myrok said. The crosshairs came to a stop low on the dome's horizon. Centered in the green crosshairs was a large bright star that stood out against the others. "We've confirmed it," Myrok added. "That's the star in the codex chart."

"How far?"

"It would take us more than a year under conventional propulsion to reach the inner orbits where the gate should be." He made a huffing sound. "This is what happens when you're the first to go somewhere." He shrugged. "We're going to make a tertiary [jump] which will bring us a lot closer. There's something which actually makes it easier for us, though. All the incoming data indicates that there isn't a single planet orbiting."

"Not one?" Cale asked.

"Not one. Nothing of significant mass. Maybe we'll find what amounts to a giant hunk of rock or ice, but nothing big enough to cause us any trouble when we remerge. We should be able to get in close enough to start searching for the gate right away."

"Any chance we could remerge with the gate and destroy it?"

Myrok grinned. "Sure, there's a chance. But there's probably a better chance you'll spontaneously combust in the next five minutes." He got up from the seat. "You should head back to your cabin. Coordinates are set, and the launch sequence is on to make the [jump] in six hours."

Cale remained in the observation lounge for a time, however, losing himself again in the stars. So far from Lagrima, from Conrad's World, from everything in his life. In some other time as well as some other place.

They had made the first leg of their registered itinerary, transuding to Winter's Eye and docking at the orbiting transit station. There they'd sold and offloaded the cargo slated for sale to that world, but instead of arranging for the purchase of replacement cargo, they'd sold off the rest of what they still carried—intended for other worlds and better prices—trimming the ship substantially. Three weeks later, with no signs of a Sarakheen or other ship trailing them, they'd left the system and made the [jump] which had brought them here.

This last [jump] would bring them near the gate. Until now, he'd tried not to think of the possibility that the gate no longer existed, or never had. Or that they had not accurately read the codex's holographic chart and the gate was located at some other star that they would never find. He shook his head at himself—it was far too late for doubts or second thoughts.

He got up from the seat, opened the floor hatch, and lowered himself through it.

The ship [jumped] again . . .

. . . and once more remerged into real space.

The sun blazed before them as the star's image filled the wall screen in the bridge. A bright silvery light tinged with . . . red . . . orange . . . Cale sensed movement from Myrok's hand and the image shrank, the sun pulled away from them until it was no more than a fourth of its original size, letting the surrounding night and stars appear on the screen.

"Not much to see, really," Myrok said. "A sun. Nothing unusual about it, nothing new for us. We're just a lot closer now."

"And the gate?" Cale asked.

"We're searching for it. Nothing yet. It doesn't help that we don't know what we're looking for. If the Jaaprana wanted us to find it, you'd think they would have been more specific about just what it was." He snorted. "*Gate.* What the hell's that supposed to mean?"

"I don't think they were interested in making it easy for us. Or for anyone else."

"Maybe so. I'd settle in for a while, if I were you. We might find it in a day or two, or it might take us weeks, even months."

"Or we might never find it," Cale admitted.

"I'll just pretend you didn't say that," Myrok replied.

Cale dreamt of Harlock and Cicero. Harlock had leathery wings tipped with feathers, one of the wings broken and dragging in the sand, and Cicero swayed and chanted out visions to his enraptured companion as they crouched before a burning shack. Cale felt disembodied, as if he were only observing from nearby but not actually present in any real way. He knew somehow that Cicero was having visions and relating them to Harlock through the chants, but Cale couldn't make out any of the words.

A bell chimed and Cale looked around, searching for the source of the sound, but the area around them was a wasteland, flat and empty and uninhabited except for the three of them—or the *two* of them, since he wasn't really there. The bell chimed again. Neither Harlock nor Cicero responded.

Then Cale realized that he was dreaming, that the chiming came from outside his dream, and that he needed to waken. But Cicero's chanting held him, and now Harlock turned to him, acknowledging his presence. Harlock's expression told Cale to stay, that Cicero had messages for him, messages from some other place and time that were meant for him and him alone.

The bell chimed again, and Cale sensed an insistence to it. He forced himself to pull away from Harlock and Cicero and dragged himself up and out of sleep, struggling until at last he was able to open his eyes to the darkness of his cabin and the chiming of his door.

Weariness weighed him down, but he managed to get out of the cot and stagger to the door, pressing the square panel that opened it.

Myrok stood in the pale blue corridor light that marked night on the ship. "Found the gate," he said.

TWO

"Well," said Myrok a bit later when they'd gathered in the bridge, "we *think* it's the gate."

There wasn't much to see at first. They were still days away from reaching it, and all that appeared on the wall screen, even magnified by the ship's telescopes, was a vaguely hexagonal shape surrounded by a glistening halo.

"That thing is impossible," Myrok said.

Captain Bol-Terra nodded his agreement, tugged at his ear, but didn't speak.

"What do you mean?" Sidonie asked.

"It's not orbiting the star. No orbit, no angular momentum, it's just holding a static position approximately thirty-three million kilometers away. The mass of the star should have sucked that thing in as soon as it got there."

"I don't understand," Cale said. "Couldn't it have some kind of propulsion to keep it in position?"

Myrok shook his head. "It could, but it doesn't. It would need acceleration, maybe not much because of its small mass, but some. And we can't pick up any traces of propulsion, no indication of any kind that an engine is firing. We do, on the other hand, get impossible mass readings from the thing. Fluctuating around a quantity you might expect from an object of its size, but rising to nearly as high as a small planet and going all the way down to zero." He shrugged. "At least that's what we think we're reading. And before you ask, no, we have no idea what could produce those kinds of fluctuations, or what they mean, or if they have anything to do with the gate being able to maintain its position."

"So what do we do now?" Cicero asked.

Myrok and Captain Bol-Terra looked at Cale with raised eyebrows.

"Nothing," Cale said. "Approach, and see what happens as we get closer." He paused, looking around the cabin. "Unless someone has another idea or suggestion."

No one did.

Myrok led Cale silently through the ship to one of the cargo holds, this one now empty like all the others, and shut the door behind them. They stood on a narrow platform of grillwork and looked out over the dark and empty hold lit only by a few firefly lights that barely kept complete darkness at bay. The walls were covered with huge bundles of meshed cable, long coils of rope, collapsed metal bands.

"I think we've got a serious problem," Myrok told Cale in a low voice, as if someone might hear him even in this empty room. Cale waited, and Myrok went on. "A few hours ago a message pod was launched from the ship."

"What's a message pod?"

"A miniature rocket, in essence. Nothing but a small conventional engine for initial thrust, a scaled-down Barlis drive to make a [jump], and a transmitter. The closest thing we have to interstellar communication. They contain recorded messages, and they have specific [jump] coordinates programmed to take them to their destination system. Once they remerge into real space, they begin transmitting their message."

"And someone launched one from this ship?"

Myrok nodded and breathed deeply. "I only discovered it by accident. Then I did some system searching and found that there'd been another launch several days ago, soon after we made the first [jump]."

"What does it mean?" Cale asked.

"I was hoping *you* might have some idea," Myrok answered.

Cale didn't reply for some time, his gaze sweeping the darkness and faint lights of the cargo hold as if some answer lay within the shadows. "There's no way to learn what the messages were, is there?"

"No, but I can guess. So could you."

Cale looked at him. His stomach tightened and he felt

a halting flutter in his chest. He was afraid to voice his thoughts.

"This star's coordinates," Myrok finally said. "That would be the first message. Maybe confirmation in the second, or confirmation of the gate's existence. Something like that." He paused, looking steadily at Cale. "I'm thinking you might at least have some idea who the messages are for. Who is being informed of where we are. Maybe even what we're doing, although *I* don't even know that." He gave Cale a half-smile.

"The Sarakheen," Cale said.

"Aww, shit," Myrok said with a sweeping turn of his head, nearly closing his eyes. "Are we going to have those freaks on our asses, then?"

"Probably."

Myrok made a choking laugh. "Well, you warned us. You told us there would be a lot of risks." He looked at Cale. "Are the Sarakheen looking for this gate, too?"

Cale shook his head. "No. They want the codex, the book. Not for the star chart. For the text."

"What's in it? The secret of eternal life?" He laughed again.

"They don't want what it says. They want what it can do." He told Myrok about the four different languages, including one of the Jaaprana, and the Sarakheen's belief that the codex would allow them to translate all the alien manuscripts they'd acquired over the decades.

"And what are *we* doing with the book and the gate?" Myrok asked.

"I'm taking the codex through the gate. I'm taking it to them, to the Jaaprana."

"I thought they were all dead."

"As far as I know, they are."

Myrok shook his head slowly. "You're as crazy as the Sarakheen."

"Maybe," Cale replied.

They remained silent for a time, both leaning on the platform rail and regarding the empty hold.

"Someone on this ship is working for them," Myrok declared.

"Yes."

"Can't believe it's one of the crew." He turned to Cale. "One of your friends?"

Cale reluctantly nodded. "Could be." He'd been considering that possibility, and couldn't reject it.

"I don't think we should tell anyone about the message pods," Myrok said. "I'll do some more digging. I might be able to figure out who's burning us."

"Any way to estimate how long before the Sarakheen get here, if that's who the messages were for?"

"Not a chance," Myrok answered. "Too many variables, no way to even guess. Two days, two months. Two years, if we're lucky, but I know we're not."

"No," Cale agreed, "we're not."

Cale told Sidonie about the message pods while they sat in her cabin, drinking hyslip tea. She got up from her cot, paced the cabin several times, then sat back down, staring into her cup.

"They'll be coming after us," she said at last, looking up at him.

"They *are* coming after us," he corrected. "They're on their way."

"And Blackburn with them."

Cale shrugged. "Maybe, maybe not. He doesn't worry me."

"It doesn't really change anything, though, does it? There's nothing we can do about it."

"No."

Sidonie sighed heavily. "It would help to know who sent the messages. Might make a difference what we do from now on, when we reach the gate." She paused looking at him. "Who we take with us when we go through."

"Yes, but we might never know."

She gave him a hard, wry smile. "Oh, we'll find out, eventually. Maybe when it's too late, but we'll find out." Then, "Have you considered the possibility that it's me?"

"No."

Her smile disappeared. "You shouldn't be so trusting, Cale."

Cale slept poorly now. Anticipation, he supposed. Anxiety . . . doubt . . . fear . . . He took to wandering the ship's corridors in the dim blue illumination of shipboard night, exploring the distant reaches of the ship, the cabins and passages and holds he'd never before seen. One night, in the dining cabin, he encountered Harlock standing before the cabin's single window, though it was covered by the exterior panel so Harlock could not see a thing.

"Harlock, you want me to open that for you?"

Harlock slowly turned his head until he faced Cale, expression vacant.

"You can hear us, can't you?" Cale said. "Do you understand? Do you understand any of what we say?"

Harlock's expression didn't change, but his attention remained fixed on Cale, as if he were waiting for him to say the right words, and that when he did, Harlock would reply, would speak to him as though he'd been speaking all his life.

"I wish I knew what you were thinking," Cale said. "Something's going on in that mind of yours, something worth understanding."

Harlock remained silent, eyes blinking infrequently, watching Cale. Cale stepped forward and reached past him to activate the exterior panel, which slid aside so that the star-filled night appeared through the clear glass, silver against black.

Harlock looked out the window for a moment, then turned and ambled off, no longer interested in the window now that it was open, no longer interested in Cale.

Five days later they maneuvered into position some two hundred kilometers from the gate, aligned as the codex instructed so that the gate was centered in the disk of the sun. Surprisingly, they discovered they had settled into what Captain Bol-Terra called a "gravity trough," which meant that once they'd positioned themselves before the gate, they, too, required no more energy to avoid being drawn toward the gate or the sun behind it.

On the bridge's main view screen, six metallic satellites formed a hexagon against the reddish silver of the sun. A faint haze of luminescent particles surrounded the satellites, flickering and flowing between them.

"That's a gate?" Aliazar said. "I don't understand."

The haze brightened and the particles coruscated with heightened intensity.

"What . . . ?" Aliazar began.

THREE

The gate opened like some great and monstrous yet mechanical eye.

The six satellites spread slowly outward from the center, and the luminous particles coalesced into silvered ribbons linking the metal orbs even as they moved farther away from one another.

The sun darkened, or rather a new and solid darkness manifested within the gate, filling in the space between the satellites and the ribbons of force, a deep and utter blackness so complete it blotted out the sun, obliterated the star that all knew shone directly behind the opened gate, that all knew should have shone *through* the open gate. A blackness absolute like the path of banishment from this universe.

Around the gate, the sky appeared warped and slightly out of focus. Starlight lengthened and distorted and took on a sense of movement against the deep blue and black of interstellar space.

Just as unexpectedly as it had opened, the gate closed. The silvered ribbons of force twisted and became seemingly taut, and the satellites drew inward once more toward one another until they were as before. The ribbons fragmented, then dissolved, reverting to the insubstantial haze of glowing particles—the gate hung dormant, a luminous hexagon with the sun shining behind it once again.

"We're supposed to go through that?" Aliazar said.

"You insisted on coming," Cale replied with a smile. "Remember?"

"No," said Aliazar.

"Aliazar has a point," Cicero put in. "I wonder myself what you have in mind."

"I'm not sure, to be honest," Cale said. "But I never intended to go in blindly. We'll send probes through first, see what happens. After that . . ." He finished with a shrug. "The plan is to go through in a lander, not the entire ship. We'll have plenty of time to think about it."

Cicero smiled halfheartedly. "The less we think about it the better."

"Worried?" Sidonie asked. They were alone on the bridge, looking at the cluster of satellites on the view screen.

"Not yet," Cale answered.

"I am."

Cale put his arm around her and felt the tension shivering through her.

"I'm supposed to be comforting *you,*" she said.

"That's silly."

"No it's not, Cale."

He breathed deeply once and nodded. "You're right, it's not." He silently regarded the shining formation that was a gate to some other place, perhaps some other time. "You'll go with me?"

"Of course. Being scared won't stop me."

"I wouldn't mind if you stayed," he said. "I might even . . ."

"No," was all she said.

"Who else do you think will go?" Cale asked.

"Aliazar and Harlock."

"Not Cicero?"

Sidonie shook her head. "Before we left Lagrima I would have said 'yes,' but he seems to have aged, lost interest somehow. I don't know. I just don't think so."

He wasn't sure why he'd asked the question. It didn't seem to matter anymore, even though he still didn't know what waited for him . . . for *them.* He felt very much alone. He knew he would have felt even more alone without Sidonie, but he no longer thought the presence of others would make much difference. This was *his* task, his commission, and in the end it was his alone.

The first probe emerged from the bay doors and floated away from the ship. Oblong and shiny and sprouting antennae, the probe wobbled slightly until the attitude rockets fired, tiny silent bursts of flame, and it stabilized. They watched from the bridge as a few more brief ignitions appeared and the shining metal probe headed directly toward the gate.

As the probe neared, the gate opened as before, the satellites dispersed uniformly, the haze of particles once again coalescing and forming the more substantial ribbons of light and force between the satellites and in turn engendering that deep and yawning blackness within their boundaries.

Readouts and tracking graphs lit up one of the smaller view screens off to the side, displaying the data being transmitted to them by the probe. The gate seemed to welcome the probe, laying itself open and shining brightly though at the same time it had once again blotted out all signs of the sun behind it.

The probe flew directly toward the center of the gate, the center of that black emptiness. For a long time there was no change but for the diminishing appearance of the probe as it moved farther from them and nearer to the gate; even the displays on the view screen pulsed with regularity.

Everything stopped for a moment, the readouts froze, all motion seemed to cease as the probe reached the gate and encountered the darkness. Cale's breath, too, stopped, long enough for him to wonder if his heart had ceased to beat before the readouts came back to life with a burst of color and then immediately died, darkening completely as the blackness swallowed the probe.

"We've got another problem," Myrok said to Cale later that day.

Cale had been lying down in his cabin, trying to sleep but unable to slow his thoughts enough to do more than fitfully doze. He sat on his cot and regarded Myrok with exhaustion.

"We get a transmission from the probe?" Cale said.

"No, nothing. Not even a hint of a signal. It's gone for good." Myrok shook his head. "We have visitors. Less than fifty million kilometers away and headed straight for us."

"Shit."

Myrok nodded. "Looks like you were right about who the message pods were bound for. The propulsion signature indicates it's a Sarakheen starship."

"How long before they get here?"

"That ship's damn fast. Five days, maybe four."

Cale sat in silence for a time, staring at the floor and thinking. He looked up at Myrok.

"No more probes," he finally said. "Probably wouldn't learn anything useful, anyway."

"You're going through the gate?" Myrok said.

"No choice," Cale replied. "Never really was. But we can't put it off any longer. I've got to go before the Sarakheen get here. I've got to go *now*."

Cale and Sidonie sat side by side in the lander's two pilot seats, Sidonie running through the systems checks with him, reviewing the controls, trying to teach him as much as possible so he could assist her or take over if necessary.

"I told Myrok and Bol-Terra to get as far away from the gate as possible once we leave," Cale said, "but I don't think they'll go anywhere."

Sidonie smiled. "Better for us, isn't it?"

"I suppose. I worry about what the Sarakheen might do to them."

"Likely nothing," she said. "They want the codex, and they'll know it's gone with us."

"You're probably right."

The ship's intercom snapped, and Myrok's voice sounded inside the lander.

"You there, Cale? Sidonie?"

Sidonie switched on the mikes. "We're here."

"So are the Sarakheen," Myrok said, voice tight yet controlled. "They made two tertiary [jumps], both a lot more directed than we could ever manage. I don't know how the hell they did it, but they did, and now they're less than a day away."

The lander moved slowly and carefully toward the open gate with minimal thrust, little more than a controlled drift, the view screens swelling with that dark blank emptiness where the sun should have been. The satellites and ribbons of force and the stars still visible at the edges of the screens were incredibly bright against that hole in the universe that was the darkness looming before them.

Captain Bol-Terra's voice came through the com system, clear and distinct. *"How's everyone doing? You look good from here, right on course."*

"We're fine," Sidonie replied. "So far nothing unexpected."

Cale looked around the lander cabin, glancing briefly at each of his companions, everyone in shock suits but with their Metzen Fields deactivated. All were silent and motionless, gazes fixed on the view screens. Only Harlock appeared relaxed, though he, too, watched the screens with surprising intensity.

Cale felt a soft bump and turned back to the view screens. Nothing had changed, and he looked at Sidonie. She attended to the instrument panels, making slight adjustments.

"What was that?" Cale asked.

"Don't know. We've got some resistance. The probe never ran into any, but we've sure got it, and we're not moving forward anymore. I'm increasing the thrust."

The lander's vibration became more noticeable, but the sense of forward progress returned, the gate growing larger on the screens.

"What's happening there?" Bol-Terra asked. *"We're picking up ignitions from you, and gravitational fluctuations from around the gate."*

"A field of some kind is giving us resistance . . . maybe gravitational from what you're saying. But we're countering it." As she spoke, though, she increased the thrust again.

Cale watched her, resisting the urge to talk, to interrupt her, and he was grateful that the others in the lander remained silent. There wasn't anything they could offer her.

Sidonie increased the thrust again only to have the resistance do the same. It was not quite a standoff, however, for they continued to move closer and closer to the gate, though their progress was barely noticeable. Sidonie ignited the two emergency boosters, and the lander shook with the added force.

"Maybe you should abort," Bol-Terra suggested. His voice carried more concern and urgency than the words did, while at the same time the transmission began to falter.

"Not a chance," Sidonie said. "We're pushing through, and we're doing it now. What's the status on the Sarakheen ship?"

"Ten hours out," Myrok responded. *"That's assuming deceleration. It's . . . occurred to m . . . that . . . might decide to foll . . . through the gate. If they do they . . . just maintain . . . tion . . . a few hours . . ."*

The front screens were now completely filled with the blackness, no hint of light. The engines roared at full thrust and the lander shook, and though it felt as if they were held immobile, the side screens and the tracking graphs showed their painfully slow but steady progress forward. Sidonie glanced at Cale and shrugged, trembling hands on the controls. There was nothing more to do.

". . . losing you." Bol-Terra's voice was now barely audible, distorted and broken. *". . . luck . . ."*

The nose of the lander broke the plane of the gate and the black emptiness before them seemed to ripple with a lighter or darker blackness . . . perhaps a different *kind* of blackness . . . something not exactly seen but rather felt or otherwise sensed. Harlock cried out, a loud and desperate wail. The lander pitched and shuddered, and Cale felt it was on the verge of coming apart. The resistance disappeared altogether and the lander hurtled forward.

FOUR

* * *

FIVE

. . . where . . . ?

. . . what happened . . . ? . . . what happened to . . . ?

<non>

SIX

Cale awakened in an unnatural darkness, an uneasy silence. He could see nothing, not even his own hand as he held it just inches from his eyes. He could hear nothing, not even the slightest whisper of movement or breath. Were the others here with him? He wondered briefly if he'd become deaf and blind.

He tried to sit up, and lost consciousness once again.

The lander shook, as though buffeted by a storm.

Complete darkness again or still. Then either his vision returned, or the lander's power (some of it), for the dim blue cabin lights came on and the instrument panels came to life and Cale could see the others around him . . .

Sidonie at the main controls unconscious, eyes closed and face slack and head lolling to one side.

Behind her, Cicero with eyes blinking, murmured unintelligibly.

Aliazar slumped in his seat, also unconscious.

Only Harlock seemed unaffected, gazing mutely at the black view screens before them as though seeing something imperceptible to the rest of them.

The lander continued to buck and shimmy, but with the view screens dark it was impossible to know what was happening. Cale adjusted the screen controls without success. He pressed the switches to move the two screens to the left and the right and requested the protective shielding be retracted from the steelglass forward windows. The safety authorization sounded and the shielding slid back from the high and wide windows.

The view through the glass was as featureless and dark as that on the view screens.

"What . . . what is this?" It was Sidonie's voice, quiet and bewildered.

Cale turned to see her sitting upright and alert, moving her hands uncertainly toward the controls, her attention shifting back and forth between the screens and the view through the windows. She activated the exterior lights, but nothing changed—either the lights didn't work, or they had no effect on the darkness surrounding them.

"Are you all right?" Cale asked.

"There's nothing out there," she said. Then, in a whisper, "Nothing."

The shaking eased, gradually became little more than a resonant vibration, and finally ceased altogether. The view remained black.

The lander hovered completely motionless, as if they were suspended outside the universe.

Just as the lander hovered, Sidonie's hands, too, hovered not quite touching the controls.

"I don't know what to do," she said.

"Engines?" Cale asked. "I don't hear or feel anything."

Sidonie shrugged. "Instruments indicate the engines are running, everything go. But there's no acceleration, no fuel consumption." She shrugged again.

A heavy stifling quiet, a stillness that encased the lander. Cale sensed the void pressing in on them, yet he felt no fear, no concern that the pressure and the void would overwhelm and crush the lander and all of their lives with it. There was an assurance to this pressure, a security to the grip in which the void held them. Without knowing why, he felt certain that they were safe.

Time passed strangely, with an extreme slowness that somehow dispelled any possibility of tedium or impatience. They remained in their seats, watching for something to appear within the black and featureless view before them, rarely speaking.

The windows and screens lit up with a blazing white flare, a bright wash like sheet lightning. Cale jerked, startled by the flash, and pulled out of the trancelike state into which he had fallen. He sat upright as the light faded and the screens and windows went dark again. Then dark blue color appeared, and hints of distant lights, and suddenly the lander's engines resumed their roaring, the sudden acceleration shoving him back and deep into his seat as the craft blasted forward into the darkness.

Aliazar cried out, a wordless shout harsh and frightened. Gravity manifested itself and the lander dropped, falling suddenly, then slammed into something with a crash and caromed upward as Sidonie gave it a burst of lift.

"Lights!" she called out.

Cale searched the panels before him, trying to remember, then recognized the switches and hit the lander's exterior floodlights as the vehicle crashed into something *above* them.

"Shit . . . shit . . . shit . . ." Sidonie muttered, hands moving frantically across the controls as the lander fell once more, now listing and pulling to the right.

The windows and screens came to life with the shadowed images of rock spread out before them, though overhead and to the sides loomed only darkness. What had they hit overhead? They hurtled along over blackened stone, broken and jagged, the ground coming up at them once more.

Cale glanced down at the instrument panels, then returned his attention to the uneven terrain, feeling utterly helpless. The lander bucked and swerved and rose in a looping arc, pulling up and away from the rocks. The floodlights beamed elongated cones away from the craft that vanished into blackness, illuminating nothing.

The lander slowed and dipped again, falling to the right. Cale watched Sidonie at the controls, trying to follow her efforts, remembering now that the engines had been at full thrust when they'd broken through the gate. She was trying to cut back on the thrust while compensating for damage that must have occurred when they'd first bottomed out. They pulled up, hung for a moment weightless, then pitched forward and descended, this time slightly more smoothly and less precipitously, though still pulling so hard to the right that Sidonie could barely keep them close to a straight course.

The lights showed a rocky plain that abruptly ended several hundred meters ahead. They hurtled forward and passed the boundary, the ground dropping away and becoming one with the darkness above and around them. The lander continued to list, but Sidonie gradually brought it under control, nearly leveling the flight and easing back on the velocity.

Darkness surrounded them again. It was not black and empty like the void of the gate, however, and Cale thought he could detect distant glimmers of light or vague shapes beyond the reach of the lander's floodlights.

The forward thrust engines died, and the lander dropped. Sidonie cursed and hit all the vertical thrusters, jolting the lander but halting their descent. Varying the power to the verticals, she brought the craft around in a wide bouncing turn and headed slowly and awkwardly back toward the rocky ground they'd left behind. As the solid ground approached, Cale could see that the cliff edge was straight and even and stretched unbroken and without apparent end in both directions, and the wall that fell into the deeps was smooth and featureless, reflecting the floodlights like polished metal.

Despite the damage and the pronounced list, Sidonie managed to set down as more rough landing than crash, the craft bouncing and scraping and sliding before coming to rest. The cabin became profoundly quiet except for the harsh whisper of ragged breaths.

"Everyone okay?" Sidonie asked, surveying the interior. Cicero and Aliazar nodded, while Harlock simply blinked at her without expression.

"What's the chance of making it back out in this condition?" Cale asked.

Sidonie shook her head. "Might be able to limp it along back to where we came from, but we don't even know if this gate is two-way, do we? Or if it would take the same kind of thrust to get through going back, in which case we wouldn't have a chance. We shouldn't even think about it now. We try to do what we came here to do, deliver the codex, and then we worry about getting back afterward."

"How do we do that?" Cicero asked.

"Do what?"

"Deliver the codex."

Sidonie just shrugged, and Cale said, "We go outside. I assume we'll be able to figure out where to go once we're out there."

Cicero smiled. "That's optimistic of you."

Sidonie returned her attention to the lander controls. "Outside temperature is cold, but not bad, hovering around freezing. Atmosphere analysis is running, but we'll be using the Metzen Fields anyway." The Metzen Fields would enclose each person's head like an invisible helmet, providing air and insulation.

Sidonie reached across the control panels and switched

off the exterior and interior lights. Harlock moaned quietly, but gradually the surrounding environment became dimly visible through the windows, illuminated by a faint ambient light of background radiation. The lander rested on rocky plain that paled into a strange and utter darkness in the direction from which they'd entered this place, ended abruptly at a cliff in the opposite direction, and stretched unending for miles to their right and left.

"All right, let's activate the Metzen Fields," Sidonie said.

Cale twisted the flange on his suit collar . . . and nothing happened. He worked at the switch, resetting it and twisting again. He looked at Sidonie, who shook her head at him in dismay.

"Cicero?" Sidonie said.

"My field doesn't seem to be working."

"Not mine neither," Aliazar said from the darkness behind them. "What's wrong?"

"None of them are working?" Cale asked. "How can that be?"

Before Sidonie could think of an answer, or could tell him she had none, a ringing alarm sounded and red light flashed on the control panel.

"What the hell . . . ?" Sidonie switched on the interior lights and got to her feet, turning around toward the rear. "The outer door . . . Harlock!"

The inner airlock door at the rear of the cabin was open, and Harlock had worked the manual override for the outer door, which now slid open as he turned the wheel. Cold air rushed in as their own air rushed out, and when the opening was wide enough Harlock stepped through the doorway and dropped to the ground outside. After a brief hesitation,

Aliazar ran out after him, calling his brother's name.

"Damn it!" Sidonie snapped. She ran to the main panel to seal off the interior door and flipped the switch. The door slid shut and the alarm ceased.

There was little to be done or said. Cale and Sidonie and Cicero remained in the lander, watching Aliazar and Harlock. Cale switched on one of the exterior floods, which illuminated their two companions and cast long shadows across the rocky ground. Harlock seemed quite content and worked his way to the cliff edge, where he stood and looked out into the yawning darkness. Aliazar joined his brother and tugged at his arm and appeared to plead with him, but Harlock would not budge.

It was only a matter of time before they joined those two, Cale thought, certain Sidonie and Cicero recognized the same thing. Unless the atmosphere outside held certain death for them, they had no choice but to risk it. They could not stay here indefinitely, and returning the way they had come did not appear to be a viable option.

Fifteen minutes later Sidonie glanced at a set of readouts that had begun to blink and said, "Preliminary analysis indicates a breathable atmosphere. Harlock and Aliazar will be glad to hear that."

Cicero chuckled and got up from his seat. "Shouldn't we go tell them?"

Cale retrieved the rucksack with the codex and worked his arms through the shoulder straps, adjusting them. Sidonie activated the lander's rooftop beacon—a slowly pulsing orange lantern that cast an eerie illumination about the vehicle—and switched off the exterior floods and the interior lights.

"Harlock's walking off," Cicero said as he stood at the window.

Cale and Sidonie joined him, and observed Harlock making his way across the plain, angled slightly away from the edge of the abyss. He hiked steadily, but in no hurry, and Aliazar followed.

Sidonie opened the interior door, and the three of them disembarked.

SEVEN

They followed Harlock for no reason other than that he seemed to have an actual destination in mind, or was guided by some hovering cynosure recognizable to none but him: his own personal Star of Bethlehem. Intentionally or not, he led them on, shambling across the broken and yet unnatural terrain, hunched forward as if still harnessed to the cart Cale had seen him pulling all those years ago across the desert. Aliazar followed his brother as in those days, but hatless and on foot, now.

The way was dimly lit by an ambient silver blue light. Cale walked behind Aliazar, the rucksack with the codex on his shoulders; Cicero came next, and Sidonie last. Pilgrims on their way to a holy shrine. Disaster survivors looking for rescue. A little of both, Cale supposed.

Sidonie shone a powerful hand light into the darkness on all sides, casting long shadows and illuminating blocks of quarried stone, shattered glass, and spiky shrubs of oxidized metal that had never lived and never would, yet would endure for centuries. No hills, no cavern walls, an endless lifeless plain. Whenever the light shone ahead of Harlock, he would stop and turn back to her with a grimace, and would not resume until she had aimed the light in another direction. Eventually she switched it off and followed in the dim illumination.

They marched on in this way for hours in silence, and Cale wondered if they were all afraid that any question, any word at all might bring them to a halt, might engender some discussion of whether or not to go on, might result in their turning back when they all knew there was little or no hope in that. Occasionally he turned around and searched for the tiny pulsing beacon atop the lander, and he always found it, but each time it was smaller and dimmer. Soon he would not be able to see it at all.

At one point during their march they heard a muted roaring and crashing and screeching from far behind them. When they turned to look, there was a dulled flicker of light in the distance, back from the direction of the lander.

"The Sarakheen?" Sidonie wondered aloud. No one replied, probably because there was no one else it could be. They stood watching and listening, but when they saw and heard no more they turned and went on, hurrying to catch up with Harlock, who had not paused in his private and resolute march.

* * *

Sometime later, a high wall rose in the distance ahead of them, a solid darker shadow blotting out all other shadows. As they neared it, the wall loomed over them, a massive presence, the demarcation between one unknown place and another.

Harlock kept on without pause, and walked purposefully toward an opening in the wall, a high arched doorway. He stopped before it and leaned forward, reaching hesitantly toward it, then pulling back his hand as the others came up beside him.

The open doorway revealed the same thorough and palpable darkness as that which had waited for them beyond the gate. Cale moved to the side of the opening and put his gloved hand against the wall. He felt a surprising warmth through the glove. He stared into the darkness of the doorway, but it had no dimension, as if the wall was infinitely deep or had no depth at all. Harlock swayed and hummed before it, head cocked as though trying to make a decision. Cale looked at Aliazar.

"No, he's not going to have a vision," Aliazar said, answering the unspoken question. "This is too quiet." He reached up and gently laid his hand on his brother's shoulder, but Harlock did not seem to notice, and continued to hum and sway.

Cicero spoke, lightly but seriously. "If Harlock goes through, we follow."

Aliazar glanced at Cicero, then looked back at Cale. "He's right," Cale said. "That's what we do."

They remained like this for some time, watching and

listening to Harlock. He stopped humming, stood straighter. He appeared to focus on something on the other side of the darkness, something again imperceptible to the rest of them. He sighed deeply, stepped forward and into the doorway, and vanished.

Aliazar hesitated only a few moments, then followed his brother and he, too, disappeared.

Cale looked at Sidonie and Cicero, and they both returned his gaze without questions spoken or unspoken. They were waiting to follow him. He turned back to the doorway, gripped the straps of the rucksack to hold the codex tight against his back, then stepped through.

One step, was all. He stood on the floor of a vast and wondrous chamber, an immense cylinder that appeared to be several miles across and far more than that high, the upper reaches disappearing into a darkening mist. A steady vibration emanated from the floor, gently penetrating his bones, and a deep and low thrum enveloped him. There was more light here than back on the plain they'd marched across, though here, too, it infused the air itself, pale and blue. The walls held row upon row of wide horizontal metal lockers of a silver-bluish cast set within niches of polished black stone—thousands, tens of thousands . . . probably hundreds of thousands or more, Cale thought.

The Graveyard of Saints?

Harlock sat cross-legged on the floor, head tilted back, gazing up raptly at the endless curved wall, at the innumerable metal vessels. Aliazar stood beside him, silent and awestruck, mouth open.

Cicero stepped through the doorway and stopped at Cale's side, and a few moments later Sidonie followed. Cale expected the doorway to disappear or transform, but it remained unchanged, an arched darkness revealing no sign of the unnatural plain they had walked upon for hours.

"What *is* this place?" Cicero whispered, but with nothing in his voice to suggest that he expected an answer.

"The Graveyard of Saints." Cale approached the wall and touched one of the metal lockers. The surface was so smooth his gloved fingers slipped across it without traction. The container, like all of the others, was about three feet high and at least ten feet wide. He had the distinct feeling that if there had been a handle on it—and he were strong enough—he could have pulled the locker out of the wall like the drawer of some immense and indestructible cabinet.

"Where's the light coming from?" Sidonie asked.

"It was dark when we first came through," Aliazar replied. His voice was tentative, as if he were afraid to speak aloud. "The light kind of poured in from the walls, it . . ." He trailed off.

"Now what?" Cicero asked. This time it was clear that he *did* expect an answer to his question.

"We look for the shrine."

"Shrine?" Aliazar asked.

"That's what the codex says. We come to the 'Graveyard of Saints,' and look for the shrine. When we find it, we place the codex inside."

"And then what's supposed to happen?"

"The re-genesis of the Jaaprana." Cale shook his head. "We don't know what that means. Some kind of creation, perhaps. Or resurrection."

"Then maybe it's not such a good idea to do it," Aliazar said.

"It's why we're here," Cale told him.

"But that sound, I feel it going all through me, that hum . . . this is a terrible place . . . we should just leave . . . we should go back . . ."

"You pleaded with me to come along, remember?"

Aliazar nodded. "Maybe it was so we could stop you, maybe that's what Harlock meant, we had to be here to keep you from doing it."

Cale smiled. "It'll be all right, Aliazar. Whatever happens."

"How do you know?"

"He *knows,*" Sidonie said to him, her tone certain and somehow reassuring.

Aliazar looked at her, then at Cale, then finally turned back to his brother, who appeared entranced by his surroundings, hands pressed against the floor before him as if he were actively taking in the vibrations and letting them work their way through his body. "You mean even if we all die, it'll somehow be all right," Aliazar said to Cale.

"Yes," Cale replied. "I suppose that *is* what I mean."

"You sound like some kind of crazy holy man."

"I'm not, Aliazar. I'm just someone who found the codex."

Aliazar nodded, still looking at his brother. "Okay. We find the shrine."

"Maybe there," said Cicero.

He pointed to a section of the wall in the distance that gave off a faint rosy hue. Cale, Sidonie, and Cicero started toward it, and a few moments later Aliazar followed, leaving Harlock behind, still seated with his long arms stretched out to either side and his hands pressed against the floor, humming quietly.

The ground beneath their feet appeared to be a dark bronzed metal, textured with tiny bubbles and pockets, and each step seemed to add to the vibration that came up from the rough surface. The thrumming continued without interruption, and now Cale thought he could sense a subtle oscillation to it, perhaps even some complex rhythm.

The light came from within a deep alcove, the only irregularity other than the doorway in the cubicled rows of metal containers. A diffuse pinkish light emanated from an opaque panel on the back alcove wall. A shelf at chest height ran along one side wall, while the opposite wall consisted of dulled rectangles of various sizes that might have been dormant lights or other displays. On the back wall, amid the rosy light, was a narrow ledge, and at its center an angled platform with a shallow recess that looked as if it would hold the codex.

"I hate this place," Aliazar said, his voice almost pleading.

Cale sensed fear coursing through him with its own personal and intimate vibration, but it was accompanied by excitement and anticipation that overpowered it and allowed him to act as if he was not frightened at all.

He removed the codex from the rucksack and carried it into the alcove. The air was colder and drier and the skin on his face tightened. Breathing became difficult, as if he was forced to consciously direct his lungs to work, to expand and contract. He approached the platform and examined it. The metal surface was dark and shiny with swirls of reflective burgundy hues. The recess appeared to be the same size and shape as the codex. Cale lifted the codex, and set it into the depression.

The codex sank immediately into the platform with a smooth low whirring sound, then slid back into the wall, disappearing completely. The whirring intensified, resounding from the walls and inside his head, and the rosy light brightened. Tempted to back away, but remembering the words of the codex, Cale stood waiting for its reappearance, though now he was doubtful.

A grinding rumble sounded, echoing within the alcove, like the roar of machinery coming to life. He took one unconscious step backward, then stopped himself. The codex reappeared, and rose up out of the depression, and continued rising until the depression was flush with the surface. The metal-bound volume slid down the angled platform and dropped over the edge. Cale reached out and caught it, held it away from his body, and quickly backed out of the alcove.

They all stepped back from the shrine, then as the grinding roar grew louder, they retreated even farther and watched from what seemed a safe distance. Cale put the codex back in the rucksack. They stood and waited for whatever was to come.

Hours passed. Cale suspected that if there had been anywhere else to go, the others might have left this place. As for himself, he was determined to see it through no matter what happened.

They ate sparingly from their nutrition packets and sipped at their water tubes. They listened to the background thrumming as if it were some kind of celestial music, and they listened to the steady machine rumble emanating from the shrine. They watched the rosy light of the alcove, preparing themselves to witness the emergence of . . . something. Presumably the Emissary, whoever or whatever that was. They paced and stretched their limbs and sat, then rose and paced again. They didn't speak.

Sudden quiet. All sounds ceased. When the background thrum resumed, they instinctively backed away a bit farther, but the grinding machine roar remained silenced. The rosy light faded until the rear of the alcove became dark and heavily shadowed. A harsh sliding sound reached their ears, a door opening perhaps, and an even deeper darkness momentarily filled the alcove. Then came the sound of heavy and uncertain footsteps.

An incredibly tall and imposing figure stepped out of the shadows, eight and a half, perhaps nine feet in height, with massive arms and legs and wearing armored clothing and gloves, face and head covered by a shielded helmet with caged eye holes and scales of brightly colored metal layered along its side. The alien staggered slightly, as if unsure of its footing, then firmly planted the heavy black boots, straightened, and stood still, helmeted head facing Cale and his companions. He was enormous, and reminded Cale of the high doorways in the ruins on Conrad's World.

He? Cale wondered why he thought of the alien as male, and wondered if it was a label that even made any sense. Because he saw no signs of mammaries? Which, even if they existed, could be easily obscured by the armored clothing?

Was this then the Emissary mentioned in the codex? It had to be.

No skin or hair or eyes or any other evidence of organic life was visible, everything covered or shadowed by helmet and armor, clothing and tinted shields. Cale wondered if it was possible the alien was not a living creature at all, but an animated construct. He quickly dismissed the notion as he registered the harsh breathing he now realized had been manifest since the alien had first appeared, the sound obscured by the ever-present thrum all around them.

The alien stepped forward and Cale and his companions backed away once again, keeping their distance. Cale told himself he shouldn't be afraid, but he'd reacted unconsciously. The alien, the Emissary, stopped. It deliberately reached one hand toward them, then lowered it. It came no farther.

They remained thus for long moments, no one moving, no one speaking. Then Cale, remembering his instructions, took several steps toward the alien. He held up the rucksack, showing it to the alien, then set it on the ground, preparing to remove the codex. He knelt, his movements slow and deliberate, and worked at the fabric bindings, keeping his gaze on the Emissary.

The alien put its massive gloved hands to the helmet, as if preparing to remove it, but before it could, the quiet was broken by a long and anguished wail. Cale turned to see Harlock on his feet, howling as he faced the mysterious doorway through which they had all entered this place.

The doorway was unchanged, black and dimensionless, but Harlock continued to wail, head swinging from side to side, hands clawing the air before him. He howled out a final, harsher cry and dropped to his knees, covering his face with his hands as the doorway took on a nacreous sheen that imbued the darkness with a kind of life.

Blackburn stepped through the arched darkness and

halted. He was soon followed by the Sarakheen called Justinian, then moments later by three other figures. Cale looked back at the alien, who had lowered his hands without removing the helmet and now faced the newcomers, standing straight and alert.

Blackburn and Justinian and the others took some time to get their bearings, breathing heavily as if they had just climbed a steep hill. They ignored Harlock, focused on Cale and his companions and the Emissary, and started toward them. As they approached, Cale saw that the three others were Sarakheen as well—two women and one man, artificial limbs and plated skin exposed. The male Sarakheen lagged behind the others, bleeding heavily from a gash across his forehead. All of them carried weapons—stone-burners, laser rifles, hand pistols. Blackburn carried a multicharge shattergun under his arm, held loosely but still pointed generally toward Cale and the others.

The group stopped when it was only twenty feet away, and the bleeding Sarakheen dropped to his knees, pressing his one flesh-and-blood hand against his forehead.

Blackburn smiled. "Well met again," he said to Cale, followed by a nod to Sidonie and another to Cicero. He gave Aliazar a quizzical look, then turned to regard the alien. "Look at that," he said. "A Jaaprana alien. *Alive.*" He shook his head in wonder. "However did you manage that, young Cale?"

EIGHT

The alien did not move except to occasionally turn its head from one group of humans to the other; once it looked out at Harlock, who sat upon the ground with hands and arms outstretched as before.

"We didn't expect this, I will admit," Blackburn said. He looked at Justinian. "Does this change anything?"

The Sarakheen processed the question, then slowly shook his head.

Blackburn looked at Cale and stretched out his free hand. "Now. The codex."

"How do you plan to get out of here?" Cale asked.

"That's not your concern," Blackburn replied. "I've always admired your courage, Cale, but this time it's carried you too far. This time it won't be enough, and I don't believe you'll be coming back." He adjusted his hold on the shattergun. "The codex," he repeated.

"No."

Blackburn nodded once. "I thought it would come to this."

A quiet strained tension took hold. No one spoke, no one moved. Cale held Blackburn's stare and wondered if the man would really kill him. Probably.

Surprising them all, it was the Emissary who moved first, taking two long and heavy steps forward. The alien held out its gloved hands palms up, brought them together and closed them in a prayer-like position, then opened them. The hands remained open for a time, then the alien repeated the motions, and Cale realized it was miming the opening of a book.

"I'll be damned," Blackburn said with a harsh laugh. "That creature wants the codex, too. But what for? The Jaaprana wrote the damned thing, didn't they?"

"Re-genesis," Justinian said. The Sarakheen fixed his gaze on Cale. "That's the word, isn't it? The word they use in the codex?"

"What the hell are you talking about?" Blackburn asked.

"Yes," Cale said, returning the Sarakheen's gaze. "That's exactly the word."

Justinian gave a brief nod of acknowdgement, then slowly shook his head. "We can't let that happen, Cale. You can't give it to them." He gestured toward the alien. "Look at it. Look. Can you imagine that race loosed upon the galaxy? Millions of *them,* descending on our worlds with their advanced technology and their physical superiority?

Disaster. Give them a few decades, maybe less, and they'll turn the human race into their slaves . . . or make it completely extinct."

Cale regarded the Emissary, who had lowered its open hands and now took a step back. Wary, perhaps, Cale thought. With good reason.

"We don't know that," he said. "The codex says we would live together, learn from each other."

"Of course that's what it *says.* They need us, at least a few of us, to bring it to them. They're not going to reveal the truth."

Sidonie moved to Cale's side. "That's why you want the codex," she said to the Sarakheen. "To keep it from the Jaaprana, to prevent them being revived."

"It's more than enough of a reason."

Blackburn shook his head in confusion. "What about the translation of all the Jaaprana texts you have?"

"I'm sure it will do that," Justinian said. "That will be an added benefit, no doubt. But no, that's not the real reason we're here."

"How do you know about this?" Cale asked.

"One of our people found it, many decades ago. Or another version of it. Not on Conrad's World, on Vox Romanus. I wouldn't be surprised if there's more than one, written by a number of different Jaaprana who stayed behind on each of their worlds. This woman found it, and read it, and lost it. Later she became one of us and brought with her the tale of the codex."

"And you've been searching for it ever since," Sidonie said.

"For each and every one that might exist," Justinian corrected her.

Blackburn stepped in front of Justinian and glared at him. "You told me that the translations would allow the complete integration of man and machine. That's a lie?"

"We have no idea what's in the texts we have," Justinian admitted. "But I'm sure we'll learn a great deal from them. That's not what's important, however. What's important is preventing the Jaaprana from being revived."

Cale could feel the sense of betrayal and anger building in Blackburn, and sensed also that Blackburn didn't know how or where to direct it. Blackburn wanted to survive this, and believed the Sarakheen were his best hope for that. Cale once again almost felt sorry for Blackburn. Almost. He couldn't afford to let sympathy or pity affect any action or decision right now. He glanced at the Emissary without turning his head; the alien seemed to be intently observing the interaction among the humans, as if deliberating before making a judgment. Cale was afraid of what that judgment might be.

"Who betrayed us?" Sidonie demanded to know.

"Don't tell them," Blackburn said with bitterness. "Let their suspicions eat away at them."

"There's no need for that sort of thing," Justinian said. He looked at Sidonie. "No great 'betrayal.' Your Captain Bol-Terra kept us informed. His cooperation was easily acquired—a combination of a sense of duty to the human race, and a substantial sum of money to reinforce it. Nothing complicated, nothing mysterious."

Cicero spoke up for the first time since Blackburn and the others had arrived. "You have no regard for the human race," he said to Justinian. "You know the Jaaprana are not a threat to us. You see them as a threat to *your* superiority, *your* plans to dominate all non-Sarakheen humans."

"At this moment," Justinian replied, "our 'true' motives don't matter. We are taking the codex, whatever our reasons may be."

"It matters," Cicero insisted. "It determines who will get the codex."

Justinian shook his head with a faint smile. Before the Sarakheen could say anything else, however, Cale caught a flicker of movement off to the side and turned. Aliazar had slowly and quietly made his way to the rucksack, and had opened it. With smooth and quick movements he pulled the codex from the rucksack and hurried with it toward the alien.

Blackburn raised the shattergun and aimed it at Aliazar and the alien.

Justinian's artificial hand lashed out and grabbed the barrel of Blackburn's weapon and pushed it skyward.

Aliazar held out the codex, and the alien reached forward and down and took it reverently but firmly from Aliazar's hands.

Blackburn stepped back and tried to wrench his shattergun out of the Sarakheen's grasp. Justinian would not release the barrel, however, and they stood with the weapon between them like some rigid and inorganic umbilical, and neither man would give way.

"You used me," Blackburn said. "You used me and you lied to me."

"All true," Justinian agreed. He cut his eyes toward his fellow Sarakheen and nodded once. "But we're done using you."

The wounded Sarakheen rose and came up behind Blackburn. Blackburn did not see him. When the Sarakheen raised his artificial arm and hand, Cale called out a warning. Blackburn turned, but it was too late. The Sarakheen swung his hand and arm down like a club and crushed Blackburn's skull. Blood spattered from the big man's head and he released his grip on the gun. Blackburn collapsed and pitched forward without uttering a word, surely dead by the time he hit the ground.

Feeling sick, Cale stared at the dead man, at the crushed head and pulped skin matted with blood and bits of bone and gray matter, at the deep red blood pooling thickly around his head and neck. Blackburn.

Blackburn, who had come riding into Cale's life that rainy day nearly twenty years ago, and who had at times shown a genuine liking and concern for him.

Who had been able to watch with equanimity the slaughter of Lammia's village.

Who had bound Cale when searching for the codex, yet did not kill or even harm him.

Who had forced him to watch three men butcher one another before offering to buy the codex.

Who would have willingly left them all here to die.

Who had seemed invincible, even immortal.

Blackburn, whose death now engendered in Cale a surprising sense of loss.

Blackburn.

No one moved. Cale wondered what the alien thought of what had just occurred. He finally turned to Justinian and stared into the Sarakheen's cold and shining eyes, wondering if either of them was alive.

"Why?"

"Just what I said. He'd fulfilled his purpose, and we were

done with him. He was going to create problems, soon if not right now." He gestured toward the alien while keeping his gaze fixed on Cale. "Now retrieve the codex from that thing, and bring it to us."

"Why didn't you let Blackburn fire?"

Justinian looked at the alien and said, "We may yet have to do it ourselves, but only if it becomes absolutely necessary. Firing a weapon in here might produce unwanted results." He turned back to Cale. "The codex."

"Get it yourself."

"What happened to Blackburn can happen to any one of you . . . or all of you."

"What kind of threat is that?" Cale asked. "You plan to strand us here, so we're dead either way. Now or later, and now might be a lot easier on us."

"If you're still alive you have a chance to find your way out. If you're dead . . . then you're just dead." He took his stone-burner and aimed it at Cale. "I'll kill you one at a time, and see if that doesn't become a viable threat to those still alive. I think I'd better start with you, Cale."

Without hesitating, Justinian pressed the stone-burner's igniter. Cale tensed with a quick intake of air, squinting his eyes. Nothing happened. Justinian glanced down at the burner and pressed the igniter again. Still nothing. Cale held his breath, afraid to move. Justinian looked up, then shifted his gaze to the alien.

Cale turned to look. The Emissary set the codex at its feet and withdrew a pair of coppery tubes from a banded pocket on the side of his armored suit, the tubes linked in several places by wire mesh. The alien held them so the tubes pointed at Justinian, and pressed them together. The wire mesh glowed in the alien's hands, then a golden stream of particles flared from the coppery tubes. Cale felt and heard an electrical buzz, and watched Justinian and the closer of the two Sarakheen women crumple to the ground like animatrons that had been suddenly deprived of all power.

The other Sarakheen woman raised her laser rifle, aimed it at the alien, and pulled the trigger. Just as with Justinian's weapon, nothing happened. In desperation she threw the rifle at the alien, who deflected it deftly with one arm. The Sarakheen who'd killed Blackburn stood motionless, as if paralyzed. The alien squeezed the two linked tubes together once more. Again the golden stream flared, an electric vibration washed over Cale, and the two remaining Sarakheen crumpled to the ground.

Cale turned to the alien Emissary, wondering if they were next. But the alien returned the tubes to their place, then turned its masked head toward Cale and the others. It didn't otherwise move, as though waiting for something, the codex still at its feet.

Cicero walked over to the four Sarakheen, and knelt by Justinian. "He's breathing," Cicero said. "He's still alive." He rose and checked on each of the others. "They're all still alive. Apparently the alien isn't quite as willing to kill as the Sarakheen were."

Harlock was on his feet now, and shuffled toward them. Although he seemed in no hurry, he appeared to be focused and intent. When he reached them he went by Cicero, then Cale and Sidonie, and then finally walked past Aliazar without even the slightest acknowledgment. He continued on and stopped only when he stood directly in front of the alien

Emissary, less than a foot away. Though Harlock was well over six feet tall, he was dwarfed by the massive figure before him.

The alien put its hands to its helmet as it had earlier, but this time completed the action and removed it, revealing head and face. Its skin was dark and leathery, and its large golden eyes were protected by clear lenses that appeared to be embedded in the sockets. Instead of hair, layers of large and curved dark multicolored scales covered its head and brow, whorled into structures on either side that Cale assumed were ears. Segmented folds of skin formed a wide mouth.

Harlock straightened, raised his head as high as possible, then bowed it slightly forward. The alien turned the masked helmet around, lifted it, and lowered it over Harlock's head.

"Wait!" Aliazar ran a few steps toward the two and stopped, shifting from one foot to the other. "What are you doing?"

The alien looked at Aliazar, its large and golden eyes never blinking, but did not otherwise react. Then it returned its attention to Harlock and pressed the helmet more firmly over his head, adjusting it slightly.

"Stop!" Aliazar cried, though he did not step any closer. "That's my . . ." His voice trailed off, and then he finally finished in a whisper, "My brother." He glanced frantically from Cale to Sidonie to Cicero, to his brother and the alien, then back to Cale. "What's it doing to him?"

Cale could only shake his head. When Aliazar looked back at his brother, the alien gestured with its hand for him to come forward. Aliazar hesitated, and the alien gestured again.

"Go," Sidonie said quietly.

Without looking back, Aliazar nodded and hesitantly approached the alien and his brother. Movements slow and deliberate, the alien gently took hold of Aliazar's hands, then guided them to Harlock's arm, pressing hands and arm together. Aliazar stared with fear at the helmet covering Harlock's face and gripped his brother's arm.

The alien made some adjustments to the helmet, snapped a band tight around Harlock's neck. It knelt beside the codex, opened it, and removed a shining and complexly patterned strip of metal from a pocket inside the front cover. The alien stood, inserted the strip into a slot just above the helmet eyes, then pressed a flange on the side of the helmet and stepped back.

Harlock snapped his head back and cried out, the scream muffled by the helmet. He fell forward to his knees, pulling Aliazar down with him, arching his back and howling.

"Harlock!" Aliazar grabbed his brother's shoulders, trying to hold him still, but Harlock twisted and jerked, howling out a distorted wail of anguish. Then he pitched forward and onto his belly, pressing his hands against either side of the helmet, moaning. Aliazar held on to his brother's arm, rocking from side to side and making a keening sound.

Harlock's moaning gradually eased, and after a time ceased completely. He freed his arm from Aliazar's grip, then rolled onto his back and lay still, only his chest and stomach moving, rising and falling with each harsh and heavy breath.

Aliazar scrambled to his feet and lunged at the alien, swinging his fists as he struck the alien's body. "What have you done to him?! What have you . . . ?" His words choked away as he pummeled the alien without apparent effect.

Cale felt utterly helpless. He thought the alien intended Harlock no harm, but saying so wasn't going to comfort either Aliazar or Harlock.

The alien was surprisingly gentle with Aliazar. Gloved hands took Aliazar's shoulders and eased them back, and Aliazar took to punching at the alien's arms. The alien bent down to one knee, bringing its face level with Aliazar's, and still holding his shoulders, looked directly into Aliazar's eyes.

Aliazar returned the alien's gaze and stopped flailing at it. They remained like that for a time, as if some wordless communication was taking place between them: the alien somehow reassuring Aliazar. Or at least that was the message Cale imagined came from the alien's eyes.

Aliazar pulled back and the alien released him. He knelt by his brother's side and placed a hand on his chest. Harlock's breathing had eased, deep and slow and regular now.

The alien leaned over, took Harlock's hand, and with Aliazar's aid helped him to his feet. It turned to Cale and the others and began to speak, its voice a string of deep, melodic phrases broken by long harsh gutterals. Moments later Harlock, too, began to talk, speaking in his own language the words of the Emissary. . . .

NINE

"He is damaged," the alien said through Harlock's voice. "The damage is of a . . . quality that more easily allows the . . . functioning of the translator . . . which is why I selected him. More critical matters wait, but it is also important to prevent further violence. I must proceed unimpeded." The alien stopped, apparently waiting for a response.

"What critical matters are waiting?" Cale eventually asked.

The alien turned to Harlock, but after several moments the only sounds that emerged from him were two or three unintelligible noises. Then nothing more.

The alien motioned at Cale with its hand, and Cale concluded he was being asked to repeat himself, so he did. Once again Harlock could only produce a few harsh sounds. The alien spoke again.

"There are difficulties with the translator," the alien said through Harlock's voice. "Or perhaps the damage. I need to know if you understand me since I cannot understand you. Do you have a . . . gesture . . . to indicate the affirmative?"

Cale nodded deliberately, with some exaggeration.

"Then you understand me when I speak."

Cale nodded again.

"And the gesture for negative."

Cale shook his head.

"This will have to suffice," the alien said with Harlock's voice. "You brought the manuscript with you, you delivered it to us, so you have read it."

Cale nodded.

"Then you understand what is to next occur."

First Cale nodded, then he shook his head, then shook his head again. The alien hesitated, then resumed speaking, followed once again by Harlock's voice.

"I am the Emissary, and I am charged with initiating the re-genesis of our people. It is my duty first to determine whether or not it is secure to begin. If it is not secure, or if I would perish before the re-genesis could begin, then all would wait for another Emissary to be awakened by another of the manuscripts such as the one you brought—for there are others to be found, others to be awakened.

"Once re-genesis has begun, the process is . . . self-sustaining and will continue until all are"—a long hesitation by Harlock, then the alien spoke briefly again, and finally after another hesitation Harlock completed the sentence—"revivified. This will be followed by our return to our worlds. Our worlds and yours. Our people and your people will meet at last. We hope the interactions will proceed without violence, or with minimal violence, for some probably cannot be avoided, as we have already witnessed."

The Emissary paused and motioned expansively toward the walls surrounding them. "Here we are, within our vessels, waiting for rebirth. Waiting for resurrection: for we have died and been disintegrated and been entombed and then re-created in this place outside of time that is not a place. Revivified . . ." the Emissary/Harlock repeated, "so that we may once again procreate and . . . continue."

At this point the alien stopped and looked at the still unconscious Sarakheen. It strode over to them, took them by the arms one by one and laid them together, then took several flexible bands from one of the pockets in its suit and strapped one around each of their heads.

"You need be informed of no more," the alien said, returning to them. "You may observe, but you must not interfere or you will be incapacitated also. When the ships leave, you may accompany any of them and return to one of your worlds. You need not remain here to die." After a long pause the alien resumed, its words again spoken by Harlock. "Have you understood all that I have said? Do you agree not to interfere?"

Cale and the others all nodded.

"I begin."

The Emissary picked up the codex and carried it to the alcove, set it on the long shelf along the left wall, and opened it again. This time the alien manipulated the binding so that the entire spine came away from the leaves, then picked up the top metal sheet with the stenciled markings and held it up, studying it. Apparently satisfied, the alien crossed to the opposite wall of the alcove and inserted the sheet into a narrow slot, holding it flat. An internal mechanism took up the sheet and pulled it steadily into the wall until it had completely disappeared. The Emissary returned to the codex, picked up the second metal sheet, carried it to the slot, and fed it, too, into the wall. The alien stepped back and studied the inert wall.

The wall came to life with a pulsing hum and brightly shining strips of ruby light. The alien intently observed the lights as several flashed on and off, some brightened or dimmed, while others glowed with a sustained radiance. Then at some change in pattern or frequency or some other indication, the alien returned to the unbound manuscript's stack of metal leaves. One by one the Emissary fed the stenciled sheets of metal into the wall until it reached a sheet that was not stenciled but etched with black ideograms of a human language. The Emissary laid the sheet back onto the stack and turned to the wall.

A great rumble took hold of the vault, a heavy vibration and a deep penetrating sound, and the lower rows of lockers became suffused with a phosphorescent violet light from within the walls. The Emissary appeared to take satisfaction from this development, for it exited the alcove and walked past the group of humans, continuing several hundred feet out from the curved chamber wall. The alien stopped and slowly turned a full circle, surveying the chamber, the glowing rows of lockers, the beginnings of . . . re-genesis.

Aliazar took his brother's arm and gently eased him to the floor. Harlock sat and cocked his head as if listening to this miraculous event as well as watching it. Cale regarded the two brothers with both sadness and affection.

Cale looked at Sidonie and Cicero, who stood transfixed, then he walked over to Blackburn's body and knelt beside it. The pooled blood was thick and dark and in the bluish light appeared unreal. One side of Blackburn's head was completely crushed; his face was relatively unmarked, however, though his open eyes were glassy and lifeless. Cale was bewildered by the sense of grief he felt for Blackburn, for this man who done so many terrible things in his life—certainly far more than Cale would ever know.

Blackburn. Cale remained at the dead man's side and looked up and all around that vast chamber, studying the bands of violet light encircling them, listening to the deep and resonant thrum, and waited for the future to change.

Several hours later, a lambent azure light issued forth from the upper walls like a thick yet ghostly fluid and flowed down and over the lighted lockers, reminding Cale of the blue light that had flowed up and out of the stone altar that had held the codex. The light coated the lockers like a protective film, glowing more brightly now as if to signify burgeoning life within.

A new tension charged the air, and the Emissary stood alert now, attention shifting all around that immense chamber as though uncertain where the next stage in the process would begin.

It seemed to begin everywhere at once. A new sound added itself to the deep rumbling, a sliding electrical hiss as the lockers on the bottom row emerged not quite simultaneously, extending several feet from the wall so that the corners of one nearly touched the next. Within two or three minutes it appeared that all those on the bottom row had emerged, several thousand polished metal caskets forming a miles-long ring around the interior of the chamber. The containers began to open in near unison, hundreds upon hundreds of lids rising all around them, hinged at the rear so the metal plates tilted up and back against the walls and the lockers above them, revealing thousands of pale spectral forms.

Lit by the surrounding blue light, large tall figures much like the Emissary rose uncertainly from the lockers, stiff and awkward and naked, though whether a distinction of sexes existed among them Cale still could not determine. Their skin was dark and mottled, with strips of fur or thick hair along their torsos and upper legs. The massive scaled heads twitched and jerked, huge eyes blinking spasmodically. One by one they leaned over to retrieve bundles of dark cloth, and all around the vault the aliens pulled loose robes over their heads before carefully climbing out and standing barefoot on the chamber floor.

Three or four thousand robed aliens now stood around the perimeter of the vault, most of them facing the Emissary, others studying the humans with indeterminate expressions and unfathomable intentions. They stepped away from the lockers, their movements still stiff and weak and unsure.

The lockers dimmed and drew back into the walls, until they were flush with the other lockers above them. They did not stop there, however, they kept receding, forming dark and empty hollows in the walls. The next row of lockers lowered slowly and smoothly into the new vacancies, and all the rows of lockers above them dropped one row as well, filling in all around the vault. Those lockers now on the floor level slid out from the wall as had the first, with that electrical hiss that filled the air and washed across the floor, surrounding them. The lids opened, and several thousand more aliens rose unsteadily from their coffin-like drawers, pulled on robes, and climbed out onto the vault floor, joining the others.

Over the following hours, this entire procedure repeated itself six, seven, eight more times until twenty-five or thirty thousand robed aliens stood gathered in an enormous circle and the rows of lockers ceased their movements. The aliens appeared stunned, bewildered, yet one by one, throughout the chamber, they turned their attention to the vast empty ground before them as though waiting for something. The Emissary, too, stood looking out toward the center of that great vault, and Cale was certain they all waited for the same thing.

The wait soon ended. A loud and terrible noise sheared the air, like the wail of some massive and wounded beast. The chamber floor began to open, at first a long rectangular slit through the center and running nearly from one wall to the other, not quite reaching the circle of aliens. It widened in sections as a series of panels pulled away, sliding back and under the floor, the opening now vaguely oval in shape with its rectangular edges, becoming wider and wider as more floor panels slid away.

No light appeared from the opening, and from where he stood Cale could not even guess how deep the darkness went. The wailing faded, and soon was gone or so faint it was obscured by the deep background rumbling that never ceased. A new sound soon took its place, however, a resonant drumming that shook the floor, shook Cale's bones, and seemed to presage the coming of . . . of whatever it was the aliens waited for. Cale sensed the increased anticipation among the thousands of waiting figures.

A huge and hulking form outlined with starlike gleams appeared in the floor opening, indistinct at first and rising slowly. The ambient bluish light of the vault was absorbed in some places, but in others reflected from polished metal, from glass, from projections like antennae and from projections like enormous weapons and from others that bore no familiar shape at all but in size and prominence appeared critical and essential to the workings of the great starship that now rose within the chamber.

Cale felt overwhelmed by the immensity of the ship, which dwarfed the *Night Traveler* and any other human starship he had ever seen or heard of. Shaped like some monstrous creature of the deeps, it had the form of a hunched leviathan with massive appendages, squat legs that supported its bulk on the platform that now settled into place with a resounding boom, shaking the vault.

The entire ship now stood visible to them all. At least a mile in length, and nearly half that in height and width, with huge cylinders arrayed around its stern. Massive serpentine cables lay draped across the ship's midsection, and great gouts of smoke or steam or other vapor issued forth from long horizontal vents on both sides, rising toward the upper reaches of the chamber.

Illuminated openings appeared in the ship's belly, like caverns lit by smoldering fires. Platforms emerged, slowly lowered, and came to rest on the chamber floor. Within moments the aliens began to move toward the ship. They walked deliberately toward the platforms, most still weak and awkward. A few lagged behind, as if unsure of what to do or where they were, perhaps even unsure of *who* they were; but others spoke to them and urged them along, and eventually all followed and joined in the boarding.

The Emissary spoke, and Harlock's voice said, "You may join them. You may board the ship and travel back to one of our worlds, which will likely be one of your worlds also. You will not be harmed, and you will be provided for."

"What about Harlock?" Aliazar said, scrambling to his feet and looking up at the alien, who was nearly twice his height. "What about my brother?"

Harlock made a few gurgling sounds, then stopped.

"I do not understand your meaning," the Emissary said.

Aliazar pointed to his brother, then leaned over and attempted to remove the masked helmet. The Emissary put its hand on Aliazar's shoulder and gently pulled him back, speaking once more.

"The mask cannot be removed," Harlock's voice said. "He would immediately perish." The alien made an odd scooping motion with its hand that must have had some meaning but which was indecipherable to Cale. "There is great benefit. He will accompany me, and he will serve us all, he will aid in the communication between our people, he and others like him."

"He'll die anyway!" Aliazar said with anguish. "He'll die of thirst, or starve." He made drinking motions, then brought his hand to his mouth and chewed imaginary food and made an exaggerated swallow, tracing a path with his finger down his throat to his stomach.

"He can take food and drink," the Emissary said. The alien knelt in front of Harlock and pushed a depression on the right side of the helmet. An opening at Harlock's mouth appeared and the Emissary pointed toward it.

Aliazar dug into Harlock's suit and found the end of the liquids tube, then stretched it and brought it to his brother's mouth. Harlock sucked greedily at it, leaning forward. When Harlock had finished drinking, and ate one of the nutrition packets that Aliazar fed to him, the Emissary eased Aliazar to the side and pushed the depression again, closing the mask.

"You have a strong attachment to this person," the alien said. When Aliazar nodded, the alien continued. "You may stay with us and help care for him, and help with our efforts to interact with your people."

Aliazar nodded again. The Emissary turned back to Cale and the others.

"Do you not wish to board the ship?" the alien asked. "Eventually we all will leave and there will be no one here. There is no way to survive in this place. As well, you cannot leave this place the way you entered. Do you understand this?"

Cale nodded and held up a hand, hoping the alien would understand the gesture. He glanced at the ship, saw that more than half of the aliens had boarded, then turned to Sidonie and Cicero.

"I want to see more," Cicero said. "I'd like to stay at least for the next ship, I'd like to see what happens with this one."

"If there is another ship," Sidonie said.

"The alien implied there would be others," Cicero replied. He gestured at the walls where row upon row of lockers still rose up into the darkness. "There are going to be a lot of other aliens, and a lot of other ships." He breathed deeply once. "We'll never have the chance to see anything like this again in our lives. We can always go with Aliazar and Harlock when the alien takes them."

Cale looked at Sidonie. "I'm with Cicero," he said. "I want to experience this as fully as possible."

She nodded. "Then I'll stay, too."

Cale turned to the Emissary and tried to mime as simply as possible the launch of the ship, the resurrection of more aliens, the appearance of another ship with more aliens boarding it, and then himself and Sidonie and Cicero boarding.

"I understand," the Emissary said. "You wish to stay and board one of the other ships. Is that accurate?"

Cale nodded.

"Yes," the Emissary said. "There will be many other ships and you may board any of them." The alien joined them, then slowly looked around the vault and added, "This is wondrous to behold."

They stood together and watched the remaining aliens board the starship. When the last of them had stepped onto the platforms, railings came up and surrounded them, then the platforms ascended and delivered them into the ship's interior.

More time passed with little change, then another rumble disturbed the air and the far wall seemed to crack and split. The crack widened, and Cale realized that somehow the walls were moving and separating from one another, the entire vast chamber opening to whatever lay outside. A stab of fear spiked through him as the gap widened and stars appeared against the blackness of space and he imagined all the air rushing out of the vault and sucking them out with it. But he felt no change to their atmosphere, and the fear eased as he realized that some invisible force maintained the integrity of the chamber.

The walls continued to move, sections on either side of the widening gap overlapping the remaining walls. Before long the gap was large enough for the ship to pass through, and the walls gradually came to a standstill.

Cale could not stop staring at the stars glittering in the blackness of space somehow kept at bay, the stars shining through that expansive opening, the stars beckoning to him, calling him to whatever might be home.

The starship began to move, the platform beneath it sliding forward as if on a track leading to the opening. As the bow of the ship reached the gap in the walls, a shimmering ripple appeared in the air around it, and Cale imagined that the ship was now passing through an energy barrier of some kind, whatever barrier protected the vault from the vacuum of deep space.

The ripple expanded as the ship moved through it, surrounding the craft with an incandescent corona. The ship was a long time moving through that barrier, partially outside and partially inside, but steadily progressing until at last the starship's stern with its huge cylinders passed through the barrier and the rippling corona dwindled and disappeared.

The platform supporting the ship fell away as though hinged at the vault's perimeter and the starship drifted free, cut loose from any kind of mooring. It drifted with almost no motion until dozens of tiny thrusters fired, silent and strangely insubstantial flickering streams of light pushing the immense ship away from the chamber with almost painful slowness. Some minutes later the thrusters cut out and the starship continued to move slowly away.

Brilliant and silent explosions of swirling light appeared in the massive cylinders at the ship's stern. The sky around the engines seemed to twist, stretching out the light of the surrounding stars. The swirling flames of blue and white and deep red brightened and flared so that soon the ship itself was hidden, and there was nothing to be seen but the flames and the stars.

The starship accelerated, picking up speed and growing smaller in apparent size. As it did, the platform that had dropped away came up and retracted and the walls began to move again, this time advancing toward each other, slowly but steadily closing the gap. When the walls had completely closed, cutting off all signs of the great starship and the stars outside, Cale felt a sense of loss, despite knowing he would see it all again.

The Emissary turned away from them and looked at the nearby wall. Once again the lower rows of lockers became outlined with a glowing light from within the walls, once again the deeper and louder rumble began.

Cale stood side by side with Sidonie and Cicero, Aliazar and Harlock just a few feet away, and watched the next stage of the resurrection begin. Nothing would ever be the same for human beings again.

EPILOGUE

Months later, after making their way back to Lagrima, Cale and Sidonie found his mother working in the greenhouse that had been so long abandoned but now showed a few tentative signs of new life: a cleared worktable; a mound of fresh dirt on the floor nearby; half a dozen small plants in ceramic pots lined up on a shelf. Cale's mother stood at the table with a gardening trowel, a soil-filled pot, and a seedling that she carefully worked into the soil, carving out a place for it with the trowel. Sidonie placed her hand gently and briefly on Cale's shoulder, then without a word retreated into the House, leaving him alone with his mother.

Neither spoke at first. Cale waited for her to turn toward him or acknowledge him in some other way. She finished with the seedling, then seemed to study it. Though she did not look at him, she did finally speak.

"I've been told you're responsible for all the . . . what? Distress? Consternation?" She paused, thoughtful. "Perhaps panic is the best word. Releasing millions of aliens upon the various worlds of human beings." She shook her head. "Who would ever have imagined such a thing?"

"Father started it," Cale said.

His mother looked at him with a frown. "What do you mean?"

"When he took me with him, he was searching for what I found years later, searching for what became the key to resurrecting the Jaaprana. He started it, and I suppose I finished it. Of course, in one sense it's only just begun."

His mother was silent, then she turned away and poked absently at the dirt in the pot before her. She set the trowel beside the pot and gazed out through the broken panes and across the still barren garden. "How did you know they wouldn't try to destroy us?"

"I didn't," Cale answered. "I believed they would be well-intentioned, but I couldn't be sure."

"And you revived them anyway?"

"It felt like the right thing to do."

"The right thing for who?" she said with a strange smile, still not looking at him.

"For us. For them."

She nodded. "There *has* been bloodshed, of course, but most of it seems to be our own doing. The Jaaprana are showing remarkable restraint." She turned to him. "Yes, Cale, it was the right thing to do." Then she turned away as though unable to look at him for very long.

She went to the outer door of the greenhouse and opened it, stepped outside, and sat on the old wooden bench next to the weed-choked path.

He walked through the greenhouse and out through the open door, and sat next to her, leaving a wide space between them. The air was warm, and a breeze rustled the dead leaves on the ground and rattled the few dry branches that still sprouted from the dirt. Yet he also smelled the subtle odor of damp earth from his mother's new plantings and the faint aroma of a few young buds and blossoms.

"I should get to know you, Cale." She pulled at the fabric of her trousers just above the knee, then released and smoothed it, pressing hard with her fingers.

"There's time, now," he said.

She nodded, but said no more. They sat beside each other in silence, the skies clear and the sun shining down on them with warmth and light.

ACKNOWLEDGMENTS

I again thank my wife, Candace, for all of her contributions to this book. She read the entire manuscript several times and made innumerable suggestions and corrections, improving it markedly.

I'd also like to express my deep appreciation to the four people I've worked for during the past ten years: David Ballew, Mike McCarthy, Ken Pedersen, and Russ Reid. In addition to being fine employers—generous, respectful, and always appreciative—they have been incredibly supportive of my writing career, providing me with all the flexibility I could ever ask for, and constantly encouraging me over the years. Thank you.